a floof to a kill

An Utterly Addictive Cozy Murder Mystery

The Murderwell Mysteries
Book One

b. g. wood

also by b. g. wood

THE MURDERWELL MYSTERIES

A Floof to a Kill

And Then There Was Nun

The Whispering Bones

The Intruder

To Kill a Rockingbird

book extras

View location photos, extra content, and "persons of interest" at murderwell.com/bonus

one

. . .

"Is all that we see or seem but a dream within a dream?"

— Edgar Allan Poe

AT SOME POINT, the gentle rocking motion of the car stopped, dragging Gina Biletti out from the cozy embrace of sleep. She blinked her eyes open, registering the sudden stillness. For a moment, Gina was a kid again, waking in the backseat of her parents' car during family road trips to DC or Pennsylvania. The sensation was so vivid, it conjured a wave of forgotten memories.

"Are we there yet?"

Her friend Danielle smiled at her as she shut off the engine. "You were really out, babes."

"Uh, I know. Jet lag."

The car was parked in a half-filled lot. All around them, the majesty of the Columbia River Gorge unfolded, an expanse of sky and clouds and a wide, slow-moving river.

"Where are we?" Gina asked.

"Scenic overlook," Danielle said. "I just need to pee."

"In the parking lot?"

"No. There." She motioned behind them.

Gina turned to see a squat stone structure with a domed roof. It was octagonal, like a two-story lighthouse, or some ancient temple. And it perched on a rise directly behind them, encircled by the parking lot.

Danielle read from her phone. "This is called the Vista House. Built in the early 1900s. A primitive rest stop."

"Wonderful."

"Do you need the bathroom?"

"I'm good." According to the clock on the rental car's screen, it was less than two hours since Gina had landed in Portland, Oregon.

"Okay. Be right back."

Danielle disappeared and Gina found herself alone, still fighting off the dregs of sleep. This whole situation had 'surreal' written all over it.

Last night she was pacing around her apartment in Manhattan, trying to decide whether to sublet it or just give up the lease. It would have to be one or the other, since there was no way for her to afford the rent now that she wasn't working.

It was as if life had decided to throw her a surprise party she didn't want. Only a few days away from turning forty-five, her divorce papers from Erik were still hot off the press, and she'd been downsized out of her job.

"Welcome to your Second Act," her therapist had quipped, spinning her turmoil into an opportunity for reinvention. But Gina felt she was still in the wings, waiting for her cue for the First Act.

Stop your bitching, Gina told herself.

She was here, clear across the country. Somewhere in Oregon. Thanks to Danielle. Going on some kind of mystery adventure. Emphasis on *mystery*.

A few days ago, a round-trip ticket to Portland appeared in her email inbox. It was a first-class ticket.

Thirty seconds later, Danielle had called. "Don't ask any questions. Zero. I'm serious."

"Really? You do remember who you're talking to, right?"

"That's actually two questions. Can you count? I said zero."

Ever since Gina and Danielle had met during freshman orientation at Dartmouth, Gina's penchant for asking questions had been a running joke between the two of them. But that was just the way Gina was wired. A lot of times, her inquisitiveness got her into trouble, but eventually, she channeled it into a rewarding career as a consumer behavior researcher for prestigious marketing and advertising firms in New York City.

But that was all in the past. She needed to live in the present.

And that means getting my ass out of the car and enjoying the scenery.

She unbuckled her seatbelt and emerged from the car, stretching her weary muscles. Beyond the parking lot, the majestic Columbia River Gorge sprawled out, a breathtaking vista that went on and on.

The parking area itself was neat and orderly, half-full of cars that glittered in the sunlight. A stone wall, waist-high and sturdy, provided a separation between the lot and the roadway below. A few telescopes were dotted along the edge, inviting visitors to drop a quarter and have an even closer look at the scenic beauty of the valley.

Gina drew in a lungful of the cool, crisp air and shut her eyes. Not exactly the shore at Narragansett, but she could sense the water below. Or maybe it was her imagination.

Her reverie was interrupted by the sound of kids playing. Or screaming, if you wanted to get technical. Just a stone's throw away, a gaggle of children clambered up the wall, their laughter echoing off the rock face.

Gina didn't have children herself, and actually never

really spent too much time with kids—other than the occasional holiday with her rambunctious nephews. Well, ex-nephews now.

But even to her untrained eye, it looked like there was some trouble happening. A small girl with wild, curly hair was perched precariously on the wall, teetering, her arms outstretched like a tiny, unstable airplane.

That wasn't good.

Close by, a red-haired boy, roughly twelve, jostled about, dangerously close to the girl.

Holy crap! He's going to push her off!

"Stop!" Gina's voice cracked in panic.

The little girl shrieked, her arms flailing like windmills.

Fear pulsing through her veins, Gina barreled into the throng of kids and dove for the little girl.

Just in time, she snagged the edge of the girl's sweater, yanking her back to safety, just as she was about to go over the edge.

Sobs erupted from the kid as Gina eased her back down on the solid ground of the parking lot.

"What the hell are you doing with my daughter?"

Gina turned to find an irate woman storming across the parking lot.

"She… she was going to fall," Gina said. Her body trembled from the adrenalin surge.

Ignoring Gina's explanation, the woman took her daughter's hand and marched her back towards the Vista House without even a 'thank you.'

"You're welcome," Gina called after them. "Just saved your kid's life and all. No biggie."

The woman didn't respond, but the little curly-haired girl turned back, offering Gina a shy smile and a timid wave.

Gina returned the smile. *Well, at least the kid might turn out okay.*

When she turned back to the throng of kids, she saw they

had mostly dispersed. There was no sign of the creepy little redheaded boy.

She peeked over the edge of the wall, just to confirm there were no tiny bodies strewn below. It really was a serious drop. Definitely enough to badly injure, or even kill someone.

Was that boy actually trying to push the girl off the wall? Or was it just kids rough-housing?

Taking a deep, steadying breath, Gina tried to calm her racing heart. Thank god she didn't have kids. They'd be the death of her.

THERE WAS no way Gina could fall back asleep, so she and Danielle caught up as they drove along the curving, scenic two-lane road that meandered through the Columbia River Valley. They skirted past waterfalls and drifted under leafy canopies forming natural tunnels over the road.

"You're really not going to tell me anything about where we're going?" Gina asked.

"It's a surprise," Danielle replied, a smile playing on her lips. "Plus, you need to sign an NDA before I can say a word."

"An NDA? I thought we were going away for a girls' weekend."

"We are." Danielle grinned. "But the place that we're staying isn't open to the public."

Gina's eyebrows lifted. "Ooh, a brand-new hotel?"

"Not exactly."

"Is it a client?" Gina asked.

Danielle co-owned ERF/LaTour, a high-profile PR firm in Silicon Valley, and had a regular spot on the dance card of tech bigwigs, celebs, hedge fund hotshots, and other assorted high-rollers.

"Yes, but that's all I'm going to say. Except that this weekend, you're on the LaTour payroll."

"What are you talking about?"

"That's how I'm allowed to bring you," Danielle said. "We're coworkers now. Boom!" She smacked a high-five into Gina's palm.

"Co-workers? What am I supposed to be doing?"

"I don't know, Gina. Whatever it is you do. Market research."

Leaning back into her seat, Gina pondered the mystery hotel and the mystery temp job.

Eventually, the winding two-lane road connected back to I-84—the main highway that ran along the Columbia River. They passed through a couple of cute towns—Hood River, the Dalles—which made Gina want to stop and explore. But apparently they were on some kind of schedule, and it was getting tight.

As they made their way east, the landscape changed, from lush greenery to bare, rolling hills the color of sand and rocky cliffs, stark and captivating.

"We're still in Oregon, right?" Gina asked. It looked more like Arizona or Nevada.

"Oh yeah. Eastern Oregon. Or Central Oregon. I'm not sure what it's called."

"It's a big change."

"Well, we're on the east side of the mountains now. The Cascades. It's very dry out here. Not booze dry. Dry, dry."

"So we're going to some sort of oasis?" Gina was still fishing.

"Let's talk about something else. At least until we get to the train."

"Train? You're kidding me."

"That's why we're in a rush. If we miss the train, we'll have to spend the night in Hood River or something."

"That's not necessarily a bad thing. It was cute."

"The place we're going to is cute, too. Super cute."

"Yeah, I'll be the judge of that."

Danielle playfully rolled her eyes. "Speaking of which, did I tell you about my new bae Kayto?"

"*Bae?* No one really says that anymore."

"Whatever. They're a DJ—and smokin' hot. There are some pics on my phone. Check 'em out."

"I'm good." Gina tried to keep her tone upbeat. For as long as she had known Danielle, her friend was never short of romantic partners. Male. Female. Whatever. They flocked to Danielle like she was a human pheromone factory. And it wasn't even that Danielle was spectacularly beautiful, either. She was pretty, sure, and always looked put together, but it was more her vivacious personality than her looks that attracted people.

"We're going to Majorca for Thanksgiving," Danielle said. "Sant Llorenç des Cardassar. Kayto's got a gig there. It's for a reality show."

"Should be fun."

Danielle shot Gina a mischievous look. "Admit it, you're jealous."

"Jealous? No way."

"Yes way. Big time."

"No. Well, maybe. A little."

"I told you. Come to SF for a week. I'll take you to some parties. You'll hook up for sure."

"Hook up? Danielle, I'm forty-five. I don't want to *hook up*,"

"I'm forty-five too. It doesn't matter. Age is just a number. Besides, forty-five is the new twenty-five."

"What does that even mean?"

"It means that you need to chill, girlfriend."

"I can't chill. I just got divorced." Gina felt tears welling up. She turned away and looked out the window at the dusty hills.

Danielle put her hand on Gina's arm. "I get it, honey. It sucks. I mean, it's good for you because Erik was a real dimbag. But it still sucks."

"Yeah, it does," Gina whispered, her voice barely audible.

Their conversation faded into silence. Lost in her thoughts, Gina found herself enveloped in a whirlpool of emotions.

All the crap with Erik came flooding back, like a bout of acid reflux. Not being good enough for his family. Not producing grandkids for them. Not conforming to their Southern ideals of what a proper wife should be.

And worst of all was how two-faced Erik had turned out to be. For fifteen years he had claimed not to buy into his family's b.s.—and 'traditions.' He voted intelligently, seemingly shared her values, and didn't exhibit a whiff of racism. But it was all a lie.

A pulse of anger beat at Gina's temples. She had been through all this in her mind a million times. Raging. She needed to just stop. *Stop and move on!*

Of course, telling herself that was a lot easier than actually doing it. Still, she needed to try, so she took a deep breath and cleared her mind.

"Is there a town with a Starbucks coming up?" she asked. "I really could do with a flat white."

Danielle laughed. "Look around. Does it look like there's a Starbucks around here?"

It did not, in fact, look like there was a Starbucks around. The landscape they were traveling through was vast and barren, with low hills covered by an ocean of wheat-colored grass and sparsely dotted with bushy trees. There were no signs of civilization anywhere.

"They'll have something to drink on the train," Danielle said. "Don't worry. I think we're close."

"Close? Are you serious?"

Danielle glanced at the map on the car's touchscreen. "Twenty miles more. This is exciting. Isn't it?"

"Are you seeing what I'm seeing?" There was literally nothing but the empty two-lane road they were on, besides an occasional stretch of ancient wire fence with little pillars of stacked stones.

"Just be patient for a little longer."

Gina sighed and adjusted the vent to get some air. She didn't even try to check her phone because they had lost service half an hour ago.

"You know this road we're on was built on the Oregon Trail," Danielle said.

"Doesn't surprise me. I could see myself dying of dysentery here."

"Ha ha. Did you know that before Oregon was a state, the territory was claimed by both the United States and Great Britain?"

"I did not know that," Gina said.

"Yeah. Great Britain. Interesting, huh?" She had a mischievous twinkle in her eye.

Just about ten minutes had passed when Gina noticed, with a hint of surprise, a paved road branching off from the main road. Until this point, she'd only seen dusty paths that seemed to lead into a vast nothingness. But this was different. This was a bona fide road, spotless and well-kept, carving its way through the expansive hills.

"What's this land used for?" Gina asked.

"Farming, I think."

"What kind of farming? Tumbleweeds?"

"Wheat, I think. Sheep, maybe. I don't know. I'm sure there will be someone we can ask."

"On the train, right?"

"Yes, hon. On the train. I think we've established that."

"Just checking."

They continued to wind their way up into the low, broad

hills—maybe up onto a plateau of sorts. It was tough to get the lay of the land here, where everything looked the same.

Eventually, Danielle turned off onto another road that looked even newer and was actually lined with streetlights.

Odd, thought Gina.

A guarded gate appeared ahead, flanked by a squat, ultra-modern security booth with an imposing flat white roof and large black windows. A flock of CCTV cameras were perched on its roof like vigilant crows.

"Get your ID ready," Danielle said.

"ID? Are you serious?"

As they neared the barrier, Gina squinted to make out a massive, three-story warehouse beyond the gate, ensconced within a fortress of black security fencing.

A smiling guard emerged from the booth. "Just in time for the 4:15. ID and tickets, please."

Danielle handed over Gina's ID along with her own. She also extended her phone, which displayed some kind of QR-code.

The guard checked the documents and scanned Danielle's phone. "Just the two of you today?"

"Yes, sir."

"All right. Head to the main entrance on your left. Someone'll be there to welcome you and lend a hand with unloading." With that, he stepped aside and the barrier ascended.

"I have to say, I'm intrigued," Gina said.

"I knew you would be. Just wait. It gets even better."

They drove through the gate and towards the warehouse, passing by a massive block of electrical transformers that looked big enough to power a small city. The lot surrounding the warehouse was filled with dozens of vehicles, including some trucks and what looked like horse trailers.

"So whatever happens," Danielle said, "I need you not to act surprised. Okay?"

"What do you mean?"

"Just what I said. Whatever you see or hear, take it all in stride. Don't react."

"You're freaking me out a bit here."

Danielle smiled. "Nothing to be scared of, babes. And I'll explain everything as soon as I can. Just for now, poker face. Can you do that?"

"I can try." But Gina knew herself better than that. The truth was that she didn't have much of a filter. What you saw was what you got. And she was definitely not one to keep her feelings inside, so this was going to be some kind of challenge. That was for sure.

They pulled up in front of a series of glass doors beneath a wide rectangular awning. It all looked very modern and utilitarian, like the entrance to an IKEA.

A man with a luggage cart emerged from one of the glass doors and met them at the car. He smiled and said, "Welcome to Aune Station."

Aune Station? Gina had assumed that the whole thing about taking the train was just one of Danielle's jokes, but now she wasn't so sure. Still, where was the train? Or even a hint of a station? All she could see was the looming warehouse.

"Please remove any personal electronic devices from your luggage and we'll get you checked in."

"What kind of electronic devices?" Gina asked.

"Tablets, phones, cameras, computers, or any recording device."

"It's part of the NDA," Danielle explained.

"I just have my phone and Kindle," Gina said. Now she was even more intrigued.

"Perfect. I'll take both." The porter busied himself with their luggage, slapping on electronic tags and transferring their belongings onto the cart. "Looks like you're staying at Haverford Hall. We'll send your bags straight up there. Just follow the umbrella logo, okay?"

Gina glanced in the direction he was pointing. There it was, an umbrella symbol etched neatly into one of the glass doors. She racked her brain for any hotel logos featuring umbrellas, but drew a blank.

"What about the car?" Gina asked.

"We'll keep it safe and secure until you get back."

"You have everything?" Danielle asked.

"Yeah, just my purse. Do we need to tip this guy?"

Danielle shot her a grin. "All taken care of."

With that, they entered the big warehouse building with the umbrella logo.

two

. . .

A BLAST of air-conditioned air hit Gina as she passed through the automatic doors. She found herself in what appeared to be a travel terminal of some sort. There were ticket counters and a display screen that said the next train to Maidenwell was departing at 4:15.

Maidenwell. She had never heard of that city. Maybe it was in Canada. That would explain the need to see her ID. Although she hadn't brought her passport.

A greeter approached them and asked, "First-time visitors?"

"Yes," Danielle said.

"Right this way."

The greeter led them to a ticket counter, where an older woman smiled up at them. Her name tag read 'Agatha.' Beside the printed name was a little umbrella logo like the one on the door. It was rendered in an old-fashioned engraving style.

"Welcome, first-time visitors," Agatha said in a lovely British accent. "You are in for a treat."

"Yes, we're very excited," Danielle said.

"Let's get started with tickets and ID, shall we?"

The process took nearly fifteen minutes, filling out tons of digital forms, liability releases, non-disclosure agreements, usage contracts, credit card info—even medical and trusted contacts forms. It was creeping Gina out.

The forms all referenced 'The Regenschirm Group AG,' but didn't mention any specific hotel or resort other than the mysterious Maidenwell.

"Well done," Agatha said, as she closed the final input screen on her computer. "Now we'll just get some quick photos."

"I'm not really ready for any photos," Gina said. "I've been traveling for the past twelve hours. My hair's a mess and—"

"All done!" Agatha chirped.

"What?"

"They're candid shots, love. How about you, Ms. LaTour? If you wouldn't mind stepping right there where your friend was standing—"

"Of course." Danielle shifted Gina around and smiled her thousand megawatt smile at Agatha, taking a perfect photo, Gina was sure.

"I'll just get your keycards initialized, and in the meantime, perhaps you could gather all your personal electronic devices, phones, computers, et cetera. Back in a flash." She disappeared through a door in the rear of the ticket booth.

"What is she talking about?" Gina hissed to Danielle. "We took all of our devices out of our luggage."

"No phones inside," Danielle said.

"You're crazy."

"I'm not. It's part of the experience."

"What the hell is this? Westworld?"

Danielle laughed. "Trust me, hon. It'll be worth it." She took out her own phone, checked it one more time, then powered it off and slid it across the counter.

"I don't know if I can leave my phone," Gina said. "We've been through a lot together."

Danielle rolled her eyes and plucked Gina's phone from her hands, then slid it out of reach.

"It'll do you good, Gina. Think of this as a detox. A digital detox."

Agatha returned with the keycards—which turned out to be more like smaller, thinner phones—with silver edges and a highly-polished mirrored back. But unlike any keycards Gina had seen before, these had super-sharp, high-resolution touchscreens. It looked way better than her phone.

"Please keep these with you at all times," Agatha said.

"Even when we're showering?" Gina joked.

"That's up to you, love," Agatha said with a straight face. "Whatever tickles your fancy. But do keep it with you when you leave the room. Everything in the village works by keycard."

Gina had no idea what the woman meant by that.

"Next up, security—right through there," Agatha said. "And do have a lovely time in Maidenwell."

They walked through a door that led to a screening station with a full-body scanner. This wasn't too different from the airport security Gina had passed through at JFK this morning. It was just crazy how much they had to go through just to visit this Maidenwell place.

A theory had formed in Gina's mind. She guessed Maidenwell was a new resort that was a client of Danielle's. They were getting a sneak peek before it officially opened. That would explain the secrecy and NDAs, although it still seemed way too extreme to Gina. Hopefully she'd find out soon if her hunch was correct.

Once they passed through the security screening, they were ushered down another corridor, which ended in a door labeled 'Waiting Room.'

There Gina finally saw another passenger. He was a distinguished-looking African American man wearing a coat and tie. From his salt-and-pepper hair and goatee, Gina guessed the man was a bit older than she.

"Good day." The man held the door open for them. "Do you know if we're supposed to board now?" He had an interesting accent. Not quite French.

"I'm not really sure," Gina replied. "We just got here and —" She stopped talking when she saw what was outside the waiting room's large windows.

It was an old-fashioned steam train parked at a quaint train platform. The train looked like something out of *Harry Potter*, with red lacquered wood cars with gold trim. The locomotive was a sleek, streamlined machine with swooped art deco lines.

"Oh my god, that's fantastic!"

Danielle elbowed her.

A voice over the PA said, "All aboard the 4:15 to Maidenwell."

"I guess that answers that," the distinguished gentleman said. "After you, ladies."

They exited the waiting room onto the platform, where a portly train attendant helped them aboard.

"Amazing," Gina gushed.

"Remember, nothing is supposed to surprise you," Danielle said.

"That's going to be tough."

There were three train cars in all. Gina and Danielle were ushered into the first car, where a handful of other visitors were already seated, talking among themselves. As Gina followed Danielle to a seat towards the front of the car, she did a double-take.

A willowy woman about a decade younger than Gina sat with a little boy and an older woman. Both the younger woman and the boy had the same shade of red hair. And in a flash of recognition, Gina realized this boy was the same one who had pushed the girl in the parking lot of the rest stop.

She hurried past, ignoring the woman and the kid, and joined Danielle in a row of facing seats at the other end of the car.

"This is even better than I imagined," Danielle said. "The craftsmanship is amazing. You know this entire train was shipped over from England?"

Gina sat down across from her friend and leaned over. "You wouldn't believe who's on this train."

"Madonna?"

"No, not Madonna. That creepy little kid I told you about."

"The murderer?"

When Gina had told Danielle what happened in the parking lot, they had joked that Gina had thwarted the plans of a budding serial killer. Or half-joked.

"He's here with his—"

The words caught in Gina's throat as she felt a tap on her shoulder.

"Can I help you?" Danielle asked.

Gina turned in her seat. Speak of the devil.

The red-haired woman stood over her. She was tall and thin. "I'm Mason's mom," she said. "He told me how you saved that little girl in the parking lot. I just wanted to thank you."

Gina was so flustered, all she could manage was an 'umm.'

"Noelle Garland." She stuck her hand out. "Pleased to meet you."

Gina shook it automatically. "Gina Biletti."

Danielle quickly inserted herself into the conversation. "And I'm Danielle LaTour. We're with ERF/LaTour. The PR firm."

Noelle smiled. "Wow. I knew the auction was a big deal, but I didn't think they had their own PR firm."

"Actually, we work for Maidenwell."

"Of course. Well, I'm here on behalf of the IAOF—to certify the animals."

"You're a vet?" Danielle asked.

"I am."

"No offense, but you look young to be a vet," Gina blurted.

"I'll take that as a compliment." Noelle smiled.

A voice sounded over the PA asking travelers to return to their seats for departure.

"Nice meeting you, ladies," Noelle said. "I'm sure we'll bump into each other at the various events." She headed back to her own seat.

"Well, that was awkward," Gina said.

"You think?"

"What's this about an auction?"

"I'll tell you later, hon."

"Tell me now. I've already signed the damned NDA."

"Fine. It's an alpaca auction."

"A what? You're messing with me."

"No, the owners of the top alpaca ranches in the country are all here. This is the most significant alpaca auction in the last ten years. It's an exclusive event. Super exclusive."

"Hold on, rewind. Who even knew there was such a thing as an alpaca auction? In Oregon, of all places? I thought alpacas lived in South America."

"That's where they are from originally, but there are hundreds of alpaca ranches around the world. It's a big business. They have their own shows, and there are champion alpacas that go for the big bucks. Including Florrie."

"Florrie?"

"He's the one being auctioned off, and whoever wins him

will basically control the fate of the alpaca industry in North America."

"This is all way over my head. I thought alpacas were just cute animals. That sometimes showed up at weddings."

"They are, but—"

At that moment, the train sounded its horn and rolled forward, pulling out of the station.

"Next stop, Maidenwell," the voice over the PA said. "For your enjoyment and edification, may I direct your attention to the screens in front of you, where we have a brief presentation about our little village."

Gina watched in amazement as video screens emerged from hidden compartments in the fine woodwork of the train compartment.

Danielle moved into the seat beside Gina and whispered in her ear. "We produced this video. It's really good."

"If it's about DNA and mosquito blood and bringing back the dinosaurs, I'm leaving."

"Shut up."

"Welcome to the village of Maidenwell," the video's announcer said, over footage of what looked to be a quaint English village.

"Located in Eastern Oregon, Maidenwell has a unique history. In the early 1900s, the town of Drummond's Crossing was known as an important regional center for the sheep and wool industry, producing nearly 3,000 tons of wool per year throughout the first decade of the 20th century. However, with the diversion of railroad traffic to points west, Drummond's Crossing began to decline."

"I was expecting them to be talking about alpacas," Gina whispered.

"Shhhh!"

"In 1918, timber baron John Mayhew Haverford purchased the town and surrounding land and embarked on a most unusual project: a very special gift for his British-born wife, Elizabeth. To help ease his wife's homesickness, John Haverford recreated the

North Yorkshire village where his wife grew up, brick by brick, importing tons of fixtures and building materials from the UK. It took a team of several hundred workers nearly two decades to finish the village, which was re-christened Maidenwell."

"Wow, that was some gesture," Gina said. "During the whole fifteen years we were together, Erik never got me anything nicer than an Instapot."

"Maidenwell was a faithful recreation of an English village, with shops, cottages, a town square, a 16th-century church, and, of course, Haverford Hall, a Tudor-style country manor with lavish gardens. The Hall served as the Haverfords' summer residence until John's death in 1963. Sadly, the village fell into disrepair in the 1970s and was largely abandoned. At one point in the late 1980s, Maidenwell was occupied by the controversial Yeechee religious cult, until the arrest of the cult's leader for tax evasion in 1988."

"I've read about the Yeechees," Gina said. "I didn't know they were in Oregon."

"Yeah."

"In 2010, Austrian business magnate, visionary, and philanthropist Matthias Loneskum formed the Regenschirm Group, dedicated to sustainable living and the preservation of traditional habitations throughout the world."

Ah! Now things are making sense, Gina thought.

More footage of Maidenwell showed a picturesque village with ivy-covered stone cottages, narrow cobblestone streets, flowering gardens, and a park-like expanse in the center of town. It looked exactly like something out of a BBC mystery show, or maybe the cozy wizarding village in *Harry Potter*. But it definitely didn't look like Oregon.

The video continued with an aerial tour of the village, tucked neatly in a lush valley, hugged protectively by mesas crowned with rimrock cliffs. Gina found out that despite the larger area being classified as high desert, the valley cradling Maidenwell was graced with its own little weather system—a micro-climate that served up conditions much cooler and damper than its surrounding landscape.

"And, although the village appears to be hundreds of years old," the video's narrator continued, *"behind the scenes, Maidenwell is a showcase of the most advanced municipal systems, powered by Regenschirm's HyperCiv technology. Here's founder Matthias Loneskum."*

Gina inched forward in her seat. "You filmed Matthias Loneskum?"

"Yeah. I've worked with him directly several times. He's an interesting guy."

"That's an understatement."

Matthias Loneskum was one of the top three billionaires in the world, a titan in the tech world, but very eccentric. Although he was now in his early forties, he was still regarded as an *enfant terrible* of Silicon Valley.

He smiled and looked directly into the camera, and as he spoke, Gina felt like he was speaking directly to her and no one else.

"The best, most unique places in the world to live are small towns, villages, hamlets," Loneskum said. Gina detected only the barest hint of his Austrian accent.

"But people are leaving these small towns, and—sadly—these treasured places are dying. But not if we have anything to say about it. Our mission at Regenschirm is to breathe new life into our oldest villages, and make them the most advanced, livable, and desirable places from which to launch the new economy. We can do that thanks to our HyperCiv Smart Village technology, a suite of AI-powered utility systems that can be retrofitted into villages of up to three thousand residents—non-invasively, without ripping up streets, or negatively impacting the existing architecture of a village."

"I don't get this," Gina whispered to Danielle. "What does he mean by retro-fitting?"

"It's technical. I'll explain how it works later. Just keep watching."

"We're reinventing the village and allowing its residents to reap the rewards. With no-cost residential energy, no-cost residential utilities, the most advanced recycling system in the world, and a green electric mini-grid that powers nearly everything in Maidenwell. Including the train you're riding on."

"I thought this was a steam train," Gina said to Danielle.

"Fully electric. All that steam? Fake."

"Wow. Just wow."

"But that's not all." Matthias Loneskum paused dramatically. *"Because when it comes right down to it, what's really important are people. Without its citizens, a village is just a collection of buildings. That's why our five-year Maidenwell pilot program provides a universal basic income for all residents, and why we've attracted a diverse group of artists, craftspeople, writers, makers, farmers, growers, and dreamers to be the very first residents. A good portion of what's consumed in Maidenwell is made in Maidenwell. And the excess is sold via our frictionless social commerce platform."*

The video changed to shots of various people working in home offices and quaint little workshops. Most were young and looked like they spent a lot of time on Etsy.

"HyperCiv has been described as the Tesla of urban renewal, but actually, I prefer to describe Tesla as the HyperCiv of electric cars. I can't wait to share Maidenwell with the world." He grinned at the camera and Gina felt a little shiver run through her.

"Actually, it might be another year before he shares it with the world," Danielle whispered.

"Why? Trouble in paradise?"

"Nothing like that. He's just really buttoned up. Careful. Everything has to be just so."

"Anal retentive."

"Shut it."

The video cut back to shots of the village again and

continued for several more minutes. Gina learned that, in addition to this picturesque little village, Matthias Loneskum had also built a 160-acre data center to serve his various tech companies. It was located two miles outside of Maidenwell. Both the village and the data center were powered by one of the largest non-utility emission-free fuel cell installations in the country.

When the video finished, she leaned in close to Danielle. "So… a little English village that's also a high-tech wonderland—"

"Behind the scenes," Danielle said. "Just behind the scenes."

"And alpacas," Gina continued. "Anything else I'm missing?"

"Not really. What do you think?"

"What do I think? I think you have the best job in the world. And I kind of hate you for it!"

Danielle smiled at her. "Hey, don't forget that we work for the same company. At least this weekend."

At that moment, the train slowed to a stop.

"This isn't supposed to happen," Danielle said.

"Maybe the train battery needs a recharge."

"Sorry for the delay, ladies and gentlemen," the voice said over the train's PA. "We are stopping to accommodate some late arrivals."

At that moment, Gina heard the sound of a helicopter outside of the train. She got up and peered through the window. It was a helicopter! A sleek ultra-modern-looking model with an elongated cabin. And it was setting down in a flat meadow not one hundred feet away.

three

. . .

"THAT'S NOT MATTHIAS LONESKUM, is it?" Gina asked.

"No way. He's in Portofino this weekend. I'm not sure who it is."

A few minutes later, three people emerged from the helicopter. A burly, bald man with a beard, dressed in an expensive-looking suit, led the way. He was followed by a tall, thin, chic-looking woman in a designer jumpsuit and wearing overly large sunglasses. Finally, a young man trailed after the bald man and the woman. He wore jeans and a sport jacket and struggled with two suitcases and a backpack.

The trio was met by four train attendants. One escorted the newcomers to the train, while the others made their way to the helicopter. A minute later, the three helicopter passengers entered the train compartment, led by the bald man, who boomed greetings to some of the passengers.

"Good to see you, Orville," he said as he pushed past the distinguished-looking man Gina and Danielle had met in the waiting room.

"Stanley." The distinguished-looking man nodded.

"I guess they're letting anyone into this auction. Ha!" He clapped the other man on the shoulder and pushed past.

Gina noticed him glance toward the red-haired veterinarian, but he didn't greet her. He just looked away with a frown.

The woman from the helicopter pulled down her sunglasses and surveyed the car with an expression of distaste. "Where's our compartment?" she asked an attendant.

Gina tried not to stare. The woman was very beautiful, but in a hard way—with pulled-back hair and severe-looking make-up. She had a long neck and held herself upright, almost like she was posing for a photographer who wasn't there.

"Please feel free to take any open seat, ma'am."

"Open seat? I'd like a private compartment, if you don't mind."

"This isn't the Orient Express, dear," the bald man said. "It's a twenty-minute trip."

"Sixty-three minutes, actually," the young man from the helicopter said. He appeared to be in his late twenties, with a pale complexion, dark eyes, and model-like cheekbones. He looked like a brooding vampire from a romance novel.

"Well, in that case, go find the bar car, Ian," the bald man said. "What are you waiting for?"

"I don't think there's a bar car on this train, Mr. Schaeffer."

"Nonsense. There's always a bar car."

Danielle leaned over and whispered in Gina's ear. "That's Stanley and Vanessa Schaeffer. They have the largest alpaca ranch in the country."

"Am I supposed to be impressed?"

"She's very wealthy. Her family owns a huge meat-packer in the Midwest."

"Who knew you could get rich from sausages?"

The bald man—Stanley—grumbled about being parched and eased into a seat across the aisle from Gina and Danielle.

The young man sat opposite him and consulted a notebook. "Apparently there's a pub in Maidenwell. 'The Feathers,' it's called."

"What kind of name is that for a pub?"

"No idea. I've never been to England."

"Me neither. And I can't, for the life of me, understand why Loneskum would want to build an English village."

"My understanding is that his mother, Frau Loneskum, likes the architecture."

"Actually," Danielle leaned over and inserted herself into the conversation, "Matthias Loneskum didn't build Maidenwell. The village was built in the early 1900s."

"You don't say?" Stanley smirked. "Are you the town historian?"

"No, Danielle LaTour of ERF/LaTour PR. This is my associate, Gina."

"Stanley Schaeffer." He puffed out his chest. "But you probably already knew that. My wife Vanessa. And my assistant Ian."

"Pleased to meet you."

"So you're doing PR for the auction?"

"Not specifically. We're actually here doing some preliminary background work for some other projects."

"Well, best keep your eye on Schaeffer Family Farms. We're going to be the winner of Florentine, no doubt about that. I have an ace up my sleeve." He leaned in conspiratorially. "Her name is Magdalene. Perhaps we should speak after the auction. You could have a scoop about how we're single-handedly transforming the alpaca industry in the United States."

"More like single-handedly destroying it!"

Gina turned to see a young woman advancing towards

them. She was in her twenties with pink-tipped hair cut in a sharp, neat bob. Her eyes flashed in anger.

"You will never get your hands on Florrie!" the young woman said.

"Becca, dear! Please!" An older woman, tall and horsey-looking, quickly followed the young woman. "You're embarrassing me!"

"Maybe you want to rethink that decision to give your ranch to your niece, Catherine," Stanley Schaeffer said to the horsey woman. "She's a little hot under the collar, I'd say. Not a good look. Especially in front of the press."

"I'm not really the press," Danielle said.

The pink-haired woman—Becca—spun to face Danielle. "You need to hear the truth about what he wants to do. Factory farming. Alpaca slaughter."

"Culling the herd," Stanley said, getting right back into Becca's face. "It's called good stewardship and breeding for positive genetics. Follow the science, little lady!"

"You want to raise alpacas for dog food!" Becca spat. "Dog food!"

"Becca, please!" her aunt said. "Stop it!"

Finally, the train attendant shooed everyone back to their own seats.

"They were thirty seconds away from throwing punches," Gina whispered to Danielle. "I didn't know there could be so much drama about alpacas. Llamas maybe. But not alpacas."

Danielle rolled her eyes. "Let's just enjoy the scenery."

As the sun sank lower in the sky, the train wound its way through valleys and across the top of mesas. Gina found herself almost dozing off again from the gentle rocking of the train.

"I better stretch my legs," she said.

"Don't go far, okay? We're almost there." Danielle returned to reading her book: some sort of lurid mystery, judging by the cover.

Gina's joints creaked as she stood up. Way too much sitting today. She made her way towards the rear of the car, smiling at the other passengers. Most ignored her.

She passed through the door at the end of the car into the gangway connection between cars. A woman stood in the vestibule, smoking. It was Vanessa Schaeffer.

"Oh, sorry," Gina said. "I didn't know anyone else was out here."

"It's fine. I just needed to get away from the plebes for a bit." Vanessa stretched her back, kind of like a cat. Then she looked out over the landscape.

"Does this connect to the next car?" Gina asked.

"Door's locked. I don't think they want us to mingle with the others."

"That's odd," Gina said.

"This whole place is odd. Cigarette?" Vanessa dug into her purse.

"No thanks. I don't smoke anymore. Not since my twenties, anyway."

"You sure? It's like riding a horse. You just have to get back on again." She smiled at Gina.

"Tempting, but no."

"I shouldn't either. It's just that—without a few choice vices—I don't think I could go on." She shifted her body again, feet turned out. Almost like a ballet dancer.

"Is everything okay?"

"Oh, the usual. My husband is a wretch. I want to murder my mother. Our business is—" She cut herself off. "Look at me. About to spill my guts to the press." Vanessa contemplated her cigarette. "I really need something stronger."

"I'm not actually the press," Gina said.

"So you say. But you *do* work for a PR firm."

"Yes. Well, technically, I'm a contractor. And I'm new. It's Danielle's firm."

"Uh huh. Well, I can see how you lull people into trusting you so you can get the dirt."

"It's really not like that at all. Actually, my specialty is market research—"

"Whatever you say, Tina."

"It's Gina, actually."

"Of course it is."

At that moment, the train's horn sounded—an old-fashioned melodious steam horn. Although, who knew? It actually might have been digital audio.

"I think we're arriving," Vanessa said. "Which means I'm that much closer to a cocktail." She tossed her cigarette onto the tracks in a shower of sparks and glided past Gina back inside. "See you around. Tina."

That was weird, Gina thought. *Rich people.*

She stood by herself for a few moments, taking in the view. Low hills were bathed in the golden light of dusk and the few lone trees cast long, dark shadows. The sun seemed so different out here in the west. Almost as if it was a sister sun to the one they had back east.

The air was crisp and cool—verging on chilly—but it felt good. Gina didn't really want to go back inside. But she knew she should. She probably wasn't even allowed to be out here.

THE TRAIN EASED to a stop in front of a little station with a lit-up sign that read 'Maidenwell.' The station house was a narrow stone building with a slate roof. On the platform stood a dozen men and women, their faces lit by the glow of the tablets they held.

"I thought we weren't allowed to have electronic devices," Gina said.

"No, we're not allowed to *bring in* personal electronics,"

Danielle said. "I'm sure you can borrow one if you really need it."

"Who are all those people?"

"Hospitality staff, I'm guessing."

As they exited the train car, a tall 30-something woman approached them. "Danielle and Gina?"

"Yes."

"Welcome to Maidenwell. I'm Millicent, your driver."

"We get a driver?" Gina asked.

"Don't get too excited," Millicent said. "I'm not much of a driver, and we're just going up to Haverford Hall. It's a five-minute trip, but the car is pretty cool. Follow me, please."

"What about our bags?" Gina asked.

"They're on their way as well. Should be up in your room within the hour."

Millicent led them down a lit walkway that circled around the train station and led to a gravel lot. Under the glow of the lot's cast-iron lamps, Gina saw what looked to be a fleet of a dozen antique cars. She knew little about old cars, but these appeared like vintage Ford Model Ts.

"We're actually riding in one of those?" Gina asked.

"Yes, it's perfectly safe." Millicent led them to one of the old cars, painted a dark green color with gold pin-striping and the umbrella logo emblazoned on the side doors. "Isn't it cool? Looks a hundred years old, right?"

"If not older," Gina said. "You're sure it's okay?"

"Absolutely. This vehicle is actually only two years old."

"What?"

"It's a recreation of the 1909 Renault Landaulette, but fully electric."

Gina and Danielle climbed into the rear passenger cabin and sat in a plush rear seat that looked like a high-end upholstered loveseat.

"Buckle up, please," Millicent said.

Gina was pleased to discover that the vintage car actually

had a normal seat belt, with a shoulder strap and everything. Maybe it had airbags as well. Who knew?

The car silently exited the parking lot onto a winding lane flanked by low stone walls.

"I'm sorry you won't be able to see much of the town," Millicent said. "It's getting dark earlier now. During the summer, it stays light until nearly nine at night."

"So do you live here year round?" Danielle asked.

"Yes, but I've only been here eleven months."

"You like it?" Gina asked.

"Yes, very much. It's very mellow and the people are super nice."

"And you're a full-time Uber driver?" Gina asked.

Millicent laughed. "Uber doesn't exist in Maidenwell. I just drive during events. Most of the time, I do letterpress printing and bookbinding. And some paper making."

"Really?"

"Yes, they set me up in one of the craft collectives. It's called the Barrelworks. Stop by and I'll show you around."

"Barrelworks," Gina repeated. "I'll remember that."

"Ugh, I'm totally failing as a driver. I'm supposed to be giving you the Grand Tour."

"Don't worry about it," Danielle said.

"Well, I'll loop around. This is the Village Green coming up. Basically, the center of town."

It was too dark to make out much, but Gina got the sense of a central square with buildings set around it.

"That tall tower at the end of the Green is St. Mary's," Millicent said. "It actually dates from the 16th century and it was brought over from England, brick by brick."

They drove past a church with a square tower that took up one full side of the Green. Then they passed by all kinds of cute little shops and cottages, all made of rustic-looking stone blocks.

"On your right is the inn. The White Horse." A long, two-story building stretched parallel to the road. "It's pretty nice, but not quite as nice as where you'll be staying."

"Oh?" Danielle asked.

"Haverford Hall is our own little Downton Abbey. It's pretty amazing. And right up the hill."

As they entered a small roundabout, Millicent pointed to a picturesque building on the corner. "The Feathers. I bet you'll be spending some time there."

"The pub, right?"

"Gastro-pub, actually. The food is amazing. All farm-to-table, organic. Lots of great veggie options, too."

They continued to drive through the village, winding their way along narrow cobblestone streets.

"How many restaurants are in town?" Gina asked.

"Six counting the bakery, but it's only open for breakfast."

"And how many people live here?"

"Roughly 500, the last I heard. Plus, a bunch of people are visiting for the alpaca auction. That's what you guys are here for, right?"

"Not specifically," Danielle said. "We're with Maidenwell's PR firm."

"Oh, interesting. Does that mean we'll finally be allowed to talk about the village?"

Danielle smiled. "Not quite yet. We're just doing some preliminary background work right now. Hopefully soon, though."

They cut back along the edge of the Green, and then drove to the outskirts of the village along a road that switchbacked up a hill. Below them, the lights of Maidenwell twinkled in the October evening.

"We're coming up on Haverford Hall," Millicent said. "It's where Yvonne Loneskum lives, at least part of the year."

"Is she Matthias Loneskum's wife?" Gina asked.

"Mom," Danielle said.

"And we're staying with her?"

"Not *with* her exactly," Danielle said. "Haverford Hall has been converted to a guest house. Like a high-end hotel. I think Frau Loneskum has her own wing, though."

"She does," Millicent said. "And, yes, the Hall is very large. Something like thirty guest rooms, but don't quote me on that."

"And it's old, too, isn't it?" Gina asked.

"Weren't you paying attention to my video, hon?" Danielle teased.

"Kind of."

"The Hall was built in 1919," Millicent said, sounding like a tour guide. "But it was a recreation of a Tudor country home from the 1700s. Like everything here, the Hall's been fully renovated and modernized, so it just looks old."

Gina couldn't see much detail of the estate, but the structure they drove towards was an impressive stone manor house with a large forecourt. It really did look like a smaller version of the house from *Downton Abbey*. A few other cars were parked in front, unloading passengers.

"Well, this is it," Millicent said. "There are attendants inside who will show you to your rooms."

"Thank you," Danielle said.

"Do you have an app or anything for a tip?" Gina asked.

Millicent laughed. "No need. It's all taken care of. But let me beam you my info. I'm driving all weekend long and would be happy to give you a proper tour."

"Beam?" Gina asked.

"Our keycards," Danielle said.

"Just hit accept," Millicent said.

Gina fished out the keycard she had been given when they checked in at the train station. An alert window read: "Incoming contact details from Millicent Ryan. Accept?"

She pushed the 'yes' button.

"Now you can text me whenever you need a ride," Millicent said.

"Our keycards can text?"

"They're actually more than just keycards. That's just what we call them. They're like little phones. Play around with yours."

They said goodbye to Millicent and crunched along the gravel forecourt to a pair of painted double doors. They stepped into a well-lit entrance hall with fluted marble pillars and a bright-red runner carpet. Gina felt as if she had wandered into a museum.

The hall opened up into a lobby of sorts, with a two-story vaulted ceiling and imposing arches. Gina couldn't help gasping at the opulent antique furniture, the gold-framed oil paintings, and an Oriental rug that was three times as big as her whole apartment back in New York.

"Babes, mouth closed," Danielle joked. "Don't drool on the settee."

"I'm trying not to."

They made their way to a discreet desk in one corner of the lobby. There, a gentleman checked them in by scanning their keycards. Then another attendant led them up an enormous staircase to the third floor and through a maze of hallways filled with more paintings. None of the guest rooms seemed to have numbers on them.

"Give it to me straight," Gina said to the attendant. "Do people actually get lost in this place? I mean, really lost. Like you need to send in a search party."

The attendant chuckled. "Not that I know of. Besides, you can always use your keycard to find your room."

"Ah, the magic keycard strikes again."

"It is very useful."

The attendant showed Danielle to her room first, and then Gina to hers—with Danielle tagging along.

"If there's anything you need, just call or text the front desk," the attendant said—and then left them.

"Are you sure we're not supposed to tip them?" Gina asked.

"It doesn't work that way, hon. Let's check out your room."

The room was magnificent, with decorative woodwork on the ceilings, a big four-poster bed, a stone fireplace, and green silk wallpaper embossed with intricate designs.

"Not too shabby," Gina said. "Not too shabby at all. I could get used to this."

"Notice what's *not* here?" Danielle asked.

Gina looked around the room. Everything looked so perfect. "No idea."

"A TV."

"Ah. Let me guess. They didn't have TVs back in the 1700s."

"They didn't have keycards, either, but there you go. It was a deliberate choice."

"Well, if someone is watching TV in a place like this, something's wrong."

"Now you're getting it. You know what else they don't have?" Danielle walked back towards the door out to the hallway.

"An umbrella stand? That's ironic."

"No." Danielle opened the door to the hallway.

Gina looked it up and down. It looked like a normal door. Then it hit her. No security chain. No deadbolt. "That can't be."

"No locks," Danielle said.

"Why wouldn't you have locks in a hotel?" As a lifelong New Yorker, this definitely did not compute.

"We're not really in a hotel. We're in Frau Loneskum's residence. And, apparently, it's an old Austrian tradition."

"Well, that's messed up."

"You can always prop a chair under the doorknob."

"Thanks. Now I know I'll sleep better."

Danielle left Gina to freshen up and chill out for a bit before they set out for dinner. While she was in the bathroom fixing her make-up, another attendant delivered her luggage.

This place certainly is efficient, she thought. Maybe it was the Austrian influence.

Gina wandered over to an ornate desk with a table-top mirror on it and looked at her reflection. Even with her fresh make-up, she thought she looked old and tired.

Well, she was tired. That was for sure. Her internal clock was still stuck in New York time. It was nearly 10 p.m., and normally, around now, she'd be thinking of curling up with her Kindle.

She saw a little leather folio on the desk and opened it up. There on engraved stationery—maybe from Millicent's shop—was a welcome letter from Yvonne Loneskum and a schedule of events. Before she could read through them properly, a knock on the door sounded.

four

. . .

"OKAY, babes? Ready to hit the town? Or village, as the case may be?" Danielle had changed her clothes and was looking refreshed and spectacular.

"Sure, but I have to warn you—I'm starting to peter out a little bit. Jet lag."

"Don't talk to me about jet lag until you've flown from LA to Prague."

"Did you see this?" Gina held up the papers from the desk.

"Yes, I'd thought we'd head down to the little happy hour downstairs. It's in the drawing room."

"I'm actually kind of hungry."

"I'm sure there will be snacks there. Good ones. Come on. It will give us a chance to snoop around."

As they left Gina's room and made their way back down towards the lobby, they saw another guest leaving her room—a woman Gina remembered seeing on the train. She was short and blonde and wore oversized pink plastic glasses that screamed *I'm Quirky. With a capital Q.*

"Are you looking for the happy hour, too?" Gina asked.

The woman turned in surprise, like she had just seen a ghost.

"Uh, yes. Yes, I am."

"Us too," Danielle said. "It's supposed to be in the drawing room."

"Which one? I think there's a dozen drawing rooms in this place." She introduced herself as Frankie Roth.

"The artist?" Danielle asked.

"Yes." Frankie smiled at them, seemingly pleased to be recognized.

Danielle turned to Gina. "Ms. Roth is a big deal in the art world. She started the Modern Cubist movement."

"Frankie, please. And the style is actually called *Nouveau Cubism*. There's a video on my website explaining it all."

"An artist, huh?" Gina said. "You should be the one telling us where the *drawing* room is. Get it?"

"What?"

"Sorry," Danielle said. "She's making a stupid joke."

"Oh." Frankie made a face. "I think I saw you on the train."

"Yes. Danielle LaTour and Gina Biletti. We're doing PR for Maidenwell."

"Ah, that explains it."

"What?" Gina asked.

"Nothing. Shall we?" Frankie motioned them forward.

THE DRAWING ROOM was a long rectangular room filled with several dozen people, including a pianist in formal wear providing spirited background music. Gina loved the decor—fabric wallpaper the color of tangerines and cream-colored wainscoting. It was all very elegant. Oversized oil paintings hung from wires attached to a picture rail high on the walls, and an ornate crystal chandelier glittered above their heads. A fire in the immense marble fireplace helped make the big room feel a bit cozier.

"I don't think I'd ever get tired of this," Gina said.

"It's nice to see how the other half lives, huh?" Danielle said.

"What are you talking about? You are the other half."

"Not like this."

Servers floated around with trays of hors d'oeuvres, and all the guests seemed to have glasses of wine—except for them.

Gina spotted a bar area towards the far end of the room and made a bee-line towards it.

"The Pinot or the Chardonnay?" The server was a guy who looked like he was barely out of college. "We also have water."

"Pinot, definitely," Danielle said.

"I'll try the Chardonnay," Gina said.

Before the server could pour their wine, a woman in a rich purple dress swooped behind the bar, pulled the server aside and began to berate him. Even though the woman was trying to keep her voice down, Gina pretty much heard everything.

"It's not just *Pinot,* you moron. It's the *Ribbon Ridge Reserve Pinot Noir*. And the Chardonnay is the *Bogwood Bay Heritage Estate Chardonnay.* You got that?"

"Yes, ma'am."

"And where are the damn sell cards?"

"Uh, I'm not sure. Cheryl was looking for them in the kitchen."

The woman in purple whipped around, no doubt scanning the crowd for the hapless Cheryl. Then she turned back to the server. "What are you waiting for? Get these guests their wine. Now."

"Yes, of course, Ms. Seville."

The woman in purple took a few steps back and glared at

the server, watching him like a hawk as he poured Gina and Danielle's wine.

If her face hadn't been locked into a perpetual frown, the woman in purple would have been exceptionally beautiful. She was African American, with flawless skin and big eyes, and her dress fit her perfectly. Her hair was swirled into a big bun of highlighted braids sitting elegantly atop her head. Gina guessed she might be in her mid-thirties.

"Here you go, ladies," the server said. "The 2017 Ribbon Ridge Reserve Pinot Noir and the 2019 Bogwood Bay Heritage Estate Chardonnay. Both exceptional wines. I hope you enjoy them."

"Thanks," Gina said.

As they walked away from the bar, the woman in purple intercepted them. "I am so sorry for the server. He's new, and it's so difficult to—"

"Don't say 'get good help,' please," Gina said. "Just don't."

"Well, I'm sure you understand."

"It's fine," Danielle said. "The wine is delicious."

"Isn't it just? 2019 was such an excellent vintage for chardonnay. Our weather was nice and cool, so the grapes had a chance to ripen gradually."

"Can I try a sip?" Gina was normally more of a red wine person, but she was curious about Danielle's wine.

"Sure."

"The Heritage Estate is unoaked," the woman in purple said. "So you'll find it's much more nuanced and well-balanced. It opens with a fleshy perfume of peach, green apple, and moss, with a gingery steel note in the background."

Gina took a sip. She really didn't taste any gingery steel, whatever that was supposed to be. "Refreshing."

"So refreshing," the woman in purple said. "Do you sense that flinty damp-stone tension at the end?"

Gina just smiled in a non-committal way. "You obviously know a lot about wine."

The woman laughed. "I should hope so. I'm the brand ambassador for Bogwood Bay Winery." She produced a pair of business cards, seemingly out of thin air. "Amadora Seville."

"Oh," Danielle said. "Color me impressed." She introduced herself and Gina to Amadora.

Gina hadn't ever heard of Bogwood Bay, but then again, she wasn't a big wine person.

They chatted politely for a few more minutes, during which Amadora Seville managed to work in the fact that her winery had won eleven awards this year. Then she spotted someone across the room and excused herself.

"Well, that was different," Gina said.

"I don't know," Danielle said. "I liked her. She's got a good energy."

"She's very pretty."

Danielle noticed someone moving through the crowd of guests. "Oh, there's the grande dame herself. I need to go say hello."

"Mrs. Loneskum?"

"*Frau* Loneskum. She hates being called 'missus.' And she hates the English. Do you want to meet her?"

"All that hate. Why not?" Gina took another swig of her wine. It tasted like Pinot Noir to her. A good Pinot Noir, sure. But she couldn't detect any weird flavors. Like moss.

Yvonne Loneskum was a striking figure, a grand dame in her seventies who stood tall and regal. Her vibrant orange hair was pulled back into a sleek bun, and she was adorned with large, antique-style jewelry that echoed her Old-World charm. She commanded the attention of a cluster of people, Vanessa Schaeffer among them, who Gina had chatted with on the train. Two other familiar faces caught Gina's eye—the scholarly guy from the platform, and Frankie Roth, the artist.

Danielle waited for an opening in the conversation and then introduced them.

"Ah yes." Frau Loneskum spoke with a distinct Austrian accent. She sounded like an old lady version of Arnold Schwarzenegger. "My son mentioned you'd be attending. You're not alpaca people, are you?"

"I'm afraid not," Danielle said.

"I don't think I've actually even seen a real live alpaca," Gina chimed in.

"In that case, my dears, we must rectify this tomorrow morning. Do come to the stables and acquaint yourselves with my pride and joy."

"You mean Florrie?" Gina asked—and promptly got an elbow in the side from Danielle.

Frau Loneskum's eyes narrowed. "I'll forgive your mistake, since you don't really know better. 'Florrie' is his barn name. His proper name is Alpengipfel Florentine."

"And what does Alpengipfel mean?" Gina got another jab in the ribs. "Ouch!" She jostled Danielle back.

"No, it's fine, dear," Frau Loneskum said to Danielle. Then she addressed Gina. "Alpengipfel is the name of my alpaca ranch in Austria. It means 'alpine peak' in English. We have exquisite mountains in Austria: the Alps. Perhaps you've heard of them?" Her eyes twinkled with mischief.

"I have indeed," Gina said.

"The auction should be interesting." Danielle said.

Gina guessed that her friend was trying to shift the conversation away from her—probably to avoid any more embarrassment.

"That is an understatement, madame," Édouard Orville said. "No one has seen an animal like Florentine for generations."

"Really?" Gina asked. "What makes him so special?"

"It's rather technical with genetics and all, but he has won International Herdsire of the Year for the past five years, and he's the finest-fleeced alpaca in the world. Every animal he's sired has also been a champion."

"Fleeced?" Gina asked.

"His fleece is truly remarkable. It is extremely uniform and yet so dense that the fleece weight is very high."

That still made little sense to Gina, but she smiled and nodded as if she was suitably impressed.

"My Florentine has been the backbone of the European alpaca industry for years," Frau Loneskum said. "And now he is here in America. Lucky you, America."

They continued to chat until the tall, horsey-looking woman from the train came up to Frau Loneskum with her niece in tow. Gina remembered the younger woman with the pink hair because she seemed to have it in for the man from the helicopter, Vanessa's husband. And Gina definitely admired that kind of spunk.

Vanessa Schaeffer did not, however. At the sight of the young woman, she murmured something about going outside for some fresh air and slipped away.

"Frau Loneskum, so good to see you," the horsey-looking woman gushed.

"You as well, Catherine."

"May I present my niece, Rebecca Hill?"

"It's Becca," the young woman mumbled.

Frau Loneskum looked Becca up and down and nodded at her. "So you shall be the new mistress of Hill Alpacas? You seem quite young."

"I've been working with my aunt for five years, since I graduated."

"Becca has a BS in Animal Sciences from WSU," Catherine said. "And she graduated with honors."

"Wonderful, dear. Well, I wish you the best of luck, Rebecca. And you as well, Catherine, with your retirement."

Catherine clucked her tongue. "Well, we'll see about the

whole retirement thing. I'm a bit on the fence about it, if I'm being honest."

Becca shot her aunt a sharp look, then changed the subject. "Frau Loneskum, I just want you to know that I will be the very best steward of—"

"Mmm, mmm, mmm!" Frau Loneskum cut her off with a wagging finger. "No campaigning outside of the auction, my dear. You know the rules."

"Oh my god." Becca blanched in embarrassment. "I'm so sorry. I would never—"

"That's quite all right, dear. No harm done. I look forward to hearing about your strategic plan for Florentine at the auction."

"Of course."

"I don't understand," Gina said. "Strategic plan?"

"This is a most unusual auction, Ms. Biletti," Édouard said. "The winner is not simply the farm willing to pay the most."

"Still drawing a blank here."

"I will judge the aspirants on their plans for my Florentine as well," Frau Loneskum explained. "Each bidder must make their case why they alone are most deserving of guiding the industry forward with Florentine's exceptional genetics."

"Well, that's different."

"I think it's very responsible of you, Frau Loneskum," Catherine said. "And we can't wait to present our plan. Well, Becca's plan, actually."

Over the course of the evening, Gina met several more people involved with the alpaca auction, and slowly got the lay of the land. Everyone seemed nice except for the boorish helicopter guy, Stanley Schaeffer. He moved through the crowd like a clumsy bull, back-slapping those he favored and casting half-muttered remarks to those he found distasteful.

That latter group seemed to include the red-haired veterinarian, who was there without her creepy son. She looked good. Especially her hair. Gina had toyed with the idea of going red herself but was concerned about ending up with a clownish, orange hue like Frau Loneskum's.

Schaeffer scowled at the red-haired vet as he openly questioned why the International Alpaca Owners Federation didn't employ a more impartial vet. Someone without ties to the various ranches competing for Florentine—or Florrie, as Gina still thought of him.

Rude, Gina thought. *She's standing right there.* But the vet just ignored Stanley and made her way through the crowd, talking to people.

As Gina picked up more and more gossip, she learned that the world of alpaca breeders was a bit incestuous. Many ranches were started by couples. Unfortunately, when love soured, so did the ranch. Sometimes, one half of the couple moved in with the home wrecker—or ranch wrecker, as the case may be—and started a new ranch.

Everyone knew everyone else and were all up into their rivals' business. Just like any tightly knit group, she guessed.

Towards the end of the evening, Gina found herself fading fast. Maybe it was the jet lag. Maybe it was way too much wine.

Across the room, Danielle was deep in conversation with the wine rep Amadora Seville, either flirting or trying to get the Bogwood Bay Winery PR business. Or maybe both.

Gina caught Danielle's eye and pantomimed putting her head down on a pillow. Danielle nodded and gave her the thumbs up.

As she left the drawing room, Gina realized she might be a little tipsier than she thought. Instead of exiting the way she came in, she accidentally went through an old butler's door and found herself in an alcove with folding tray stands, serving trolleys, and rolling catering carts.

She stood there for a moment, trying to get her bearings. That was when she noticed the young man.

He was pulling wine bottles from a box and wrapping them in his jacket. At the sight of Gina, he looked up in alarm.

The guy wasn't a waiter, that was for sure. He looked more like a guest—even without his jacket.

And then Gina recognized him.

He was the handsome young man who was with Stanley Schaeffer and his wife. From the helicopter.

"You know they have open bottles out in the main room," Gina said, trying not to slur her words. "Glasses, too. And I'm pretty sure it's not self-serve."

"Yeah, I... uh..." An embarrassed flush played over the guy's face.

"Are you stealing wine?" Gina asked.

"No. Of course not."

"Then what are you doing?"

"These aren't for me."

"So you're stealing wine for someone else?" she snorted. For some reason, this struck her as deeply funny.

"It's for my boss, okay? You're not going to tell anyone, are you?"

"Your boss is Stanley, right? You came in on the chopper."

"Yeah, that's right."

"You're Liam."

"It's Ian, actually."

"Ian. Right."

"And you're that PR lady."

"One of them, anyway." She extended her hand. "Gina Biletti. At your service. Not really."

"Seriously, can we just keep this between us?"

"I don't care if you steal wine. That wine lady was kind of a bitch."

"Thank god."

"But you owe me one, Stretch."

"You want a bottle?"

"No." *Pretty, but dim.* "It's a figure of speech."

"Right." Ian finished wrapping up his loot. It looked like he had managed to stuff a half dozen bottles in his jacket. That was quite a haul.

"There is something I don't understand," she said.

"What's that?"

"If your boss is rich enough to have a private helicopter, why doesn't he just *buy* the wine? He certainly can afford it."

Ian said nothing, but he made a little face. "Thanks again for keeping my secret." With that, he was off—bottles clinking softly in his jacket-wrapped parcel.

Weird, Gina thought. As she turned to follow him, her hip caught the edge of a rolling serving cart. It slid out from the wall. As Gina rolled it back into place, she caught a glimpse of some small plastic bottles scattered on the ground next to the wall. She picked one up. It was a bottle of eye drops for red eyes, but it was empty.

Probably some servers were smoking pot and didn't want to get busted by their boss. Or maybe it was that wine guy. If so, she couldn't blame him. Especially with a boss like that.

five

. . .

BETWEEN THE WINE and the jet lag, Gina fully expected to sleep until noon. But, according to the antique wind-up clock on her nightstand, it was close to 5:30 a.m. when she snapped awake, feeling like she had just downed a triple espresso.

She tried to go back to sleep, but her body was having none of it. Probably because it was 8:30 a.m. New York time. She wanted to text Danielle to see if she was awake, but her phone was in some lock box at the train depot an hour away—and she wasn't sure how to work her magic keycard.

After a much-needed shower, Gina took her time dressing and getting ready. Still, when she peered out of her window, it was mostly dark, with just the dim pre-dawn glow seeping through the shadows. She shut the light off in the room and let her eyes adjust to the darkness in an effort to make out the landscape surrounding Haverford Hall.

Her room faced the west side of the manor, and she could make out a line of dark trees a couple of dozen yards away. It also looked as if there were hedges and formal gardens down there, but she couldn't make out any detail.

Then she saw it.

A figure in white. A dark-haired woman. In a hooded nightgown. She looked like Princess Leia or something.

Is she sleepwalking? Or sleep gliding?

The woman *was* kind of gliding. Like a ghost. A very graceful ghost.

No, that's stupid. That's definitely not a ghost.

Still, Gina found herself mesmerized by the sight. The woman paused and looked around.

Then a compactly built person came into view, not as tall as the woman, and wearing dark clothes. Probably a short guy, judging from the way he moved. He had come from somewhere near the trees and headed directly towards the woman.

Before he could get too close, she raised her hand, signaling for him to stop. He said something, and she shook her head.

The two spoke for a minute or two—animatedly. Possibly even arguing. It was hard to tell, even with the twilight glow slightly brighter now.

As Gina watched, the woman withdrew something from the folds of her nightgown, a thick envelope or package. She couldn't make out exactly what it was.

The woman in white placed it on the ground and then turned and walked away quickly, back towards the manor house.

The man just stood there for a moment. He looked confused. Then he picked up the package and stalked away, disappearing into the trees.

Okay. Super weird.

Had she just witnessed a pre-dawn drug deal going down? She really wanted to know.

Gina grabbed her jacket and bolted from her room.

OUTSIDE, there was no sign of the woman in white or the short man. Gina stood shivering on the stone patio outside the manor house. By the time she had navigated her way downstairs and located an exit, dawn had broken and the first shafts of warm sunlight bathed the grounds.

The formal gardens were a typical geometric English arrangement with squared-off flower beds, perfectly shaped balls of shrubbery, a bevy of Greek statues, benches, and low concrete walls topped with big ornamental stone vases.

Beyond the gardens stood a row of fruit trees that looked like they had been fairly recent additions to the landscape. It was all very scenic, but Gina found herself still thinking about the short man and the woman in white.

She decided to stroll around the grounds towards the other side of Haverford Hall. The gravel lot near the front entrance was empty of vehicles, but in the distance, across the big circular lawn the size of a football field, she saw a stand of brick buildings. *Could the stables be over there?*

As she crunched along the gravel drive towards the buildings, a whirring sound caught her attention. She turned to see a small vehicle approaching her. It was about the size of a golf cart, and trimmed in green and gold like Millicent's antique car. And, of course, it had an umbrella logo on the hood. The driver was a man in a dark jacket, a white shirt, and tactical cargo pants. He drove the cart right up to her and then got out.

"Can I help you with something, ma'am?" The man was about her own age, tall and serious-looking, with graying hair and intense-looking eyes.

"Just out for a stroll," she said.

"You must be an early bird. Are you staying at Haverford?"

"Yes."

"Mind if I scan your keycard real quick?"

Panic rose from the pit of her stomach. Her worst nightmare had just come true. She had left her damn keycard in her room.

"I forgot it."

"You forgot it?"

"I know."

"They told you about the keycard in the station, didn't they?"

"Yes, they did."

"They told you how you're supposed to keep it with you at all times in Maidenwell?"

"Yes, they were very thorough. It's my bad. I didn't sleep very well, and I thought I saw some people down here in the garden, so I kind of just dashed—"

In one swift movement, the tall man grabbed a compact walkie-talkie from his belt and spoke into it. "We've got a 313 near the Winter Garden."

"Roger that," came the reply. "What's the status?"

"Guest says she misplaced her card."

"I did not *misplace* my card," Gina said indignantly. "I told you. It's in my room."

"Allegedly, it's in her room," the guy said into his walkie. "I'm going to verify. Be back in a bit." Then he turned to Gina. "Hop in."

"Do I have a choice?"

"Not really."

"I'm not trying to be difficult or anything, but who are you exactly?"

"Name's Reeve. Village Security."

"You're a cop?"

"No, ma'am. Maidenwell does not have municipal law enforcement."

"Huh?"

"The WBID contracts with private security. Us, specifically."

"WBID?"

"Windy Butte Improvement District. It's a state special tax district." Reeve patted the seat beside him. "Hop in. I'll explain while we drive."

Gina sighed. At least the golf cart didn't have any doors. So if things got weird, she could always run for it.

As they drove, Reeve explained that the Windy Butte Improvement District was a special public/private pilot program between the State of Oregon and Matthias Loneskum's company, the Regenschirm Group. WBID had a ten-year charter to develop, govern, provide services and utilities, regulate building and land use codes, and assess taxes within the district.

"So, what? Like a private government?"

"Close enough. Loneskum is a big fan of privatization."

"So I gathered."

"You don't approve?"

This guy Reeve is pretty perceptive, Gina thought. *For a rent-a-cop.* "I don't live in Oregon, so it's no skin off my nose."

"Oh yeah? Where are you from?"

Before Gina could open her mouth, he said, "New Jersey!"

"New York, actually."

"Close enough."

"What gave me away?" she asked. "And don't say my accent—because I don't have one!"

He favored her with a little half smile. "Everyone has an accent, but it wasn't your voice."

"What, then?"

He shrugged. "I don't know. Just a hunch. Maybe it was the way you were looking around at the sky when I first pulled up."

"We have a sky in New York. And besides, I wasn't looking at the sky. I was looking for the people I saw out my window."

"A man and a woman, you say?"

"Yes. He was short, and she was in a white nightgown.

Where are you driving us, by the way?" She had noticed he was taking a very roundabout route around Haverford Hall.

"Service entrance. Frau Loneskum prefers we keep our vehicles in the back. So what were these people doing?"

"It was hard to see. Buying drugs, maybe."

"What?" The golf cart lurched to a stop.

"Chill out. I'm not really sure what I saw. It looked like the woman was giving the guy some kind of thick envelope."

"You saw all that in the middle of the night from your window?"

"It wasn't the middle of the night. It was dawn. Or practically dawn. And, yes, I happened to be looking out of my window. And I happen to have very good vision."

"Contacts?" He glanced over and met her eyes.

"Nope."

"Eat lots of carrots?"

"I'm pretty sure that's an old wives' tale."

"I don't know. All that Vitamin A."

He began to drive again and turned the cart into a walled courtyard just south of the manor house. They headed down an alley edged with low brick utility buildings. One of them was an open garage filled with a line of carts parked in front of EV chargers.

Reeve pulled to a stop and hopped out. Gina did the same and looked around the curious antiquated garage. In many ways, this old garage was more interesting than the manor house itself. The high-tech chargers looked so strange, pulsing with light against the backdrop of old brick and wooden shelves filled with all kinds of vintage tools and parts.

"Is that all for show, or what?" She pointed at the mammoth, rust-ridden wrenches and collection of gears and flywheels that looked like relics from a steampunk convention.

"No, there are people sorting through that stuff. It's all vintage."

"Yeah, I can see."

"This way."

He led her back outside, across the charming cobblestone alley and toward the manor house. "This is the service block. That's the old larder. And these are storerooms. I think that building used to be a laundry."

"But it's all a re-creation, right?"

"Yes, all this was originally built in the early 1900s, but it was closely modeled on an English country house. And then Regenschirm has been restoring it even further for the past ten years."

"So weird." Gina shook her head in amusement. "A re-creation of a re-creation."

Reeve used his keycard to enter through a side door. Apparently the no-locks policy didn't extend to the exterior doors.

They navigated a narrow corridor and then to a staircase up to the residential floor. Then it took Gina a good ten minutes of wandering around to find her room.

"You know, your keycard can direct you back to your room," Reeve said with a smile. "Assuming you have your keycard in your possession, that is."

"I swear I will never let it out of my sight again!" she wailed in mock anguish. "But to be fair, no one ever trained me in the use of these keycards."

"It's pretty intuitive. Just play with it. You touch the edge to activate it. And then you can use voice or the touchscreen to do stuff. It's similar to a smartphone, but even more high-tech. I'll show you if you want."

"Yes, definitely."

Once she found the correct hallway, Gina spotted Danielle waiting outside her room.

"There you are!" Danielle said. "I've been trying to call you. Where have you been?"

"I got arrested."

"You are not under arrest," Reeve said.

"What's going on?" Danielle looked Reeve up and down.

"She was wandering around without her keycard," Reeve said.

"Who are you?"

As Reeve introduced himself to Danielle, Gina realized she had never told him her name. Once she retrieved her keycard from the dresser, they beamed each other their contact info.

"Get your stuff," Danielle told Gina. "Millicent's downstairs. We're going to get our tour of the village and grab some breakfast at the bakery."

"Yum." Gina turned to Reeve. "You want to come along?"

"Thanks, but I'm still on duty. You never know who's prowling around without their keycards."

"Ha ha."

He smiled at her. "Stay out of trouble, Gina Biletti."

As they made their way downstairs, Danielle pulled Gina close. "Tell. Me. Everything."

"There's not much to tell."

"You suck, you know that?" she laughed.

"I'm serious. He literally just picked me up because I was wandering around in the gardens without my ID."

"Babes, he *picked you up?* Oooh."

"Shut up."

"Gina's in love!"

"Again, shut up. I am officially ending this conversation."

"Whatever."

"Aren't you at all curious about why I was out wandering in the gardens at six in the morning?" Gina asked.

"Let me guess. You were sleepwalking."

Gina cut her off. "I saw a ghost."

"What?!"

"Well, she looked like a ghost. A woman in a white nightgown gliding through the gardens outside of my window."

"You were probably still asleep."

"I wasn't. The difference in the time zones messed me up. I was up at five-thirty a.m. Fully awake. Buzzing around my room."

"Been there, done that."

"I took a shower and got dressed and happened to look out the window. That's when I saw it."

"So what? Someone else was as wired as you and decided to walk it off."

"No, she met a guy."

"So did you."

"I'm serious. The woman met this short guy. They looked like they were arguing. And then she gave him a thick envelope."

"Sounds like a drug deal."

"That's *exactly* what I said!"

"What did Officer Hunky say?" Danielle asked.

"He seemed more bothered by my lack of keycard."

"You were told to keep it with you at all times, hon."

"You know me. I've never been very good with rules."

MILLICENT SEEMED happy to see them. Her green antique/modern car looked like it had just been washed, and she offered Gina and Danielle coffee from a big thermos with an umbrella logo on it.

"Yes, please!" Danielle said.

"How was your first night in Maidenwell?" Millicent asked, as they climbed into the car.

"Way too much wine," Gina said.

"Occupational hazard," Danielle said.

"You'll get used to it. We've got some great wine in town. And beer. It's kind of embarrassing."

"This coffee isn't half bad," Gina said.

"Locally roasted."

"I could get used to this."

Millicent drove around the big gravel circle and headed down the hill towards the village. In the daylight, Gina saw the full extent of the manor grounds, with walled gardens, orchards, and sprawling pastures. Soon they were in the village proper, and Gina took in all the details of the stone houses and cottages: thatched roofs, fieldstone walls, half-timbered facades.

"Wow," she said. "This is even more beautiful than I thought."

They wound their way through the village, which looked like it was fully awake—with people wandering the streets with baskets, doing their morning shopping.

Gina really felt that she had been transported to England—and possibly back a hundred years.

"That's the bakery," Millicent said, as they passed a cute two-story building with café tables and chairs arranged out on the sidewalk. "We'll just swing around the Village Green and I'll let you off."

"Why don't you come in with us?" Gina asked.

"Oh, I had breakfast already."

"Well, coffee then. Come on."

"Okay, if you don't mind—"

"Of course not. You can tell me what to get in case they are all out of black and white cookies."

As they drove around the square, Gina got a much better view of the old church. It wasn't the typical little town church you might find in small-town U.S.A., with white clapboard and steeples. This church was made of brick and stone, with an imposing square tower that looked like it belonged on a castle.

Millicent easily found a place to park, since there weren't many cars at all in Maidenwell. But there were a fair number of bicycles parked on the sidewalk. Most looked to be electric.

Even though there was a definite chill in the air, the morning sun felt warm on Gina's body. They walked past various shops, and Millicent greeted several people by name.

The bakery had a boldly painted red façade and a pair of wide floor-to-ceiling windows on either side of the front door. A sign above everything read LIBNEY CAFÉ & TEA ROOM.

Even before she had fully stepped through the door, Gina was hit by the smell of freshly baked bread and pastries mixed with the powerful aroma of roasted coffee beans. It was incredible. Inside, a long room stretched to the right and left, filled with a dozen or more tables. Towards the back, a marble-topped counter stood with a big case filled with all sorts of goodies. Wall shelves held baskets of fresh bread and rows of jams and other sweets.

"That's it," Gina said. "I'm never leaving this place."

"But you haven't even tasted anything?" Millicent smiled at her.

"Doesn't matter. Have my clothes sent down."

Everything for the next thirty minutes was a blur. A blur of gruyere and leek toasties, poached pear and raspberry almond cream tarts, brioche buns with ground pistachios and a dusting of chocolate, and the most delicious latte Gina had ever tasted.

When they were done, Gina felt like she was actually waddling out the door. "I need to walk that off."

"Me too," Danielle said.

"You? You hardly ate anything!"

"Except that salmon and broccoli quiche and about a million of those little chouquettes."

"The quiche was gluten free, so it doesn't count!"

They spent the next hour or so wandering through the village, down narrow lanes and cobblestone streets, window shopping and regular shopping at all the little shops.

At one point, Millicent motioned for them to follow her through a stone archway into a passageway between buildings. It was so narrow that Gina could stretch her arms out and touch both walls.

"You're not taking us in here to murder us, are you?" Gina asked.

Millicent laughed. "No way. This is the Tangles."

"The what?"

"Tangles, babes," Danielle said. "It's modeled after the Shambles in York."

"Still not ringing a bell."

"Just look around," Millicent said.

They emerged into an interior courtyard of sorts, and the alley passage branched into several more narrow alleys winding off in all directions. Lining either side of the alleys were compact storefronts of all sorts of businesses, from clothing stores to a pottery shop, to shops selling artisanal food and drink.

"It's our own version of Diagon Alley," Millicent said.

"I'm guessing that there's no Starbucks here," Gina said.

"No chains of any kind," Millicent said. "Everything's one-of-a-kind and locally owned."

"That's impressive," Gina said. She couldn't get over the architecture. Everything looked real and authentic, not at all like a theme-park version of an English village. And yet, it wasn't all ancient. CCTV cameras perched on rooftops. Flat-panel displays showed menus outside restaurant doors. And you paid for everything using your keycard.

Before they returned to the car, Millicent took them to her

studio, a brick building north of the Village Green and behind the big church. The Barrelworks Artist Collective was cluttered with all kinds of printing and paper-making presses, work tables, drawers filled with metal and wood type, paper-making equipment, frames, drills, and a ton of other stuff that Gina couldn't really identify.

Millicent was going to gift them both with handmade journals, but Gina insisted on paying. "I really need to practice with this keycard."

"Besides, we're on an expense account," Danielle said.

"Oh, that's nice."

"Perk of being the boss."

It was close to noon when they finally headed back up the hill to Haverford Hall. And that was when Gina saw the ambulance.

six

. . .

THE AMBULANCE WAS NOT AN ANTIQUE. It was a compact modern van with lights and flashers going. Paramedics were loading someone on a stretcher into the back of the ambulance, but Gina couldn't see who it was.

Staff members from the Hall directed their car away from the scene.

"I better drop you off, so they can keep the area clear," Millicent said. She drove around to the side of the manor and pulled over near where Gina had been wandering around earlier that morning.

"I hope everything's okay," Millicent said.

"Yeah," Gina said. "Doesn't look great."

"Well, let me know if you need anything."

After Millicent pulled away, Gina suggested they try to go around to the side entrance near the formal gardens. Now that she had her keycard, entering via the side door shouldn't be a problem.

They navigated around a low wall and walked down to the formal garden with its meticulously pruned shrubbery and Greek statues.

"There we go." Gina led the way towards a door off the manor house's stone patio.

Inside, the tension was palpable. All the staff spoke in hushed voices and several uniformed security people prowled the hallways. As they headed up to their rooms, Gina spotted Édouard Orville, the dapper gentleman they had met on their way to the train.

"What's going on?"

The man's eyes were wide with panic, and he mopped his brow with a handkerchief. "It's horrible. Just horrible."

"What?" Gina asked.

"Vanessa Schaeffer. She's dead."

"Oh my god. How?"

"They're saying she had a heart attack. When Stanley woke up this morning, she had passed. A tragedy."

The news set Gina's mind spinning. She had spoken to Vanessa Schaeffer last night, and she seemed fine. "How old was she?"

"She couldn't have been more than forty, forty-five," Édouard said. "She was in the prime of her life. Stanley is devastated. And Frau Loneskum is beside herself. They will have to cancel the auction."

"Ms. LaTour? Ms. Biletti?"

Danielle and Gina both turned at the same time. Reeve, the security guy, strode down the hallway towards them.

"Ms. Grier needs to speak with you."

"Who?" Gina asked.

"Peyton Grier. She's the District Executive for Maidenwell. This way."

Gina looked at Danielle questioningly, but her friend just nodded. *I guess I'm coming along,* Gina thought.

Reeve led them along a winding route back to a service elevator that looked way too small and rickety to be safe. Gina wasn't a fan of normal elevators, let alone this ironwork cage that seemed like it was a century out of date. But when they entered, Gina discovered the elevator was like everything else in Maidenwell. It only *looked* old. When Reeve opened an ancient-looking panel box, Gina glimpsed an extremely high-tech display panel with all kinds of diagnostic info.

His fingers danced over the touch display and the elevator soundlessly descended, moving precisely without a single shudder or bump.

The doors opened to reveal a stark, modern-looking hallway with recessed lighting. In the background, a faint hum of air conditioning sounded.

"Where are we?" Gina asked.

"Administrative block," Reeve said. "Obviously not part of the original structure."

"Obviously," Gina said.

"That's why we're tucked underground."

"Underground? How far underground?" Gina recalled the fact that Oregon was in some sort of high-risk seismic zone.

"Not far. Thirty, forty feet."

"Aren't you worried about earthquakes?"

"Not much chance of that here, on this side of the mountains."

That was a relief. *One more gold star for Maidenwell.*

They passed various office pods and conference rooms, and then Reeve escorted them into an alcove where a single administrative assistant was working at a computer on a very tidy desk. She looked up as they entered.

"PR people," Reeve announced.

"Go ahead in," the young woman said.

They pushed through into a large office with a round conference table and a stand-up desk. Behind the desk loomed Peyton Grier, a tall, severe-looking woman in her sixties with short dark hair, no jewelry, and what Gina guessed was supposed to be a power suit. If power suits were actually still a thing.

Peyton was finishing up a phone conversation, so Gina looked around the office. It was minimalistic and functional, with no personal items on display. She did notice a big wall-mounted monitor and some video conferencing gear set up near the conference table.

Peyton hung up without saying goodbye and looked directly at Gina. "Danielle LaTour?"

Gina shook her head. "I'm Gina Biletti. That's Danielle."

Peyton put on a pair of reading glasses and consulted her computer. "ERF/LaTour, right?"

"Yes," Danielle said.

"Fine. We're here to talk about the death of Vanessa Schaeffer and any implications for Maidenwell, as well as the messaging surrounding this event."

"Obviously, I have a lot of questions," Danielle said.

"I would be disappointed if you did not. Here's what we know. According to his statement, at approximately 9:15 this morning, Stanley Schaeffer knocked on his wife's door. He didn't get any answer, so he—"

"Wait a second," Gina said. "They have separate rooms?"

Peyton pushed down her reading glasses and fixed Gina with a look. "Apparently, Mr. Schaeffer's CPAP machine kept Mrs. Schaeffer awake, so she preferred her own room."

"Got it."

"Mr. Schaeffer then entered the room and saw his wife in bed, seemingly asleep. When he was unable to rouse her, he ran from the room and called for help."

Danielle had pulled a small notebook from her bag and began furiously scribbling notes. Gina felt as though she should take notes as well, but didn't have a notebook of her own. And she was certainly not going to risk Peyton Grier's ire by asking for one.

"A staff member, Roger Purl, attended to Mr. Schaeffer and followed him to Mrs. Schaeffer's room. According to his report, Purl discovered Vanessa Schaeffer in her bed and unresponsive. He attempted CPR and told Mr. Schaeffer to call 9-1-1."

"You've got 9-1-1 here?" Gina asked.

Again, Peyton Grier slid down her glasses and fixed Gina with a withering look. But Gina felt it was a fair question. After all, they were in a tiny little village in the middle of nowhere that you had to take a train to get to.

"Yes, in fact, we do," Peyton Grier said. "Maidenwell is fortunate to possess a very effective and efficient emergency services team. And they were immediately dispatched to Haverford Hall. Fortunately, Dr. Kurian was already on the premises—"

"Who's—?"

Peyton Grier cut Gina off. "Dr. Kurian is Frau Loneskum's personal physician. She had an early appointment with him."

"Must be nice to have your own doctor on call," Gina said.

"Ms. Biletti, one more outburst and you can leave," Peyton snapped. "We don't have time for your interruptions."

"Sorry."

"Unfortunately, neither Roger Purl nor Dr. Kurian could revive Ms. Schaeffer. Her body was taken to the hospital for further examination,"

Gina clamped her lips together before she could utter a word of surprise that Maidenwell also had a hospital. What else did they have? Their own international airport? Maybe an opera house?

"Medevac's on its way from Pendleton," Peyton said. "Soon it will be in the county's hands."

"Do they have a cause of death?" Danielle asked.

"Not yet, but Kurian believes Ms. Schaeffer suffered from a sudden cardiac arrest, and Mr. Schaeffer confirmed his wife had complained of some discomfort the night before."

"How old was she?" Reeve asked.

Peyton checked her notes. "Forty-five."

"She looked younger," Danielle said. "Still, forty-five is pretty young to die of a heart attack. Poor thing."

"Apparently, she was a smoker."

"Well, yes, but she was also an athlete," Gina blurted out. She couldn't help herself.

Peyton narrowed her eyes at Gina. "How do you know that?"

"I can tell. I recognized how she was standing. The natural turn-out of her feet. Also, the way she moved. It was obvious."

"Well, you happen to be correct. Ms. Schaeffer was a professional ballet dancer for twelve years. But even professional dancers can suffer heart attacks."

Gina said nothing.

"The important thing, from a PR perspective, is that there wasn't anything unusual about her death. Strictly speaking."

"Like what?" Danielle asked.

"Drugs, signs of foul play—"

"Tainted hors d'oeuvres," Gina suggested.

"Okay, that's it!" Peyton Grier's face flushed with anger. "Out!"

"But—"

"Out. Now."

"I'm so sorry for my co-worker's behavior," Danielle glared at Gina.

Gina felt herself turn beet red. "I didn't mean to—"

"Reeve, escort this woman out of here."

Me and my big mouth, Gina thought.

Reeve walked Gina to the elevator, giving her the silent treatment the whole way. But then, right before the doors closed, he said, "Smart observation about her being a dancer."

Hmmm.

That was a nice thing to say, but Gina couldn't help feeling horrible. This wasn't the first time her lack of a filter had gotten her into trouble. She had been written up several times at work for essentially not knowing when to shut up.

Hopefully, Danielle wasn't too mad at her.

Gina didn't want to go sulk in her room—not when there were acres of beautiful grounds to sulk in. So she decided to go find the stables and maybe take a look at this million-dollar alpaca before he got shipped home.

With the untimely passing of Vanessa Schaeffer, there was no way Frau Loneskum would continue with the auction. In fact, Gina wouldn't be surprised to see everyone departing on this afternoon's train.

What a mess.

As she wandered around the manor house, she thought about the poor woman. Not poor as in destitute, obviously. Poor as in unfortunate. There had been something about Vanessa Schaeffer when they chatted on the train. A sadness. Maybe even something else.

And the fact that she and Gina were the same age was brutal. But, to be fair, a heart attack could get you at any age. Still, to be struck down like that, so young. It wasn't fair.

Gina crossed the big gravel driveway and made her way towards the buildings she had seen right before Reeve had picked her up. Hopefully, she was heading in the right direction for the stables.

It seemed weird that no one else was around. Maybe everyone was back in their rooms packing.

A group of low buildings stretched out in front of her, but they didn't appear to be stables. There were no dry lots or fenced areas. As she drew closer, she saw that these were sheds and storage buildings of some sort. She peeked in through one window and saw a row of tractors, large mowers, and all sorts of professional-looking landscaping equipment. But no alpacas.

She followed a gravel path beyond the buildings down to another group of formal gardens. Several small greenhouses stood in front of a stand of fruit trees.

An older man, stooped and gray, emerged from one of the greenhouses holding a tray of little pots.

"Excuse me," Gina called.

The man stopped and looked around, trying to identify the source of the sound.

Poor thing's probably as blind as a bat. Gina waved her arms and hustled over.

"Oh, hello there," the man said.

"Hi. I was wondering if you could tell me how to get to the stables."

"The stables?"

"Yes, there's supposed to be an alpaca there."

"There are several, I wager," the man said. "But you, dear lady, are nowhere near the stables."

"What?"

"Stables are clear in the other direction: southeast of the main house." He pointed back towards Haverford Hall. "There's a wide trail that goes through the junipers. Just follow that."

"Is it far?"

"Not really. Ten or fifteen minutes by foot. I'd run you over in the quad meself, but I need to get these over to the fernery before they dry out."

"Fernery?"

"The Frau has one of the largest collections of ferns on the West Coast. Got to put 'em somewhere."

"I actually did not know that anyone collected ferns," Gina said. "I guess you learn something new every day."

"Just follow the path back through the Winter Garden. Then you'll be in view of the house. Veer around to the left and you'll see the bridle trail, clear as day. I think there are even some signs."

“Thanks.”

“Oh, and before you head back, you may want to visit our hedge maze.”

“You have a hedge maze?”

“Aye.”

“Like in *The Shining*?”

“I don’t know about that. But see for yourself. It’s right back there.” He pointed beyond the greenhouses.

“Okay, maybe I will. Thank you.”

Why not? Gina thought. *As long as there aren’t any axe murderers hanging out in there.*

seven

. . .

GINA FOLLOWED a little winding path between the greenhouses and through the grove of fruit trees. The path opened up to a lawn area and there it was, just as advertised. A hedge maze.

It looked like an immense block of dense shrubbery, a clipped green wall easily a hundred feet wide. A single dark entrance was set in the middle of the hedge wall, flanked by stone statues. As she drew closer, Gina saw the walls were at least two feet over her head. There would be no way to peek over the top to get her bearings.

Screw it, she thought. *How often do I get the chance to wander through a real-life hedge maze?*

Gina took a deep breath and walked through the opening. She found herself in a shadowy green passage leading straight into the heart of the maze. After fifty feet or so, the passage opened into a sunny circular area with a patina-encrusted metal sundial set on a white stone pedestal. There was one exit besides the way she came in.

So far, so good.

It was actually kind of peaceful in here. And quiet. Gina stood, letting the sun warm her face. Her mind wandered back to Vanessa Schaeffer. Had she been the woman Gina saw in the gardens this morning? It was so dark, she couldn't be sure.

But if she was, how did that fit with her death?

Did Vanessa go for an early morning stroll, meet the guy in the hoodie, give him a package, and then go back to her room, climb back into her bed, have a heart attack, and die?

It made no sense.

Just then, she heard a cough. And another.

Gina froze. Was someone here in the maze with her?

"Hello?" she called tentatively. "Is someone there?"

Another cough, and then a quiet "Hello" back from a female voice.

"Oh, hello." Gina had no idea who might be here in the maze with her. "Are you, um, lost?"

"Lost?" the female voice said with a giggle. "Who knows? Maybe." It was a young-sounding voice, for sure. And there was an edge of panic in it.

"Hang on," Gina said. "I'll come and find you. Keep talking."

"What do you want me to say?"

Gina left the circular area and followed a winding path, homing in on the girl's voice. "Whatever you want."

"La dee da, what a wonderful day. Wait. No, it's not. That was a horrible thing to say. I'm such an idiot."

"No, you're not. Keep talking. I'm getting closer."

The maze's path curved back on itself a few times, but then ended in a T. "Hello?" Gina called.

"Over here."

Gina followed the left path for thirty feet and was rewarded with the sight of another little room within the hedge maze. There, the young woman with pink hair sat on a stone bench. Her eyes were red, but judging by the plume of vapor in the air, it wasn't from crying.

"You found me," she said.

"Yes, I did. Rebecca, isn't it?"

"Becca, yeah."

"I'm Gina."

"The PR lady. I remember."

"Well, I'm kind of more market research."

Gina tried not to stare as Becca took a hit from her vape pen, but the younger woman definitely noticed. "It's legal in Oregon."

"Yeah, cool. It's legal in New York, too." Despite the legal status of marijuana, Gina couldn't help but think of smoking —or vaping—pot as an illicit activity. It was just how her generation viewed the substance.

"You want some?" She offered the vape pen to Gina.

"I'm tempted, but it's been a while. Plus, I'm on a bunch of prescription meds. Not sure what kind of interactions—"

"No prob. More for me." Becca smiled a crooked smile.

"So, this hedge maze, huh?" Gina sat down on the bench beside Becca.

"Yeah, I keep thinking of that old movie with Jack Nicholson," Becca said.

"It's called *The Shining*."

"Yeah, that's it. My aunt took me to the hotel that they filmed at."

"In Colorado?"

"No, it's actually not too far from where we are. Mt. Hood."

"I don't know where that is. This is my first time in Oregon."

"In the mountains. On the way to Portland."

"Do they have a hedge maze?" Gina asked.

"I don't think so. That might have been a special effect."

They said nothing for a while. Gina sat and Becca vaped.

Finally, to break the silence, Gina asked, "Were you close with Mrs. Schaeffer?"

Becca sputtered out vapor. "You do realize that Stanley Schaeffer is the Devil, don't you? The literal Devil!"

"I know you laid into him on the train."

"Oh my god, that was nothing. You need to know what he's up to. You need to get the truth out there."

"That's not really what—"

But Becca was on a roll. "What do you know about the alpaca industry?"

"Not much, I'm afraid. It's been less than twenty-four hours since I learned there *was* an alpaca industry."

"Well, there is. We have over two hundred thousand alpacas in the U.S. Thousands of farms. Most are mom and pop operations, but the four biggest are here this weekend."

"For the auction, right?"

"Yeah."

"So your farm is one of the biggest?" Gina asked.

"My aunt's ranch, actually, but she's retiring." She took another hit. "Soon, I hope."

"Who else?"

"Besides the Schaeffers? Uh, Schaeffer, singular…"

"Yeah."

"Édouard Orville and Frankie Roth both own large operations. But I wouldn't consider them serious contenders for Florrie. It's really between us and Schaeffer. Or was."

"How come just the two of you?"

"Édouard is very old school. Cautious. He's smart, but in an academic way. You know?"

"Not really, but I'll take your word for it. What about Frankie Roth? I thought she was a big deal artist."

"She is. But she also raises alpacas. Her ex-husband's alpacas. You know her deal, right?"

Gina shook her head. "Maybe I'll have one little toke."

Becca grinned at her and passed over the vape pen. "*Toke?* Like Cheech and Chong?"

"I'm surprised you know who they are."

Becca shrugged. "I watch YouTube." She showed Gina how to operate the pen.

"This design is really cute," Gina said. The vape pen was emblazoned with a pattern of cartoon leprechauns.

"That's from *Pot o' Gold*. Get it?"

"Not really."

"It was a cartoon when I was a kid. Really big in Japan and Korea."

"Okay, back to Frankie Roth." Gina took a hit, but didn't really feel anything. *Maybe I'm too old for this.*

When Becca told Gina who Frankie Roth's ex was, Gina coughed in disbelief.

"Are you serious? How did she land one of the biggest stars in the world?"

"They're both Triscologists. The Church set them up."

Gina knew a little about Triscology, mostly from the exposés she watched on Netflix. It was some sort of weird cult that believed in the power of Threes. They had gotten their claws into a lot of celebs, including Frankie Roth's ex, the biggest action star in the past twenty years, and currently the poster child for Triscology.

"Anyway," Becca continued. "She got his ranch and several thousand alpacas, but had to change the name, of course. Now it's called Roth Ranch, and she names all her sires after famous works of art."

"Wow, so she does all her art stuff *and* runs a huge ranch?"

"As if." Becca took the pen back and took a deep hit, blowing out a big plume of vapor. "She doesn't do anything personally. She's got an enormous staff. Something like fifty people just working the ranch itself."

"Really?"

"For now…" Becca trailed off.

"What do you mean?"

"I probably shouldn't be talking about it."

"Screw that, we're spilling the tea, sister!" Gina grinned and took back the vape pen.

Becca laughed. "Okay, but you can't tell anyone."

"Who am I going to tell?"

"And this is completely off the record."

"Of course. Dish!"

"Frankie Roth's nearly broke. I think getting her hands on Florrie is her last chance at keeping herself afloat."

"What? She's a mega-successful artist. She sells tons of paintings for big bucks. And Danielle says she owns three galleries."

Becca shrugged. "What can I say? My aunt knows a few people that work in Frankie's office and they've seen the books. Apparently, she has to give fifty percent of her income to the Church of Triscology. She's going to be bankrupt by the end of the year."

"That's horrible."

"It's her own choice."

"You're right," Gina said, taking another hit. "You are so right." Maybe she was starting to feel the pot. Just the slightest bit.

"*Religion is the opioid crisis of the masses*. Isn't that what they say?"

"Close enough," Gina said. "Okay. Stanley Schaeffer…"

"You mean the Devil?"

"Yeah, I want to hear everything. Everything."

"Oh my god, where do I start?"

"Maybe start with why he's the Devil. But first, do you know where the stables are?"

"Sure. They're very nice. Frau Farbissina needs to have everything just so."

"Frau Farbissina? Like from *Austin Powers*?"

"*Ja!*" Becca yelled.

Gina convulsed with laughter. She wasn't sure why. This

caused Becca to join in, and the two of them couldn't stop laughing for several minutes.

When she finally could breathe again, Gina said, "I was actually trying to see this King of Alpacas for myself when I got lost and ended up here."

"You want to go to the stables? I'll go with."

"Yeah, but only if you tell me about Stanley on the way."

"I guess. If you really want to know. But it's a disgusting story."

It actually took them a little longer than expected to find their way out of the maze, which struck both of them as pretty funny. But eventually they figured out the exit and found themselves on the lawn in front of the maze.

"I'm going to put this away." Becca waved her vape pen dramatically. "Frau Farbissina has spies everywhere. I need to watch what I say. Even about Stanley."

"C'mon," Gina said. "We're totally alone."

"That's what you think. I heard she's got cameras all over this place. It's super high tech."

"Even in the maze?"

"I didn't think of that!" Becca started laughing again.

As they made their way through the gardens and back towards Haverford Hall, Becca unloaded all the dirt on Stanley Schaeffer. Spies be damned.

Before the alpaca business, Stanley Schaeffer was the CEO of an orthopedic shoe company somewhere in the Midwest. He mismanaged his company, almost driving it into the ground, but then ended up marrying Vanessa. Her family owned slaughterhouses and meat-packing companies, and they kind of bailed Stanley out and brought him into the family business.

"Failing upward," Gina said. "I've seen *that* before."

"Yeah, the whole story is gross. And it gets grosser." Becca continued with her narrative.

About twelve years ago, Stanley and Vanessa started

buying up tons of alpacas with the idea of creating a large-scale industrialized fiber-producing operation in Idaho with a big mill. He handled the operational side while she met with fashion designers and big clothing conglomerates.

"His aim is a mega-herd," Becca said. "A million pounds of raw alpaca fiber a year."

"Is that a lot?"

"Put it this way, the wool industry produces about seventeen million pounds of wool."

"Much more."

"Yes, but all that raw wool sells for maybe thirty million. Thirty-two, max."

"I'd take that," Gina said.

"Alpaca fiber is much more valuable. A million pounds of raw fiber can sell for forty-five or fifty million. Much more if you actually produce yarn with it."

"I have to admit. Live math isn't my strong suit. I'm more at home with spreadsheets." Gina was starting to feel the effects of the pot for sure.

But Becca was on a roll. "One sheep produces nine or ten bucks of wool per year. An alpaca can produce three hundred dollars' worth of fiber per year."

"Okay, I get that. But I'm missing the whole Devil part of this story."

Becca made a face. "He doesn't care about the animals at all. He's breeding for volume and culling any animal that doesn't produce enough fiber."

"Culling?"

"Slaughtering. He's also trying to start up an alpaca meat industry. It's disgusting."

"People eat alpacas?"

"They do in South America. But it's out of necessity. A lot of indigenous people there are very poor and they don't have much food. We have no shortage of meat here. There's no reason to have an alpaca meat industry in America." Becca's face formed into a disgusted frown.

"Are you a vegetarian?"

"Vegan. You?"

"Aspirational."

As they circled around Haverford Hall, Becca told Gina much more than she ever wanted to know about exotic meats and state regulations and how most of the Schaeffers' slaughtered alpacas ended up as dog food. She also shared that Stanley's disregard for animals extended to wild animals as well. He fancied himself a big game hunter and had a photo in his office of him posing with an African lion he had murdered.

"I hate him. I really do. Both of them." Becca began to cry.

Gina pulled her close. "Hey, I'm sorry I asked. I didn't mean to upset you."

"No, you should know about it. Everyone should. It's just so senseless. And cruel. There's no reason for it."

Once she got her tears under control, Becca shared her own vision of ethical alpaca keeping. The young woman believed that every alpaca was valuable and should be cared for throughout its natural life.

"It's not just about fiber for high-end fashion, and opening up new markets," she said, wiping her eyes. "And it's not just about the animals hitting their quotas of fiber or getting slaughtered."

Becca went on to explain how she was going to take her aunt's ranch in a new direction. If they managed to win the auction of Florrie, they'd have the chance to redefine the U.S. alpaca industry and get everyone to adopt new standards for alpaca value.

Gina admired the young woman's passion and idealism, but she didn't know enough about the alpaca world to judge whether Becca's vision actually made sense. But Gina was certainly aware of consumer trends, and Becca was right.

Ethical treatment of animals was increasingly important to people. Especially the younger generations.

They walked along a wide bridle trail through stands of juniper trees. The temperature had warmed up a lot, and Gina slipped out of her sweater and tied it around her shoulders. She was definitely a little buzzed, but not so much that she wasn't fascinated by Becca's inside scoop on everyone. Although Gina did realize that she probably should steer the conversation away from animal slaughter or anything else that might trigger Becca.

"So what's the deal with Edward?" she asked. "You said he was old school."

"It's Édouard," Becca said, with an exaggerated French accent.

"Oh, excuse moi. *Édouard*."

They both laughed.

"He's all right," Becca said.

"But how does he fall on these new standards of yours?"

"I honestly have no idea. I want to think that if it comes down to supporting us or the Schaeffers, he'd support us. I know he's no fan of Stanley."

"Oh?"

"Yeah, I haven't mentioned the other thing that makes Stanley the Devil."

"Don't hold back now!"

"He's a slimy horn dog."

"What?"

"He's slept with half the women in the alpaca industry—including a lady who Édouard was with. Janette Something. They weren't married or anything, but still. They broke up because of Stanley Schaeffer."

"Who else did he sleep with? Not the Frau?"

Becca burst out laughing. "Oh my god, I wouldn't be surprised if he moved on her. But, no, not as far as I know. Let's see. Donna Gardner. Sherri St. Marie. Both of the Visnick twins. The vet that's here, but that was a while ago. And that chick from the winery. I think she's his current ho."

"Hold on, slow down. This is a lot. The wine lady from the party last night?" Gina searched her mind for the woman's name. "Amagansett? No, that's not right."

"I don't know her name, but I saw them together," Becca said. "There's definitely something going on."

"I wonder if Vanessa knew."

"Oh, she definitely did. In fact, my aunt thinks Vanessa was already planning to divorce Stanley, but he convinced her to wait after the auction. She's got a prenup and everything, so Stanley is going to be screwed. Which is something I love. Love, love, love!"

The trail ended in an open area with a block of brick buildings. Beyond them stretched several fenced pastures.

"Those are the stables?"

They didn't look like any sort of stables Gina had ever seen before. The closest building was a long two-story structure with dormer windows on the top floor, and a big arched entrance way topped by a clock tower and a cupola with a weathervane. The arched entrance way was at least twenty feet high and half that wide. It looked like you could drive a tank through it.

"Yeah, it's a little much. But all in the name of authenticity, right?" Becca said with a smirk.

"And all this is for the alpacas?"

"The Frau's got some pricey horses too. Somewhere in here."

The air felt cooler as they passed through the big arched entryway, and Gina caught a faint whiff of hay and manure. As they stood in the interior courtyard, she admired the architecture. "What are these other buildings?"

"Not sure. I've only been here once. I would guess that some are tack rooms. Maybe some used to be where they stored the old coaches. There's got to be someone around here that we can ask—"

At that moment, a weird buzzing/chiming sound filled the air.

"What is that?" Gina asked.

"My keycard." Becca fished it out of her pocket and Gina saw the card's display was lit up.

"It's a text from my aunt." As she read through it, Becca's face broke out into a big grin. "Oh my god. The auction is back on! This is awesome!"

"Are you sure?" Gina asked.

"Yeah. Maybe Stanley's greed outweighed mourning for Vanessa. Who knows? I need to go. My aunt needs me back at the hotel to prep."

"I'll come with you," Gina said.

"No, you're here. Go see Florrie! He's either right in there..." She pointed to one of the stable doors. "...or he's on the other side in the dry lot. They don't let him loose—for obvious reasons."

"Okay, I guess. I am curious about him."

"It'll be fine. When you're done, just follow the path back."

"Sounds good. Well, really nice hanging with you, Becca."

"You, too!" She pressed something into Gina's hands and winked. "For later."

It was her cartoon leprechaun vape pen.

"I can't take that!" Gina said.

"I've got another one just like it. We'll celebrate when I win Florentine!"

eight

. . .

GINA ENTERED the building through the door Becca had indicated. She found herself in a long, cheery, barn-like room divided into stalls and lit by the sunlight pouring in through high clerestory windows. The whole place smelled like fresh hay, and Gina guessed it must be stored up above in the second-story loft that extended over the stalls.

The stalls themselves all had outer doors which opened into some sort of yard behind the stable block. Some stalls had animals in them—and Gina got her first glimpse of real live alpacas.

Wow. They're just as fluffy and cute as I imagined!

A tall black alpaca nibbled at a bowl of grain and ignored her. Gina wondered if this was the famous Florrie, but as she moved closer to the creature's stall, she saw a brass stall sign. It read "Nyx." The tan-colored alpaca in the next stall was named "Joven."

Gina went from stall to stall until she finally found Florentine's name. Unfortunately, his pen was empty and the door to the yard was open. He was probably out catching some rays in the warm autumn afternoon.

She went back to watch Nyx some more. He was a beautiful animal, with curly fur that looked incredibly soft.

"Hey, sweetie. How are you? Are you enjoying your lunch? Sorry I didn't bring you a sugar cube or anything."

Nyx continued to ignore her.

"Okay, fine. Be like that. I'll find your buddy. Maybe he's friendlier."

Between two of the stalls, she spotted a person-sized door that seemed to lead out into the back area. But before she could even explore in that direction, she heard an ear-splitting cry. It was a shrill, high-pitched noise. *Eeep! Eeep! Eeep! Eeep! Eeep! Eeep!*

Whatever it was, it was coming from outside.

Eeep! Eeep! Eeep! Eeep! Eeep! Eeep!

As Gina pushed through the back door, she noticed a sternly worded sign reminding people to keep the gates closed. Outside, she immediately found the source of the shrill *beeping* sound.

It was an alpaca. His eyes were fixed on something in the next pen over and his sides were heaving like bellows.

Eeep! Eeep! Eeep! Eeep! Eeep! Eeep!

Gina moved further into the pen, trying to see what had upset the alpaca so much.

There, about forty feet away, in a fenced-off section of the pen, a little boy was whipping a terrified white alpaca with a riding crop.

The boy had red hair.

"STOP IT!" Gina screamed as loud as she could.

The boy ignored her and kept chasing after the alpaca. The little bastard was surprisingly quick and agile.

Frantically, Gina surveyed the area, trying to figure out

how to get into the next stall over. "Leave him alone!" she yelled.

Eeep! Eeep! Eeep! Eeep! Eeep! Eeep!

"Yeah, I'm working on it!" she called back to the screaming alpaca.

Finally, she spotted a gate between the two pens and ran over to it. After fumbling with the overly complicated latch, she flung it open and dashed through.

The kid had herded the alpaca into the back corner of the pen, where a gate was completely open to the pasture beyond.

"No!" Gina screamed. She felt her blood pounding in her ears.

But it was too late. The kid lashed the riding crop against the alpaca's haunches and the frantic animal bounded through the gate to escape.

Gina ran over to the kid. "What did you do? Was that Florrie?"

The kid ignored her.

She dashed to the outer gate just in time to see the alpaca racing away over a hill.

Shit.

The kid glared at her, but he still hadn't said a word.

"What the hell did you think you were doing? Huh?"

Gina looked around. *Why aren't there any stable boys or anyone looking after the alpacas? This is ridiculous.*

"Come on. I'm taking you back to your mother. And we need to tell someone that there's an alpaca on the loose. Probably one worth two million bucks."

She put her hand on the kid's back to steer him towards the stable building, but he twisted away and started towards the back gate.

Gina managed to grab the edge of his shirt and was pulling him back when—*whack!*—the riding crop whipped around and smacked against her bare upper arm, searing it with pain.

She gasped and stumbled back in shock, and the kid dashed away out into the pasture.

"You're not supposed to be in here!" a male voice barked at her.

She turned to see Stanley Schaeffer stalking towards her. His eyes darted around the pen. "What did you do?"

"I didn't do anything." She tried to rub her arm, but the pain was too intense. That little brat was stronger than he looked. "That kid let him out."

Stanley moved over to the open gate and called out in a big, booming voice. "Here, Paca, Paca, Paca! Here, Paca!"

"Do they really come when you call them?"

"Some do. But I don't think he'll go far. They're herd animals, after all." He looked disdainfully at Gina. "This is no place for horseplay. You and your little partner-in-crime could be in real trouble."

"He's not my partner-in-crime! I don't even know him."

"We'll have Security sort this out." His fingers danced over his keycard, no doubt alerting Maidenwell's Finest to the situation.

How come everyone knows how to use their damn keycards except me? Gina brushed hay and dirt from her clothes. "I'm very sorry about your wife, by the way."

Stanley barely looked up from his keycard. "It was quite a shock."

"If you don't mind me asking, what are you doing here in the stables? I would think you would be, you know, back in your room. Grieving."

He fixed her with a stern look. "Everyone grieves in their own way. But the show must go on."

"You mean the auction?"

"Precisely. It's what Vanessa would have wanted."

Before Gina could say anything further, Stanley bellowed "Tomas!" He strode to the far end of the pen and called again. And again.

"Is Tomas the alpaca that escaped?"

"What? No, of course not. Tomas is—"

At that moment, a man came around the side of the stables. He was short and dark with beautiful raven hair. "Hola!"

"Get the quad, my man! Florentine's loose."

"What? I just cleaned his hoofs." The man—Tomas—spoke with a noticeable accent.

"It just happened. This lady let him out."

"Me?" Gina exclaimed. "It wasn't me. I told you. It was the kid. He was whipping the alpaca."

"Whipping?" Tomas asked. "Florentine? This is not good."

"Of course it's not good," Stanley snapped. "If anyone traumatized my sire—"

"He's not your sire yet," Gina said. "And if he's traumatized, talk to the kid, not me!"

"*Rápido,* Tomas. Go!"

"*Dale, dale*!" He disappeared back into the stables.

"Who's that?" Gina asked.

"Tomas."

"I didn't see him at the party last night."

"You wouldn't have."

"Why's that?"

"Because he's the help. He lives here in the stables. He's Yvonne's pet. She brought him over from Peru."

"Really?"

"Yes, he's a *morochuco*. A Peruvian cowboy. Quite knowledgeable about alpacas, in his own way."

"That's pretty interesting."

"If you say so. I just hope—for your sake—that he finds Florentine. If something were to happen to him..." Stanley abruptly looked down at his keycard again.

"Don't go anywhere," he said. "Security will be here in a minute." With that he strode off, back into the barn, leaving Gina all alone in an alpaca pen. Well, alone except for a handful of alpacas, who regarded her curiously.

"Where would I go?" she muttered.

But as she took a step back towards the barn, her foot slipped. Looking down, she saw she had stepped in a blob of greenish-black alpaca poop.

Perfect.

GINA WANDERED BACK into the courtyard, looking for a broom or a brush or something to clean off her shoe. She took her shoes off and then poked around in the various buildings. They were mostly storage or utility buildings, and a few were locked. But she found some brushes in a garage-sized room filled with all sorts of bridles, harnesses, saddles, pads, and other horsey stuff. Gina even spotted a rack of whips and riding crops.

This is probably where that little monster got his weapon.

In the corner of the room, looking very out of place, was a long desk filled with multiple computer monitors and other electronic equipment. Curious, Gina ambled over.

This was the first computer she had seen in Maidenwell—outside of those in the underground offices. She tapped on the keyboard and one monitor turned on.

It took her a moment to figure out what she was seeing, but then she realized the screen was displaying a grid of views from security cameras, cycling through different locations. Gina could see inside and outside of the barn, various angles, and also the other buildings in the stable block, including one that seemed like a bunkhouse. The images changed again, but some of the views displayed a warning message: "CAMERA OFFLINE."

Weird.

She borrowed a brush and returned to the courtyard, where she sat on a bench and set to work cleaning off her shoe.

A shadow fell upon her and she looked up to see a tall man silhouetted by the sun. It took her a moment to realize that it was Reeve.

"Geez, you always sneak up on people like that?" she asked.

"I thought you were going to stay out of trouble."

"I never said that."

"So what happened here?" He took out a little pocket-sized notebook.

"Oh, so this is official?"

"Schaeffer said you let Florentine out of his pen and now he's missing."

"Schaeffer's an idiot. I told him multiple times that it was the kid who let the alpaca out. After he was whipping him."

"What kid?"

"The red-haired kid. The son of the vet."

He flipped through his notebook. "Garland, right?"

"That sounds familiar. Nicole, I think."

"Here it is. *Noelle* Garland. Her son's name is Mason. He's special needs. Apparently, he doesn't talk to anyone besides his mom and grandmother. Among other things."

"I didn't know that." Gina felt a pang of guilt for yelling at the kid. But even if he had problems, he still shouldn't be whipping an animal.

"Let's start at the beginning."

"There isn't much to tell. I walked down here with Becca to see Florrie."

Reeve checked his notebook again. "Rebecca Hill?"

"Yes. She had to leave and I went into the stables by myself. I heard an alpaca screaming outside, so I followed the sound out to the back pen. And there was the kid—Mason—chasing an alpaca with a riding crop."

"A riding crop?"

"Yeah, like from *Fifty Shades*, but not in a fun way."

"I wouldn't know about that."

Even in the sun, Gina noticed he blushed a little.

"Then what?" he asked.

"I tried to stop him, but he kept whipping the animal until he drove it out the back gate."

"Which was open?"

"Yes."

"And why do you think he did that?"

"How should I know? It's horrible to say, but he was acting like a little psycho."

"Yeah, that is horrible to say." He peered at her oddly. "Are you crying?"

"No. Why?"

"Your eyes are all red."

Shit, Gina thought. *I'm about to get busted for pot*. "It's all the dust around here. Believe me, I'm not about to shed any tears over that kid."

"That's a little harsh."

"Full disclosure: this is not my first run-in with him."

"You fought before?"

"I did not fight him. I don't fight kids. I usually have nothing to do with them."

"Why's that? Don't you like kids?"

"This isn't about me."

"Okay, but you've had an altercation with Mason Garland before?"

Gina told him about the incident in the parking lot of the scenic overlook, but Reeve didn't write any of that down. Maybe it was out of his jurisdiction.

"Shouldn't you be out, you know, actually trying to find him?" she asked. "And the alpaca."

"Now you're telling me how to do my job?" Reeve seemed more amused than pissed off.

"No, it's just that there's a lost kid and a two-million-dollar alpaca running around the countryside—"

"Relax. I've got guys on it."

"Oh, so you've got guys, huh?"

"What, did you think it was just me?"

"I don't know. I thought this was a rinky-dink little village, but you've got your own hospital, an underground administrative complex—"

"Don't forget the railroad."

"Yeah, Maidenwell's full of surprises," Gina said.

"Actually, we don't much like surprises around here."

"Like dead bodies?"

"Exactly."

They said nothing for a few moments, just looking at each other. Finally, Reeve told her she was free to go.

"So you believe me?" Gina asked.

"There are cameras all over the place. It will be easy enough to confirm your story."

"It's not a story," Gina said. "It's the truth." She hated when people didn't believe her. It was infuriating. Especially coming from the Marshal here.

She pulled on her shoes and stomped away. Which was tough with one shoe still partially encrusted with poop.

On the way back to Haverford Hall, she ran into Noelle Garland and the older woman who had sat with her and her son on the train. The two women were hustling down the bridle path towards the stables. Noelle looked angry, but her red hair was really catching the autumn light. Gina wondered if it was natural, but then remembered that her kid had the exact same shade of red. Her hair reverie was broken when Noelle got right into her face.

"You! What did you do to my son?" Noelle's eyes flashed.

"Nothing, I swear!"

"That's not what we heard." The older woman stood beside Noelle with her hands on her hips.

"Your son was whipping an alpaca, and I tried to stop him."

"That's ridiculous!" Noelle said. "Mason loves animals."

"Not this animal. He drove it out the back gate. I was trying to bring him back to the Hall when he whipped me, too. See?" She showed off the welt on her upper arm. "Then he ran away."

"You must have done something to him," Noelle said.

"He's a very sensitive little boy," the older woman said. She looked a bit like Noelle, but heavier and with short gray hair.

"I don't know what to say. That's what happened. Ask Officer Reeve if you don't believe me. He's checking the cameras."

Noelle's face fell. "This doesn't make sense. You do know that I'm a vet, don't you? Mason grew up around animals. He would never whip one."

"We should go, dear. We want to be there when they find him." The older woman held Noelle's arm and steered her back onto the path. They were definitely mother and daughter.

"Anyway," Gina called after them. "I hope he's all right."

"Thank you," the older woman said.

nine

. . .

BACK AT HAVERFORD HALL, Gina returned to her room and took a hot shower, and thought about all the crazy stuff that had happened. There was something definitely odd about Stanley Schaeffer's behavior. He didn't seem particularly upset that his wife had died. Sure, if he didn't love her anymore and was ho-ing around, that might make sense. But at least *pretend,* for god's sake!

As she was getting dressed, Gina's keycard chimed loudly. She pounced on it. A text! She finally got a text!

It was from Danielle. She was finishing up with Peyton Grier, but then they had a call scheduled to brief Matthias Loneskum himself at 4 p.m., so Danielle would be tied up until then. She wanted to meet at the pub at five.

Sounds good

Gina was amazed how easy it was to work the card's little virtual keyboard.

Lots to talk about

Now Gina needed to figure out what to do for the next few hours. Maybe she'd explore the village some more. She probably could even walk into town and not need to bother Millicent. Why not?

As she was leaving her room, she noticed an envelope had been slid under the door.

Her first thought was that she was being sent home, and this was her hotel bill.

But, thankfully, it wasn't.

The envelope contained a note from Frau Loneskum, printed on her fancy engraved stationery.

Gina read through the note. It was basically an announcement that the auction was back on for tomorrow evening at the request of Mr. Stanley Schaeffer.

That meant old Florrie was back safe and sound. Hopefully the kid was, too.

The note went on to mention other events during the day, including an examination and final histograms and EPDs (whatever they were) by Dr. Garland at twelve noon and a light dinner and drinks right before the auction at six.

Sounded like a splendid time for all. Especially Stanley. The creep.

GINA STOPPED by the lobby and confirmed that it was indeed possible to walk into the village. She learned that a footpath ran along the main road down the hill. It was a brisk ten-minute walk, fifteen if you took your time. And the pub was at the south end of the Village Green—not far from the White Horse Inn.

The guy behind the desk assured Gina she'd have no problem finding her way around. "Just look for St. Mary's tower. It's the tallest structure in the village and it sits right on the northern end of the green."

Gina thanked him and set off. Halfway down the hill to the village, she spotted someone else walking along the footpath. She increased her pace until she was able to recognize the person.

It was Becca's aunt Catherine. She was dressed in hiking gear and had a thin tubular case slung over her shoulder.

"Hello," Gina called.

Catherine turned and smiled, which made her look even more horse-like. Poor woman.

"Hello back," Catherine said. "Out for a stroll?"

"I'm meeting my friend, er, boss at the pub in a few hours, so I decided to do some exploring. What about you? Shouldn't you be back prepping for the auction with Becca?"

"She kicked me out. Wanted to focus without the old lady interfering." She shrugged.

"Well, she's very passionate," Gina said. "We had a good chat this afternoon."

"So she said. Anyway, I'm off to do some fishing myself." Catherine patted the case on her shoulder. "Apparently, the stream in town is overflowing with trout."

"Fishing? Really?"

"Yeah, just don't tell Becca. She doesn't really approve." She made a face. "Even though I release everything I catch."

"What's the point, then?"

"The thrill of the hunt, I suppose. And for me, it's a chance to practice casting."

"That's when you whip the fishing line in the air?" The only fishing Gina had ever done was from a boat in the Long Island Sound when she was a little kid. And that was mostly because her dad and three brothers were going and she didn't want to be left out.

Catherine laughed. "Yes, kind of. There's definitely an art to it. I was actually a ranked professional female fly caster. Number two in the world for several years."

"Wow. Color me impressed. I didn't even know there was such a thing."

"Yes, the sport has been judged on a professional level for over sixty years."

"I have to ask. Always the bridesmaid and never the bride. Who's the number one fly caster?"

"Actually, it was my partner."

"Oh? That could be awkward."

"It was fine."

"Is your partner here at the auction?" Gina hadn't seen anyone else with Catherine besides her niece, but she couldn't help being nosy.

"No, we're no longer together."

"I'm sorry about that. It wasn't because of Stanley, was it?"

Catherine made another face. "Why would you say that?"

"I heard that he's broken up more than a few relationships."

"There was some infidelity, I'm afraid. But Billie didn't stray with Stanley Schaeffer, thank god. The home wrecker in our case was a DJ who had a penchant for older women."

Gina decided to leave it at that and not ask any more questions. She glanced down the lane at the vista below. "That's some view, huh?"

"It is indeed."

It *was* a pretty spectacular view. The stone cottages and gardens of the village stretched out below them in a maze of narrow lanes. And, as promised, the big square church tower was clearly visible to the north. The afternoon sun bathed everything in a cozy glow.

As they drew closer to the village, Gina asked if she might tag along and watch Catherine fish.

"Really?" Catherine asked. "If there's one thing that can be more boring than fishing, it's watching someone else fish."

"Oh, come on. You've certainly fished in front of an audience before. Haven't you?"

"We don't actually fish during the competition. We cast. For distance and accuracy."

"Well, I can watch you cast, then. It would be an honor. And besides, I've got an hour or so to kill."

"Fine with me. As long as you don't spook the fish."

The road from the manor connected with a little traffic circle, and Catherine led them to the left. They passed a few cottages, and then a stretch of empty road lined with dry stone walls. Soon they heard the burbling of water and spotted an unbelievably scenic stone bridge arching across a good-sized stream.

"Wow," Gina said. "Just wow."

"Can you believe we're somewhere in the Oregon badlands right now?"

"Not at all. Possibly because I didn't know there was such a thing as Oregon badlands."

Catherine expertly surveyed the area and then led them upstream about fifty feet, where a bend in the river formed a natural pool.

As Catherine assembled her rod and reel, Gina asked, "So, these flies? They're not real, are they?"

"No, not at all. They're made of feathers, hair, fibers, thread. They're designed to look like insects, of course. That's an art in and of itself."

Once her rod was assembled, Catherine asked Gina to step back for safety. Then she proceeded to whip her rod back and forth. The thick fishing line snaked through the air in long figure eights, and then Catherine dropped the business end of the line in a swirling eddy close to the opposite bank.

"That was pretty sweet," Gina said. "All that whipping around, though. Do you ever hit yourself?"

"Not yet. Knock on wood."

Catherine showed off her casting skills by precisely

placing her fly at various points around the river, calling out her target in advance. "Rock… leaf… log…"

"Okay, now you're just showing off," Gina said with a smile.

"I know."

They hung out and Gina got a crash course in fly-casting as Catherine explained her technique.

"You want to try?"

"Me?" Gina asked. "No thanks. I've already been whipped once today."

"What?"

Gina told her about the whole incident with the red-haired kid and the alpaca.

"I had heard a little about that right before I left," Catherine said. "But I had no idea. He actually struck you with a horsewhip?"

"I've got the mark to prove it." Gina slipped her sweater from her shoulders and showed off her welt.

Catherine gently traced one finger along Gina's arm. "Does it hurt?"

"Not so much now, but it scared the hell out of me."

"And it was Dr. Garland's son who was whipping Florentine?"

"Yeah, the little piece of work."

"Why would the boy do such a thing?"

"He's a weird kid." But as Gina said the words, she felt guilty. Again. The kid obviously had some developmental problems. "But you know who I really don't get? Stanley Schaeffer. I mean, his wife just died, and he's carrying on like no big deal. I mean, who does that?"

"Stanley and Vanessa have always had a complicated relationship."

"I didn't mean to be harsh, if he's a friend of yours—"

"God, no," Catherine said. "We've had a few run-ins over

the years, but we're cordial now. Again, don't tell Becca. She thinks he's the Devil."

"I know, right?"

"Thing you need to know about Stanley is that he's all about winning."

"Winning?"

"He's gone through some tough times. Business-wise. And now he's desperate to be seen as a winner. That's the most important thing to him. More than money or women."

That's an interesting observation, Gina thought. But it didn't make Stanley Schaeffer any less sketchy in her book.

AFTER SHE SAID goodbye and left Catherine to fish in peace, Gina made her way back into the village via a footpath that ran along the shore of the stream.

As she walked, she couldn't help thinking about Stanley and Vanessa. Something was definitely off with those two. And it bothered her.

She followed a street that ran in the general direction of the church tower and soon found herself at the perfectly manicured Village Green. Leafy trees ringed the perimeter of the Green, and a wide sidewalk was dotted with benches and big iron lamp posts. On the sprawling lawn itself, several people were about, walking dogs, stretching out on blankets, playing with their kids, and doing everything you'd normally do in a park. Except look at their phones. Although maybe some people were looking at their keycards. Gina couldn't tell.

The buildings around the square were a mix of shops and residential. They were all built of the same honey-colored stone. Most stood two stories tall with sharply angled roofs and topped with chimneys—something you didn't see much of these days.

Gina checked the time on her keycard and saw that she had a good forty-five minutes before she was due to meet Danielle. She had walked past the pub and the building looked suitably quaint, with a half-timbered upper section and lots of picturesque dormer windows. A painted sign proclaiming *The Feathers* swung from an iron bracket jutting out over the sidewalk. The artwork was quite good, showing a bunch of white feathers sticking out of a crown.

Down the street from the pub was the sprawling White Horse Inn, but it was the shop a few doors further that caught Gina's attention. It was a bookstore by the name of Berenstein's. *Ah, finally. A touch of the Old Country,* she thought. *I wonder if I can get a cup of coffee in a Greek cup, and maybe a black and white cookie.*

As she pushed her way through the door, a bell tinkled gently. The bookstore was crowded with tall shelves and display tables, but no customers.

"Hello." A heavyset man with thick squared-off glasses and a big bushy gray beard looked up at her from behind the counter and smiled. "A visitor to our fair village, I see."

"You spelled Berenstain wrong," Gina said without preamble.

"I'm fairly sure I didn't," the man said. "Seeing as I've had sixty-four years of practice."

"It's STAIN, not STEIN," Gina said.

"Ah, a fan of the Mandela Theory, I see."

"I could have sworn the poor man died in an African prison."

"Perhaps he did," the man said. "All I know is that I am no relation to that family of ursines." He stuck his hand out in greeting. "Larry Berenstein. At your service."

Gina shook it and smiled. "Gina Biletti, late of the Isle of Manhattan."

"Me too. And that explains it."

"Explains what?"

"Most visitors don't burst in claiming I spelled my name wrong."

"What can I say? I'm a stickler for details, Larry." Gina liked this guy.

"Please. Call me Berenstein. It makes me sound like a rough character."

"Whatever you say, Berenstein."

"And stop hovering there. Come in. Look around. Can I help you find something?"

"I don't know. They confiscated my Kindle at the train station—"

"Heathen!"

"I know, I know. But in my defense, I wasn't about to schlep a three-pound hardcover for a weekend trip."

"Apology accepted."

Just then a big Siamese cat jumped up on the counter and arched its back into a stretch.

"What's a quaint little bookstore without a cat?" Gina said.

"Exactly," Berenstein said. "His name is Waldo."

"As in Where Is…?"

"As in Waldo Pepper."

"You lost me."

"Robert Redford? Ah, you're too young!"

"I'm not that young." Gina scratched Waldo the cat at the base of his tail. He squinted at her and purred appreciatively. "What a sweetheart."

A pang of sadness hit her as the thought of her own dearly departed cat, a polydactyl tabby named Benjamin Button.

"Yes, Waldo's an old soldier. Like me."

"He doesn't look that old."

"Sixty-four in cat years."

"I'm sensing a theme here."

"So what do you like to read, kiddo—besides children's books? You like thrillers? Jack Reacher?"

"Uh, not anymore."

"Romance? Sweet, spicy, bully, reverse harem? We've got it all."

"I am actually finding myself in the mood for a good mystery."

"A mystery, eh? We get that a lot. There must be something in the water."

"Or on the picturesque cobblestones." Gina smiled.

"Any particular flavor of mystery?"

"Nothing too bloody, but I do like my twists. Are you a mystery aficionado?"

"Yes, but I'm quite discerning. If I can guess who the murderer is before the sleuth does, I'm out."

"Me too. Let's see what you've got."

"This way, my dear." Berenstein led her to the mystery section of the shop—which was the largest section by far. In fact, he had devoted two full floor-to-ceiling bookshelves just to crime novels featuring pets.

"Any mysteries with alpacas?" Gina asked.

"No, that's a new one on me. We have a paranormal romance with alpaca shifters, but no alpaca mysteries, I'm afraid. So you're one of the alpaca people, eh?"

"No, not me. I'm just an innocent bystander."

"That's what they all say."

"Actually, I'm in market research."

"Ah, so you're the one to blame for the fact that there's nothing but superhero movies in the theaters anymore. Thanks for that."

Gina put her hands up in protest. "I've got nothing to do with that. I mostly do pharmaceutical research. Some financial products. Lots of packaged goods."

"Sounds thrilling."

"It is. Uh, *was*. I'm kind of retired now. Involuntarily." Gina didn't know why she was babbling on about her personal life. There was just something about Larry Berenstein that made him easy to talk to. Maybe it was the fact that he was Jewish and she was Italian. Her uncle used to say that the two cultures were so similar that they might as well merge all the holidays.

"Well, if you are looking for a new business venture, Berenstein's Books might be for sale in the near future—to the right buyer."

"What? This seems like a dream job. Owning your own bookstore in this perfect little village."

"Don't get me wrong, Gina Biletti. Maidenwell's fantastic. People are nice. Business is good. Especially since we don't have any competition."

"You're the only bookstore in town?"

"We are. And better than that, that Big-Online-Bookstore-That-Shall-Not-Be-Named can't deliver here. No one can."

"Really?"

"You see any UPS trucks on the street?"

"Come to think of it, no."

"Technically, you could order something and have it delivered to Aune Station and it would come in on the train, but most of us prefer to shop locally."

"I like that." Gina looked around at the bookstore, seeing everything in a slightly different light. "So, why are you selling?"

"I hit age 65, I have to move to Florida. It's Hebrew law," he deadpanned.

"We have the same thing, but we usually go to Arizona."

"Well, think about it," Berenstein said. "Here's my card."

This all seemed so surreal to Gina.

I'm in town for less than twenty-four hours and I see a ghost, I'm attacked by a junior serial killer, and now I'm offered a bookstore. What next?

She continued to chat with Berenstein and puttered around the store some more until she found a mystery novel that seemed interesting.

As he bagged the book for her, Berenstein asked, "Where are you staying, by the by?"

"Big house on the hill."

"Haverford Hall. Fancy-schmancy. You must have friends in high places, kiddo."

"Oh yeah, me and the Frau are like this." She held up two intertwined fingers. "How much do I owe you?"

"No charge."

"No charge? This is how you butter someone up to buy your shop? I'm going to need a little more than a paperback, Berenstein."

He laughed. "No, all the books here are free."

"What is this, a super-sized Little Free Library? No wonder you want to get out of the biz."

"It's not like that at all. I record all the sales, and get paid for everything. Just not by my customers directly."

"I don't get it."

"Matthias Loneskum is a big fan of books."

"Still don't get it."

"He subsidizes us. I report what I would have sold, and at the end of the month, I receive a check. We're doing very well, thank you very much. It will all be in the financial packet I send you."

"Wait, I'm still trying to grasp this concept. Everyone in the town gets free books?"

"Just another little perk of living in Maidenwell."

"This Loneskum guy's kind of like a modern-day feudal lord, isn't he? Bestowing boons upon the populace."

"I never thought of it like that, but yes, perhaps." Berenstein scratched his beard thoughtfully. "A benevolent lord of the manor."

"Hmmm." Gina found herself thinking about a million things at once. "Listen, what time do you close up for the day?"

"Five-thirty. Why?"

"Can I buy you a drink?"

"Are you coming on to me, Miss Biletti?"

"No."

"I'm old enough to be your father. And you'd be barking up the wrong tree, I'm afraid."

"It's not like that at all," Gina said. But she knew he was teasing her. "Besides, my friend Danielle will be there as well."

"Is she as lovely as you?"

"More. Lovely, that is."

"Be still my beating heart!"

"Shut up, Berenstein. Just meet me at the pub at 5:30. And thanks for the book."

"Don't thank me. Thank Matthias Loneskum."

ten

. . .

THE FEATHERS PUB was even cuter on the inside than the outside. After passing through a leaded glass entryway, Gina took in the wood-paneled and white stucco walls, flagstone floor, exposed oak beams, brass sconces, dart boards, and the long bar with a section covered in copper. The little round tables were mostly occupied—and so were the larger tables with banquette seating that ran along one wall. But then she spotted Danielle. Her friend had grabbed a table in the far corner of the pub and was waving at her.

"Hey, girl. You're a sight for sore eyes." She slid a full pint of beer towards her.

"Danielle, I am so sorry. Did I get you in trouble? Tell me I didn't get you in trouble." Gina took a deep swig, even though she wasn't much of a beer drinker.

"No, it's fine. I smoothed things over, but I have to say Peyton Grier is not your biggest fan."

"The feeling's mutual, but I still shouldn't have opened my mouth like that. You know me. When I get nervous, I blabber."

"I know, I know." Danielle patted Gina's arm. "As I said, everything's fine. Loneskum's not worried about this. It was just an unfortunate thing to happen, but people die of heart attacks all the time."

"Yeah, about that." Gina lowered her voice. "I have some thoughts."

"Well, I'm off duty. Tell me in the morning. Let's talk about something else. How was your day, dear?"

"You didn't hear?"

"I've been in a windowless office all day."

"I went to see Florrie, and I caught the vet's kid whipping him."

"What?"

"Then the kid let the alpaca out of his pen and when I tried to confront him about it, he whipped me. Look." Gina displayed her welt. She was getting a lot of mileage out of it.

Danielle gasped. "Oh, babes. Are you all right?"

"Yeah, fine. I hardly feel it anymore."

"That's crazy. I had heard that the auction was back on for tomorrow, but nothing about the alpaca being injured or loose."

"I don't think he actually got hurt. But the little monster was hell bent on setting him free. Oh, and I spoke to Stanley Schaeffer."

"When?"

"Right after it happened. And that vet with the red hair. I think she's in denial about her kid." Gina took another gulp of beer. "Oh, and I got high with Becca Hill and she spilled a lot of tea. A *lot*."

"Well, this is a firehose of information. We're going to need to pace ourselves."

"Oh, and one more thing. A guy's going to join us in a half hour."

"What? You have a date?"

"No, nothing like that. He's an old guy. From New York. Very funny. Owns a bookstore down the street. Which he wants me to buy."

"Gina, I leave you alone for a couple of hours—!"

"I know, I know." Gina wanted to wait until Larry Berenstein joined them before she shared her suspicions. Instead, she asked Danielle if she would have to work anymore.

"That's why I'm here. Tomorrow Peyton's taking me on a tour of the water reclamation plant, and then I'm meeting with the engineering team to get briefed some more on HyperCiv."

"Which is what, exactly?"

"You saw it on the video. It's the technology that powers all the utilities: the energy grid, recycling, everything."

"Yawn. I don't have to come with you, do I?"

"No. In fact, since Peyton's going to be there, I'd say you might be a liability."

"A liability, huh? That's what I always wanted to be. A liability."

"Shut up, babes."

They ordered another round and some appetizers, and Gina told Danielle about her encounter with Becca's aunt Catherine and the whole fly-casting thing.

"I had no idea there even was such a sport," Danielle said.

"Me either. But the old girl was pretty amazing with that rod."

At that moment, Larry Berenstein came up from behind Gina and patted her shoulder. "I'm not going to even ask if that was the punchline to a joke or not. I'm just going to assume it was and not ask any questions."

Gina laughed and made introductions. The server swooped in and took their orders.

"I recommend the steak and kidney pie," Berenstein said. "Specialty of the house."

"You're doing my job again, Berenstein," the server said with a grin.

"Sorry, Tal, we've got some newbies here."

"As tantalizing as cow organs might sound—and I'm sure

they're delicious—I think I'll do the sweet potato and chickpea tagine," Gina said.

"So boring," Danielle said. "I'll have the spicy jerk chicken and a burrata."

"Oh, and a round of your famous Scotch eggs, if you please," Berenstein said.

"What's a Scotch egg?" Danielle asked.

"It's an egg soaked in whiskey, of course." Gina didn't know what it really was.

Berenstein smacked his lips. "Oh, it's wonderful, ladies. Wonder. Full. You'll love it. They make it with local blue cheese, balsamic onions, and chutney."

"Well, I trust you." Danielle turned to Gina. "So, what's this mysterious conversation you wanted to have?"

"Oh, so she teased you as well?" Berenstein asked. "I thought I was the only one in the dark."

"We're all in the dark." Gina leaned in and beckoned them close. "I think that Vanessa Schaeffer was murdered."

"What?" Danielle jerked her head back.

"Shhhhh!" Gina hissed.

"Who's Vanessa Schaeffer?" Berenstein asked.

Gina quickly filled him in on what had happened over the past twenty-four hours.

"So, why do you think she was murdered?" Berenstein asked. "People have heart attacks all the time."

"Yeah, everyone keeps saying that." Gina took a drink of beer. "But there are definitely some weird things going on. Just keep an open mind, you guys. And think of it as a whodunnit."

"Alas, the real world is quite a bit messier than a mystery novel," Berenstein said. "But lay it on me, sister."

So Gina ran through everything she knew or had heard about Vanessa from Becca and Catherine: the marital problems (including what she had told Gina on the train about her husband being a wretch), the weird pre-dawn meeting in the garden—

"I'm going to stop you right there," Danielle said. "You told me you didn't recognize the woman in white."

"Sounds like a Wilkie Collins novel," Berenstein said. "Had she escaped from an asylum?"

Gina ignored him. "I didn't recognize her at the time, but the more I thought of it, the more it made sense that it was Vanessa. The woman I saw was very graceful. Like a dancer."

Danielle turned to Berenstein. "She's showing off. This morning she made a big deal of deducing that Vanessa Schaeffer was a dancer just by how she stood."

"And I was right. She has a natural turn-out."

"It was a lucky guess."

"You're just jealous."

"Go on, go on," Berenstein said, eyes alight with excitement.

"And I think that the guy she met with was Tomas, the ranch hand who works for Yvonne Loneskum."

"Tomas?" Danielle asked.

Berenstein smacked the table with his hand. "That's it. I'm out."

"What are you talking about?"

"It's all fun and games until you start involving Frau L."

"Again," Gina said, "not quite understanding."

"You don't mess with the Frau, kiddo." He gestured around him. "Everything you see. The entirety of this little experiment, oasis, whatever you want to call it… it's all because of Frau L."

"I thought it was because of her son."

"Matthias has built all of this for his mother," Berenstein said matter-of-factly.

"That's not entirely true," Danielle said. "He's a pioneer of sustainable living and the preservation of traditional habitations throughout the world."

"You sound like a friggin' press release, Danielle!" Gina said.

"Well, no matter," Berenstein said. "Matthias is a good son. Do you know that Frau L. doesn't even like the English?"

"I had heard that," Gina said. "So why build her an English village?"

"The village was here before the Regenschirm Group bought it," Danielle said wearily. "And Frau Loneskum only hates the English *people*. She loves their architecture."

Gina rolled her eyes. "Can we get back to the murder?"

"Seriously, stop saying 'murder.' It's creeping me out."

"Okay, so we have a possibly suspicious death?" Berenstein asked. "Am I understanding you correctly? A heart attack that might not be a heart attack?"

"The oldest trick in the book," Gina said. "Some kind of poison."

"Which would be one-hundred-percent detected by the medical examiner," Danielle said.

"Ah, not necessarily," Berenstein said. "Are you aware of digoxin? It's a fairly common drug used for heart problems, but too much can trigger a heart attack."

"See!" Gina said. "Someone could have injected her with that stuff. Boom. Heart attack."

"I don't even think you need to inject it. It can be slipped into someone's food or drink."

"This is crazy," Danielle looked from Gina to Berenstein and back again.

"Is it?" Gina scoffed. *"Motive, means, opportunity.* Did I get that right, Berenstein?"

"Yes, well done."

"And you think Stanley had a motive for killing her?" Danielle asked.

"Of course. She was going to divorce him. Maybe as soon as the auction was done. And she's got a prenup as well."

"Hmm," Berenstein said. "Money's a big motive. No denying that. Money and love."

"Or hate," Gina said.

"I don't think Stanley hated his wife," Danielle said.

"Still plenty of motives," Berenstein said. "We covered means already. That leaves opportunity."

"Stanley's room was right next to Vanessa's." Gina said.

"They didn't share a room?" Berenstein asked.

"I know, right? Odd."

"He's a snorer," Danielle said. "Big time."

"And how would you know, my dear?" Berenstein winked at her.

Danielle did not look amused. "It was in the police report."

"Stanley could have easily poisoned her at any point," Gina said.

"Even at five in the morning?" Danielle asked.

"Actually, there are poisons that build up in your system," Berenstein said. "It's possible that the husband could have been micro-dosing his wife for some time and it just hit a tipping point and…" He drew one finger across his throat for emphasis.

This is all falling into place, Gina thought. "So, what do we do about it?"

"Listen, Gina. I appreciate all the CSI stuff, but I can't get involved. And neither can you."

"What are you talking about?"

"Loneskum is my client. He pays me to keep him out of the news."

"But you own a PR firm. That's literally the opposite of what a PR firm does."

"Not these days, hon. We're all about reputation management. That means squashing any hint of negative news."

"I could see how murder might be considered negative news," Berenstein said.

Gina felt a flush on her face. And it wasn't the beer. "A woman's dead and we're supposed to just pretend nothing's wrong?"

"I just can't have this connected to me or my firm," Danielle said. "And seeing as you are part of my firm—at least this weekend—you can't say anything, either."

"Oh, that's not going to work for me."

"Gina, I am asking for forty-eight hours, max."

Berenstein leaned in. "What if I was the tipster?"

"Thank you, Larry, but—"

"*Berenstein*, please."

"I don't think that will work," Gina said. "They'd ask a lot of questions that you wouldn't be able to answer. It's got to be me."

"It's not going to be you," Danielle said emphatically. "No way in hell, babes."

The mood during the rest of the dinner was particularly tense. Trying to lighten everyone's spirits, Berenstein asked the two women if they noticed the pub sign on their way in.

"Sure," Gina said, mopping up the last of her tagine with a thick slab of rustic bread that tasted like crack and seemed to have the same effect on her.

"The feathers and the crown?" Danielle asked.

"That's right. Anyone know why English pubs all have these kinds of colorful signs hanging over the sidewalk?"

"No idea," Gina said.

"Well, one reason is that in the Dark Ages, most people couldn't actually *read* signs with words on them, so that's why the signs were illustrated."

"Makes sense."

"Also, in the 14th century, King Richard II passed a law requiring all pubs and inns to have a sign with a white deer on it—which was his own emblem."

"Ah, an early use of a logo," Danielle said.

"Exactly. But it also identified the establishment as one that needed to be visited by the Royal Ale Taster."

"There were Royal Ale Tasters?" Danielle asked.

"Apparently so."

"So there is a job out there for me," Gina grinned.

"Hey, I offered you a job already," Berenstein said. "Bookstore owner."

"Yes, please." Danielle drained the last of her pint. "Take her off my hands. I beseech you."

They hung out for another hour, during which Danielle convinced Gina and Berenstein to do some shots. That caused Gina to get extra loud and Berenstein to get sleepy and want to call it a night. So Danielle called for a ride and they bid Berenstein goodnight.

"Are you sure we can't drop you anywhere?" Gina asked Berenstein, as their car pulled up. Millicent wasn't available, so another driver would shuttle them back up to Haverford Hall.

"I doubt I'd fit. Besides, my place is just around the corner. A three-minute walk."

"That's handy."

"It sure is. And I'd throw in the cottage if you bought the bookstore."

"You're giving me the hard sell, aren't you?"

"Think about it."

As they pulled away, Danielle asked, "What's all this about you buying a bookstore?"

"He wants to retire to Florida, and he's looking to unload his shop."

"You're not considering it, are you?"

"Not in a million years."

eleven

. . .

BACK IN HER ROOM, as she was getting ready to curl up with her new book, Gina noticed the toilet paper hadn't been restocked.

That's going to be a problem.

She decided to wander down to the front desk.

The guy on duty was very apologetic, and he went himself to fetch some for her.

"Shall I send someone up with it?" he asked.

"I'll just take it. I've been seen walking around with worse."

On her way back to her room, she spotted someone loitering in the hallway. As she got closer, she recognized Stanley's assistant. Liam. No, Ian.

"Can't sleep?" she asked.

He seemed a little unnerved. "No, I um… Just stretching my legs."

"Uh huh." He was definitely acting sketchy. "I'm very sorry about Ms. Schaeffer. Were you two close?"

"Not really. I mostly worked for Mr. Schaeffer."

"Still, it had to have been a shock."

"Yeah, it was," he said unconvincingly.

"She wasn't ill at all, was she? No heart issues?"

"I don't think so. You'd have to ask Mr. Schaeffer, though."

Gina noticed him staring at the three rolls of toilet paper in her hands. "No, I didn't steal these. They forgot to restock my room."

"You're not going to let me forget that, are you?" A faint smile played across his face.

"Probably not. I just don't get it. A captain of industry. The owner of the largest alpaca ranch in the country. Why would he need to steal a few bottles of wine?"

"I think you're obsessed, lady."

"That hurt." Gina took a deep breath. "The lady part, not the obsessed part. I'm definitely obsessed. I'll own that."

"What, you don't like being called a lady?"

"Makes me sound old."

Ian didn't have a response to that.

Gina threw a roll of toilet paper at him.

"Hey! What'd you do that for?"

"When a woman says 'it makes me sound old,' you're supposed to say 'no way, you're not old at all!' Jeesh, didn't your mom teach you how to act around females?"

He handed the roll of toilet paper back to her. "Are you drunk or something?"

"Of course not. Just had a few beers at dinner."

"You kind of smell like whiskey."

"Those were the shots we had for afters. But again, Ian, not a polite comment."

"Sorry," he said, not meeting her eyes.

There's definitely something up with this kid, Gina thought. *Maybe I should press him a bit.*

Gina had plenty of experience getting consumers to talk during focus groups and one-on-ones. This guy didn't seem like much of a challenge at all.

"So, looks like the auction is back on," she said, trying to keep it casual.

"Yeah."

"Don't you think that's odd?"

"It was Mr. Schaeffer's call."

"I know. I read Mrs. Loneskum's letter. It just seems weird to me. I mean, the guy's wife just died suddenly. Why would he be wanting to attend an alpaca auction?"

"Florentine's a big deal."

"So I heard. He's some magical alpaca who has the power to change the industry forever. Blah, blah, blah."

"Well, he does."

"I'll take your word for it." Gina didn't know why Ian was still hanging out in the hallway, despite their extremely boring conversation, but she was going to damn well find out.

"So, is that your room?" She nodded at the door near where Ian was leaning.

"No, I'm actually down the hall a bit."

"Oh? So you just like loitering in front of someone else's room?"

"No."

"Are you a perv, Ian?"

"What? No! Of course not."

"I didn't think so. I was just messing with you. I'm sure you have a perfectly good reason for guarding that door."

"I'm not guarding it." His face reddened and Gina knew she had struck a nerve.

"That's Stanley's room, isn't it?"

"No. Could you just leave me alone? Please."

"Sure. I'll leave you alone." Gina started moving, feinting left like she was leaving the area.

But then she lunged forward and yanked open the guest room door.

"No!"

She barged inside to see Stanley Schaeffer in *flagrante delicto* with a woman in his bed.

"Oops. Sorry. Wrong room!"

As she dashed out, Gina took one more look.

Yup. He's shtupping the wine lady.

THIS PUTS AN ENTIRELY *new spin on things,* Gina thought—back in her room—as she flossed her teeth. She remembered Becca had mentioned that Stanley was having an affair with the wine woman, but at the time, she had a hard time believing it. After all, Stanley was kind of an ogre in the looks department, while the wine lady was very beautiful. And young.

Well, some women don't give a shit. They're just chasing the money.

It was sad, but true. Zero self-respect.

Even so, what she had seen added some fuel to the fire. Stanley was having an affair with the wine lady. Confirmed. It was another check in the 'motive' box.

The problem was Danielle. She had a good point. If Gina stirred up trouble and started accusing people of murder in Maidenwell—*make that MURDERwell*—it would reflect badly on Danielle and her firm.

Gina couldn't do that to a friend.

So she would just have to figure out another way to get the word out.

The key was Marshal Reeve.

He was the law in these parts. She needed to plant some seeds with him. Preferably without getting Danielle into trouble.

She found her keycard and after thirty seconds of randomly clicking on it like a chimpanzee, she managed to find the text app.

Breakfast tomorrow?

Within a minute, he texted back:

sure. bakery 6 a.m.?

Can we make it 6:30? I need my beauty sleep. LOL.

K.

Perfect.

Gina cursed the fact that there wasn't a mini-bar in her room. Instead, she curled up in bed with her book, and fell asleep thinking of murder and alibis.

The next morning, she woke up early. And, although she was a little hungover from the shots last night, a shower and a brisk walk into town managed to clear her head. Mostly.

She arrived only five minutes late to the bakery.

Reeve greeted her with a coffee and a berry scone. He did not look hungover.

"I'm glad you texted me," he said without preamble.

"Oh?"

"We have a minor problem with the security video at the barn."

Gina remembered what she had seen in the room with the computer.

"Let me guess. Some of the cameras were offline."

Reeve looked genuinely surprised. Then genuinely suspicious. "How did you know?"

"When I was looking for a brush to clean the poop off my shoe, I happened to see a computer monitor. It said there were cameras offline."

"Did you touch anything?"

"No. Of course not."

"Good."

"I mean, I might have tapped the keyboard."

"Why would you do that?"

"I don't know. Maybe because I'm naturally curious." Gina took a sip of the coffee Reeve had brought her. It was black. Of course.

"Is that why you wanted to meet this morning? You wanted to confess?"

Gina couldn't tell if the guy was serious or not.

"No. It's something else."

"What?"

She looked around the bakery to see if anyone else was listening. Then she beckoned him close. "You promise to keep this on the down-low?"

"I can't promise that, Mrs. Biletti."

"It's 'Ms.' Or better yet, 'Gina.' Or even 'Biletti.' And why not?"

"If you know something about tampering with the security cameras—"

"Would you forget the damn security cameras? This is bigger. Much bigger." She took a deep breath. *Sorry, Danielle.* "I think someone was murdered."

"What?!"

"Not so loud!" Gina hissed.

"Ms. Biletti, what the hell are you talking about?"

"*Gina.* And I have good reason to believe that Vanessa Schaeffer didn't die of a heart attack. At least a natural one."

Reeve stared at her with his intense gray eyes. She met his gaze.

Finally, he motioned for her to follow him outside.

On the street, he said, "This better not be another one of your jokes."

"I never joke about murder."

"Walk with me. And start talking."

He led her towards the Village Green and she succinctly

outlined her suspicions about Stanley Schaeffer—just as she had done with Berenstein and Danielle the night before.

When she was done, Reeve shook his head. "That's quite a story. You happen to have any actual proof? Or is it just the gossip that makes you think that Vanessa Schaeffer was murdered?"

"Gossip?" Gina sputtered.

"Yes, gossip. And hearsay."

"I would call that 'reasonable doubt' instead."

"I think you're mixing up your terminology." His stern expression softened. "Listen, Gina, I'm going to be straight with you. The fact is, we're not really in a position to investigate murder allegations here—especially without any sort of actual evidence."

"But—"

"And my marching orders from our district executive are pretty clear: keep a low profile."

"But—"

"That being said…" He lowered his voice. "Maybe I can look into some of your, uh, concerns. Off the record."

Gina realized this was the best she could hope for. "That would be great," she mumbled.

"Ms. Schaeffer's body is in Pendleton. If the medical examiner has any questions, I could maybe open a line of dialog—unofficially and outside of Maidenwell, of course."

"Sure. I could just be a concerned citizen."

Reeve had offered to drive Gina back up to Haverford Hall, but she told him she wanted to stroll around the village a bit. She wandered down the side street that led to the stream and thought of Catherine and Becca. Both women seemed to know quite a lot about Stanley and Vanessa—which made sense. According to what she had learned at the party, these alpaca people were all up in each other's business.

Maybe I should hang with Becca some more, Gina thought. *Minus the weed.*

As she stood on the walled embankment, staring at the gently flowing water, doubts clouded her mind.

What's the use, though, really? What else can I do—if no one is going to really investigate this thing?

Gina kicked a pebble into the stream, probably scaring a bunch of trout. This entire experience here in Maidenwell was so surreal. She shouldn't even be here. She should be back in New York trying to find a job—not playing amateur detective in this theme-park English village. It was crazy.

The thought of not having gainful employment terrified her. Gina had worked continuously since she was sixteen. All through high school, and all through college. There was never a time when she didn't have a job. And every time she had changed jobs, it was for a better opportunity. She had never been fired. Or downsized.

Until now.

She kicked another pebble into the water.

Her flight home was the day after tomorrow, but she didn't see much point in staying. Maybe they could take the afternoon train out of here once Danielle was finished touring water reclamation plants or whatever she was looking at. Then she could spend tomorrow exploring more of Portland than just the airport.

Gina headed back to the Village Green to see if Berenstein's shop was open. He was a good guy and it would be nice to say goodbye in person. And break the news that she wouldn't be buying his bookstore.

Unfortunately, when she arrived at Berenstein's Books, the shop was dark and locked up tight. Maybe he wasn't even open on Sundays.

Oh well, she thought. *I still have his card. I can call him when I get back home.* It would be good to keep in touch.

Gina circled around the Village Green and headed past the pub and the White Horse Inn towards the road that ran up the hill to Haverford Hall. Just as she started up the road, the church bell chimed seven o'clock. Gina had imagined that living in the village near an active bell tower would be a nightmare, but the sound of the St. Mary's bells was low and pleasant. Just loud enough to hear from a distance, but not too obnoxious.

For no particular reason, other than that she didn't want to hang out in her room all day, Gina veered off the roadside path and cut across an open, verdant clearing towards a grove of trees.

She was a little nervous that Reeve would come zooming over in his souped-up golf cart and bust her for not walking on the designated paths, but whatever.

If Gina had her bearings right, she was heading toward the rose gardens and the hedge maze. Not that she really expected that Becca would be there—smoking pot again. The girl was probably cramming for her presentation at the auction.

She entered the grove of manicured, carefully spaced trees and followed a narrow path that she hoped was heading in the right direction. Shafts of warm autumn sunlight pierced the tree canopy, creating a magic tunnel of golden leaves and dappled light and shadow. Gina paused and soaked it all in.

This is like something out of a fairy tale.

In the distance, she heard the soft burble of flowing water and wondered if she was close to Catherine's trout stream.

Gina continued along the wooded path, curving along a ridge. A low stone wall made of volcanic rock edged the ridge. Mortared into the wall was a bronze plaque. The metal was tarnished and discolored as if it had been there for hundreds of years, but the words were legible:

"NOT ALL THOSE WHO WANDER ARE LOST."
—J.R.R. Tolkien

Great. Gina looked around nervously. *That's all I need. Hobbits.*

Through a break in the trees, she glimpsed a fast-moving brook running down the slope. She guessed it fed into the trout stream.

Eventually the grove thinned out, and the path followed the brook upstream through a meadow of wheat-colored grass. The wind started to pick up here at the top of the hill, fluttering the grass like ripples in the ocean.

I'm definitely taking the scenic route, Gina thought as she huffed along the hill. A little short of breath, she stopped near a lone tree and was promptly chastised by a black and white bird with a long tail.

Eeh, eeh, eeh! it chattered.

"I know, I know," Gina said. "I need to get back to the gym. It's been a minute."

The bird hopped onto another branch and continued to admonish Gina. She didn't recognize the type of bird. Maybe it was some West Coast variety. Or who knew? Maybe Matthias Loneskum imported birds from the English countryside to add to the authenticity of Maidenwell.

Eeh, eeh, eeh!

"Okay, I'm leaving. Don't get your feathers in a bunch."

She trudged up the hill until the land leveled out. Finally. Up ahead, she saw a white stone structure that looked like a miniature Roman temple, with columns and a domed metal roof. It perched on the shore of a long ornamental pond ringed with trees.

As she drew closer, she saw that there was someone there on the shore. A woman.

Gina was about to call out a greeting when she realized

that the woman was stripping off her clothes. In two seconds, she was completely naked.

The naked woman was thin and willowy, with a mane of red hair that fluttered in the breeze. She balanced perfectly on a big flat rock on the edge of the pond.

Once she had recovered from her initial shock, Gina realized who the woman was: Noelle Garland.

She's so skinny! Gina couldn't help thinking. *Even after having a kid.* Of course, that had been a while ago. Her creepy son was at least twelve years old.

Luckily, Noelle didn't seem to notice Gina watching her. She gracefully dipped her foot in the water, as if judging its temperature.

I need to get out of here, Gina thought frantically. *This is very awkward.*

She backed away, but not before another inappropriate thought popped into her head.

I guess the carpet doesn't match the drapes.

Instantly, she regretted even thinking of that vulgar expression. She hated it whenever Erik used it—which was whenever he could. Apparently, he thought it was funny. Or clever. *So much for Southern gentility.*

As Gina ducked down to slink away, her foot slipped in the mud. She let out a loud yelp of alarm before tumbling back, and careened down the slope. Branches tore at her and then her head smacked against the ground.

Oof!

All her breath was driven out of her body and everything went dark.

twelve

. . .

AS SHE LAY THERE, unable to see, unable to move, Gina found herself in a weird dream state. She knew it was a dream because an alpaca was talking to her. It was Florrie.

"You can't keep on doing what you're doing, girl," Florrie said.

Even though he was fluffy and obviously an animal, he sounded like the gay best friend in a cheesy rom-com.

"Alpacas can't talk," Gina said.

"Uh huh. This is about you, honey, not me. Deflect much?"

"I'm not deflecting."

"You are totally deflecting," Florrie said. "What are you afraid of?"

Gina snorted a very unladylike snort. "Me? Afraid? I'm not afraid of anything."

"Lies, all lies." Florrie had very large brown eyes—that seemed to bore into her.

"Okay, maybe I'm afraid of some things. But it's all the usual stuff. Lyme disease. Dying alone. Getting audited by the IRS."

"I think you're afraid of the truth, girlfriend."

"I'm not afraid of the truth. I seek the truth. I *love* the truth."

"Maybe you love the truth in the abstract—just not the truth about yourself."

"That doesn't make sense."

"Or does it?" Florrie winked at her. "Why are you trying to get back in that rut? That's what you should ask yourself."

"It's kind of weird when an animal says 'rut,' but go on."

"You've been sleepwalking through life. Just taking the safe route."

"Really?" Gina scoffed. "This most recent route didn't turn out to be very safe. I probably broke my skull or something."

"Don't be a hypochondriac," Florrie said. "You're going to be fine."

He nestled against her chest, his fuzzy head pressing against her boobs.

"That's nice," she murmured. "I could stay like this forever." She took a deep breath, inhaling the scent of his fur. It smelled uncannily like Herbal Essence shampoo.

And suddenly, Gina was awake, her face tangled in a mass of wet, yet sweet-smelling red hair.

Noelle lifted her head from Gina's chest. "You're alive!"

"What are you doing?"

"Giving you CPR. You stopped breathing, and I was listening for a heartbeat."

Gina let out a groan.

"Don't move. I've called for help."

"I think I'm okay." Gina moved her fingers and her toes. Everything seemed to work and nothing seemed to be broken, so she sat up, breathing deeply to clear her head.

"You really shouldn't be moving around. You had a nasty fall."

Gina noticed Noelle was no longer nude, but her clothes

were wet. "I'm sorry that I was kind of creeping on you—" Gina stammered.

"What? No. You're fine." She smiled. "I didn't think anyone was around."

"What were you doing, uh, naked?"

"They told me people used to bathe in this pond. Mineral springs or something." Noelle shrugged. "I didn't bring a bathing suit."

"Well, you, uh, have a very nice body. Do you work out?" Gina cringed inwardly as the words left her mouth.

"Not really. I'm pretty busy between my practice and taking care of Mason."

"Oh, shit. Your son. How is he?"

"He's fine." She sighed. "Listen, I owe you an apology for snapping at you yesterday."

"No, don't worry about it."

"Mason is not like other kids. He has… challenges."

"What, like—?"

"He's been diagnosed with ASD."

"I don't really know what that is."

"Autism spectrum disorder. He's, uh, on the spectrum, as they say."

"Oh." Gina tried to look suitably surprised as well as sympathetic, even though Reeve had already told her that Mason Garland was a special needs child.

"He doesn't speak to anyone but me and my mother," Noelle explained.

"That's why he wouldn't tell me why he was whipping Florrie."

"Yes, and I'm sorry that he hit you."

Gina unconsciously rubbed her arm.

"Can I take a look?" Noelle asked.

"It's fine."

But Noelle leaned close, her damp hair brushing Gina's face. It still smelled fantastic. She hadn't been imagining that.

"Just a bruise, really," Noelle said. "Didn't even break the skin. No infection."

"Yeah, I barely feel it now. I think I was just more surprised than anything else."

"Well, Mason's a strong kid. He's big for his age."

"How old is he?"

"Ten."

"Really? I thought he might be older."

"Everyone thinks that."

"He has the same hair as you."

Noelle smiled. "Yes, ginger club."

Gina struggled to her feet.

"I really don't think you should be doing that," Noelle said. But she helped Gina steady herself.

"I'm fine. More embarrassed than anything else." Gina felt like her face was on fire. She fanned herself, but it didn't seem to do anything.

"Don't be embarrassed. Seriously." Noelle's big brown eyes were very kind looking. She must have a pretty good bedside manner. If animals even cared about that sort of thing.

"Can I ask you something?"

"Sure," Noelle said. "But let's sit over in the folly. You really shouldn't be moving around."

"Folly?"

Noelle motioned to the miniature Roman temple. "That's what these little decorative buildings are called. It's on your map."

"What map?"

"On your keycard."

"Who knew it had a map?"

"It's a pretty amazing piece of tech."

"Yeah, maybe for someone who can figure it out. I'm pretty hopeless with it."

"Really? I'd be happy to show you."

"You know how to use it?"

Noelle laughed. "Yeah. Geek alert."

"You?"

"I built my first PC when I was in junior high."

"Wow. I'm a Mac girl myself, but that's impressive."

"Yeah, well, I was seriously considering majoring in electric engineering before deciding to go into veterinary medicine."

"Show-off!"

Noelle took Gina's arm, and they walked over to the folly. The little temple was made of worn stone blocks. Its classical columns were chipped and pitted, but it looked sturdy enough.

Noelle led the way to a stone bench. "This is a good place to wait for the medic."

"I really don't need a medic—"

"Shhhh." Noelle placed her hand on Gina's arm again. "Doctor's orders."

They sat there together for a few minutes, not saying anything. Then Gina began to feel even more awkward.

"Can I ask you something?"

"Sure," Noelle said.

"Do you know Stanley Schaeffer?"

A weird little look played over Noelle's face. Just for a second. Then it was gone. "I used to."

"Oh?"

"He gave me my first job when I was living in Idaho."

"Really?" That actually surprised Gina because at the party on Friday night, Stanley didn't seem like he was a big fan of Noelle.

"Yeah, I worked for the Schaeffer Family Farm right out of vet school. That's the reason I specialize in camelids."

"Camelids?"

"Alpacas."

"Did you know Vanessa?"

"Yeah, but she was always less involved on the animal side, so I didn't work with her as much."

"Do you still work with them?"

"No, it's been years. I moved to California when Mason was born. I have my own independent practice now, and I consult for the IAOF."

"Is that the alpaca club?"

"The International Alpaca Owners Federation. It's a worldwide organization. I do a lot of traveling."

"Oh, and do you take Mason with you?" Gina had noticed that Noelle never mentioned a husband or partner.

"My mom takes care of him. I couldn't do it without her." Noelle smiled again. She had perfect teeth. "So why all the questions? Is this part of your job? Are you doing a story about all of us?"

"God, no." Gina immediately realized her tone might be insulting. "Not that all you alpaca people aren't super fascinating."

Noelle laughed politely. "So you're basically just nosy. Huh?"

"Yes!" Gina laughed. "I am nosy! I am so nosy!"

"I get it."

"It's just that I can't help wondering why Stanley wanted the auction to go on. I was married for ten years and if my husband died suddenly, I'd be a mess. There's no way I'd be able to do anything work-related. Of course, that was before we broke up. Now, he can go to hell."

Noelle smiled at her. "Well, I don't think I'm speaking out of turn here, because everyone who knows Stanley and Vanessa knows they've been drifting apart."

"Oh?"

"Yeah, I wouldn't say that they hated each other, but over the past few years, I think Stanley was more committed to his business than his marriage."

"Well, I think it's so sad. And disrespectful. Don't you think?"

"I try not to get involved in all the alpaca drama. And, believe me, there's a lot."

"What do you mean?"

"Did you meet Tomas yet?"

"The farmhand?"

"He's more than a farmhand. There's a rumor going around that Stanley hired him to smuggle an alpaca out of Peru."

"What?"

"Yes, Stanley's female, Magdalene, that he wants to breed with Florentine. She's got amazing genetics that happen to be very different from her sire and dam. At least the sire and dam listed on her certificate."

"That sounds extremely shady."

"Well, it would be. Alpaca smuggling is a big deal. Especially the high-end prize-winning alpacas."

"Are you sure about this?"

"That's the problem. I can't really prove anything, and if I go to Frau Loneskum with this before the auction, it could tip the scales away from Stanley. Or towards him, depending on what Frau Loneskum thinks about it. Either way, I would be seen interfering with the process in a big way and I can't do that. I'm supposed to be impartial. Just reporting on the animals' health and genetics."

All kinds of thoughts were swirling around in Gina's head. "Wow."

Noelle looked away. "I've blabbed way too much. You have to promise not to say anything to anyone, okay?"

"I promise."

"Okay." She turned back and looked right into Gina's eyes, holding her gaze. "I trust you. You have an honest face."

Gina laughed uneasily. "Really? That's the first time anyone's ever said that. Usually—"

At that moment, both of their keycards started beeping an alarm.

"What the hell is that?"

Noelle was the first one to fish out her card. "Uh oh."

Gina finally freed her keycard from her pocket. She stared down at the flashing screen.

> Public Health Emergency Alert. All guests must return to their rooms immediately. Code 94.

HAVERFORD HALL WAS IN CHAOS. Compact police vehicles crowded the parking lot. Guests and staff alike were huddled up outside, whispering and gawking.

Noelle spotted her mom and Mason and ran over to them, leaving Gina by herself.

What's going on? she wondered, as she walked closer to the entrance. *Plague? Gas leak? A rabid alpaca?*

She scanned the crowd for Danielle, but there was no sign of her. Her eyes landed on Frankie Roth instead, her funky, oversized glasses barely concealing the tears threatening to spill out.

"What happened?" Gina asked.

"It's Stanley Schaeffer," Frankie gasped. "He's dead."

"What?" Gina thought she had misheard. "What did you say?"

"Stanley. He's been murdered!"

The words hit Gina like a sucker punch. She wasn't exactly Stanley's biggest fan, but murdered? That was a lot.

Out of nowhere, Reeve burst onto the scene, barking orders for his team to usher everyone back to their rooms. As Gina was being nudged inside by a burly female security guard in a windbreaker emblazoned with SECURITY in large letters, she tried to get Reeve's attention. But he either didn't hear her or decided to play deaf.

Soon, all the guests were locked up in their rooms, instructed to hang tight till further notice.

"What? Are we under house arrest or something?" Gina asked. But the big woman ignored her.

This is ridiculous. Someone had to tell Gina what was going on. They couldn't just keep everyone locked in their rooms. Or could they?

Gina remembered what Reeve had told her about Maidenwell being some kind of self-governing special district within the state of Oregon. *Maybe they have weird laws here that only pertain to Maidenwell. Who knew?*

She spent the next half hour fumbling around with her keycard, trying to get ahold of Danielle, but got no response.

Next she tried Becca, Berenstein, even Millicent.

Nothing.

Maybe her keycard broke when she fell. No, that didn't make sense. She had received the emergency alert. Maybe someone was blocking outgoing messages.

Wouldn't that be illegal? she wondered. Who knew with these tech companies and billionaires? They all seemed to write their own rules.

After nearly two hours of cooling her jets, a staff member knocked on her door.

"They're having a briefing for all the guests downstairs."

The other guests were also ushered out of their rooms and they all went down together to the drawing room, where they attended the party on the first night. This time there was no wine being served—and no sign of the wine woman.

But Danielle was there—along with Peyton Grier and Reeve, the three of them standing in front of a single microphone. Which wasn't really necessary since the room had not much more than a dozen people in it.

"Can I have your attention, everyone?" Danielle said, clapping her hands together.

Gina looked around the room. It was mostly filled with the alpaca people she had met over the course of the weekend: Catherine and Becca, Noelle, her son and her mom, the artist Frankie Roth, Édouard Orville, and the Schaeffers' assistant Ian. There were some other folks there as well. Maybe Haverford Hall's staff members.

"We have a special announcement from District Executive Grier."

Peyton Grier approached the microphone.

"Recently, a male guest was found unresponsive in the stables. Subsequent examination determined that the man was deceased, and possibly a victim of violence."

Several gasps of alarm sounded from the group.

"We have notified the county sheriff's office, and they have requested assistance from the state's Criminal Investigations Division. Qualified personnel are now en route to Maidenwell. When they arrive, the scene of the incident will be secured and every guest and staff member will be interviewed. In the meantime, we would like to request that all guests remain in their rooms—for your own safety. Food and beverages will be provided. That is all."

She stepped away from the microphone just as a flurry of questions erupted from the group.

"What about the auction?" Becca called out.

Danielle moved to the microphone. "Due to current circumstances, the auction and all events at Haverford Hall have been cancelled."

"When can we leave?" Frankie asked.

"That's up to the CID," Danielle said.

"Danielle, you know I have to catch a plane back to New York on Tuesday," Gina said.

Peyton Grier stepped back up to the front of the room.

"We're advising everyone to clear their schedules. If you need to make calls to family or work, we can arrange that after your interviews with law enforcement. But the fact is, no one's going anywhere for a while."

thirteen

. . .

A FEW HOURS LATER, a knock interrupted Gina's nap. She hadn't been in a deep sleep, just dozing in between chapters of her book. Somehow it felt weird reading about a murder mystery while living one.

She opened the door to reveal Reeve, standing there in the hallway with a serious look on his face. Which wasn't very different from every other time she had seen him.

"I probably should have asked who it was, first," Gina said, "seeing as there is a murderer at large."

"You probably should have. Can I come in?"

"That depends. Are you the murderer?"

"No."

"Then, by all means." She stepped aside and beckoned him in with a flourish.

He shut the door behind him but didn't sit down. "Technically, I shouldn't be here."

"I know. If I wasn't still sleepy, I'd be freaking out right now."

"I figured that after our conversation this morning, I owed you an apology… for being skeptical."

"Oh, about the whole murder thing?" Gina arched an eyebrow. She didn't hate seeing him squirm a bit.

"Yes."

"That's fine. I realize not everyone is as suspicious as me. Or has seen as many *Lifetime* movies."

"You've got me there."

"How was Stanley killed?" Gina had been eager to find out the details all day long, even though she knew it was perverse and gruesome.

"I really shouldn't be talking about this."

"Then why are you here?"

"I told you—"

"Why are you *really* here?"

Finally, Reeve sat down on one of the brocade chairs. "It's going to be awhile before the state investigators arrive."

"Where are they coming from?"

"All over. Portland. Salem."

"And you're worried about losing time. Right?"

"Right."

"Because the critical time for investigation is the first twelve hours after a crime." She thumped her mystery novel. "I just read that."

"I think another brain working on this might not be a bad idea."

"And you thought of *my* brain?" Gina smiled. "I'm flattered. Lay it on me, Watson."

Reeve got up and started pacing. "We think Stanley was murdered in the stables somewhere between 6:48 and 7:30 this morning."

"That's a pretty narrow window."

"According to his keycard, he left Haverford Hall at 6:48. Then—"

"Hold on." Gina furrowed her brow. "*According to his keycard?* Are you tracking us?"

"Only in certain areas. And before you ask, not in the stables."

It still seemed sketchy to her. "What was Stanley doing there—in the stables?"

"No idea. We found him in Florentine's pen. His femoral artery had been ripped out." Reeve patted his inner thigh. "Right there."

"I hate to even ask this, but could it have been an animal attack?"

"Alpacas are herbivores."

"Maybe Florrie thought Stanley was an oversized artichoke."

"This isn't funny," Reeve said.

"I know. Sorry. I'm nervous. You know how that goes."

"Anyway, Dr. Kurian believes the wound was caused by a sharp metal object that first punctured the inside of Schaeffer's inner thigh, then ripped through it, severing the femoral artery. Judging by the amount of blood soaking the hay, he bled out."

"It couldn't have been accidental, could it?" Gina asked, even though her gut said MURDER.

"Like he caught himself on a rusty nail?"

"I don't know."

Reeve shook his head. "There was no blood trail. No sign of a murder weapon. Whatever happened to him, happened to him right there in the pen."

"So he didn't even try to get away?" Gina imagined herself with a big gash in her leg, bleeding profusely. She'd probably be as dead as Stanley, but at least she would have attempted to get to safety.

"Nothing that would indicate that," Reeve said.

"Security cameras catch anything?"

"Still out of commission from yesterday. Replacements aren't due until mid-week." He drifted over to the window and looked out.

"That's not good."

"No. We should have had back-ups. I'm guessing that a few people are going to lose their jobs over that. Maybe even me."

"Hopefully not. Still, in just about every British cop show I've seen, they always use CCTV to solve the crimes."

"Duly noted."

They were both quiet for a few moments while Gina tried to digest everything. She had been convinced that Stanley had something to do with Vanessa's death, but him being murdered turned everything upside down.

"I see those gears turning," Reeve said.

"Unfortunately, I'm still in neutral."

"So you haven't figured it out already?"

"The murders have to be related. Or we're looking at a pretty big coincidence."

"I don't really believe in coincidences. Especially when it comes to crimes."

"I'm not going to argue," Gina said. "So someone had it in for both Vanessa and Stanley Schaeffer…"

"You seem to know these people better than most. Any hunches?"

One name popped into her head, but she refused to believe it. Instead, she said, "I need to think about it."

"Okay, but keep your ears open. Talk to the others once you are able to."

"What does that mean?"

"The state investigators will probably interview everyone tomorrow. I'm not sure what will happen after that, but I doubt you'll be confined to your rooms."

"When can we leave? Maidenwell, I mean."

"That's not up to me. It is kind of a unique situation. We know the murderer is here. And unless they want to trek across fifty miles of wilderness, there's no way out."

AT AROUND DINNER TIME, Gina got her second visitor.

"How are you holding up?" Danielle entered, holding a bottle of wine and some glasses.

"What the hell? Why have you been ghosting me?"

"I haven't been ghosting you. I've been in crisis mode—in case you haven't noticed. But I brought you a peace offering."

Gina looked at the wine. It was a Bogwood Bay Ribbon Ridge Reserve Pinot Noir. "Did you steal this?"

"What? No. Listen, don't ask questions. Just crack this baby open. I don't have much time. We're supposed to be on a bio break."

As Gina poured them each a generous volume of wine, Danielle filled her in on what was going on behind the scenes. The first group of investigators had arrived and were now at the stables collecting evidence. Next, they'd move on to all the guests and anyone else who had contact with Stanley.

"They'll probably get to you in the morning, hon. But just be forewarned, they'll be collecting your prints, DNA, hair samples, urine sample—"

"Urine sample? Did someone pee on Stanley?"

"Not to my knowledge, but they're hitting this hard, trying to pin down the murderer with forensic evidence while everyone's in Maidenwell."

"Yeah, that's what Reeve said."

"Oh? So I'm not your first visitor of the day?" Danielle smiled behind her glass, and then took a long drink of Pinot.

"Apparently, he values my opinion."

"Ooh, good for you. I just assumed he found out you like to gossip."

"That too."

"So, who do you think offed Stanley?"

"Danielle, have some respect. A man died."

"I know you have some suspicions. Spill."

"Well, I have been thinking about it a lot."

"Go on."

Gina made a face. "The obvious suspect is Becca Hill."

"The young girl?"

"Yes. She was Stanley's chief competition for Florrie. I spent a lot of time talking with her and she hated him. No question about that."

"Hated him enough to murder him?" Danielle asked.

"That's the question. My gut feeling is no. Becca's passionate and idealistic, but she doesn't seem like a killer."

"Okay, who's next on your list?"

"Well, Becca said that the competition was really between her and the Schaeffers. She didn't think that Frau Loneskum would seriously consider selling to either Édouard Orville or Frankie Roth."

"Why not?"

"No idea. But we do know that Frankie Roth was bankrupt. If she managed to win Florrie, she might be able to turn her alpaca business around. So I could see her wanting to eliminate one or more of her competitors."

"I don't know," Danielle said. "She doesn't strike me as the murderous type, either."

"Most murderers aren't obvious murderers."

"If you say so. Anyone else?"

"There's the wine lady."

"Amadora Seville."

"You remember her name?" Gina asked, genuinely surprised.

"What can I say? I thought she was hot."

"Well, she was shtupping Stanley."

"What? No!"

"I saw them together."

"You did not!"

"Yeah, I accidentally/not accidentally burst into his room while they were doing it."

"Awkward."

"Yeah, I'll say."

"But why would Amadora want to kill Stanley?"

"No idea. If I was shtupping Stanley, I'd want to kill *myself*. But I'm just throwing it out there as a data point."

"Okay, anyone else? I need to get back."

"The only people left are Noelle and her mom, Stanley's assistant, and Tomas."

"Noelle's the vet, right?"

"Yeah, but she was with me when we got the call."

"What were you guys doing?"

Gina felt her face flush with warmth. "I kind of stumbled upon her skinny dipping."

"Babes! What do you mean, *stumbled upon*?"

"I wasn't doing anything weird. Just walking back up to the manor from town. I kind of got lost and then saw this lake where she was swimming."

"Naked?"

"Yeah. Then I tripped and knocked myself out and she helped me. No big deal."

"Sounds like a big deal. Are you okay?"

In all the commotion about the murder, Gina had forgotten all about her own mishap. She felt sore, but didn't think she had a concussion or anything. Still… "Yeah, but I wouldn't mind seeing the doctor. Just to make sure."

"I'll let someone know and we'll get you checked out." Danielle pulled her in close for a hug. "I'm sorry."

"Not your fault. I'm a klutz."

Danielle checked her watch. "I've got a briefing call with Matthias Loneskum in an hour and forty-seven minutes that I need to prep for."

"Is he coming here?"

"I don't think so. He's in Dubai." She drained the last of her wine and turned to leave.

"Aren't you going to ask me about Ian and Tomas?"

"Can't. You keep working on it. I've got to go. Peyton's on the warpath, as you can imagine. By the way, I had to tell her you really didn't work for me. Full time, I mean."

"Fine. I don't think I can get more black marks in her book."

"True. I'll tell them to send up a medical person to check you out."

"And maybe another bottle of wine while you're at it."

Gina's dinner arrived before anyone came to inspect her head. The food was nothing special. Just some sandwiches, although the bread seemed freshly baked.

She decided to lay off the wine, in case she really did have a concussion or something.

Then at around eight p.m., Yvonne Loneskum's personal physician showed up himself. He was a short, round man, a little older than Gina, with a kind-looking face and a little black doctor's bag. When he spoke, Gina detected a slight British accent.

"Ms. Biletti? I'm Nikhil Kurian."

"Thanks for coming to see me. So rare to see a doctor who makes house calls—or manor calls."

"Ah, yes. They said you fancied yourself a comedienne."

"I don't know about that. It might be the concussion talking."

"Let's hope not. That would be most concerning." He gestured to the chair. "Please sit."

Gina eased into a brocade chair. "I'm actually feeling okay. Just a little sore."

"Uh huh. And did you hit your head?"

"I think so. I actually blacked out for a little bit."

"How long?" He gently placed his hands on her shoulders. "Lean forward a bit."

"I have no idea, to be honest. But not long. Someone was with me."

"Oh?" Dr. Kurian felt along her spine and base of her neck.

"Noelle Garland. She's the alpaca vet. Next best thing to having a doctor there, right?"

"If you say so. And where exactly did you strike your head?"

"Well, I fell back."

"Okay, I'm just going to check—very gently." He probed around her head. "Does that hurt?"

"Not really. It feels good. I couldn't convince you to give me a head massage real quick, could I?"

Dr. Kurian ignored the question. "Any dizziness?"

"No."

"Balance issues?"

"Nope."

"Trouble concentrating or brain fog?"

"Not more than usual."

"How's your vision?"

"Perfect."

"Headache?"

"Surprisingly, no."

"Loss of taste or smell?"

"I don't have COVID."

"Ringing in the ears?"

"Nope."

He unclipped a little penlight from his shirt pocket. "Just going to check your eyes real quick. Do they feel sensitive?"

"What do you mean?"

"To light."

"Nope."

"Good. Well, so far, so good. If you would stand up, I'll check your body next. Would you like me to call for a chaperone?"

Gina smiled. "I trust you."

Dr. Kurian examined her body, but didn't find more than

some bruising. "I think you'll be fine, Ms. Biletti. But I'd be extra cautious over the next forty-eight hours. Please contact me if you have any of the symptoms I mentioned." He gestured to the nearly empty wine bottle. "Oh, and you don't want to be doing that. Bad idea."

"I know. Sorry. It was dumb."

"Switch to water. Get plenty of rest."

As he was packing up his bag, Gina said, "It must have been tough seeing Stanley Schaeffer like that."

"Like what?"

"Dead. With his leg torn open. Femoral artery, wasn't it?"

"I'm sorry, Ms. Biletti. I can't discuss that."

"Sure. I understand."

Dr. Kurian handed her a card. "Remember, if you experience any of those symptoms we discussed, you call my office. Day or night."

Gina examined the business card. "Isn't this a little low-tech?"

The doctor shrugged. "I'm a traditionalist. Besides, your keycard has text recognition. Just scan the card and you'll be good to go."

Oh, yeah, sure, Gina thought. *Just scan it. Easy.*

"And what about this visit? Do you need my insurance card?"

Dr. Kurian smiled. "Compliments of the house."

With that, he ducked out.

Gina poured out the rest of the wine into the sink, took a shower, and got ready for bed. It was weird not having a TV or her phone or her iPad. All she had to occupy her time was her mystery novel and her thoughts.

She wished she could meditate like Danielle.

About five years back, Gina had tried really hard to get into yoga. Her instructor was a sixty-five-year-old woman named Bali, who had the body of a thirty-year-old. Gina wanted a slice of that action, hoping to dodge being a forty-year-old woman trapped in a fifty-year-old's body. So she threw herself into yoga big time. Lived and breathed it. Books, classes, videos, several thousand dollars' worth of athleisure clothing.

But despite her best efforts, yoga just didn't click. She threw in the towel after a few months. Bali told Gina that she was surrendering to her restless, unsettled monkey mind.

Gina had never heard of 'monkey mind' before, but when she Googled it, she had to admit that Bali was right.

I've got a monkey mind. So what? Pass the bananas.

Still, she'd give anything to be able to just snap her fingers and reach a state of crystal-clear Zen.

Maybe then she'd be able to figure this mystery out.

fourteen

. . .

THE NEXT MORNING, Gina was escorted down to the administrative floor, given coffee and a berry scone, and parked in an office that was set up with audio recording equipment.

A minute later, two men entered the room. One was older than her, the other younger. Both were white, clean-cut, and earnest-looking.

"Good morning, Ms. Biletti," the older man said. "I'm Detective Waverly. This is Detective Falson."

Gina tapped on one of the microphones. "What are we doing, recording a podcast?"

"No, we need to have an audio record of our interview with you."

The detectives launched into their interview without much of a preamble, starting by asking who she was and how she came to be here in Maidenwell over the weekend.

She told them probably much more than they wanted to know about losing her job, getting divorced, and trying to start over—even though she had no idea what she would do with her life and it made her physically ill to even contemplate the question.

"Danielle took pity on me and wanted to cheer me up. That's why she brought me along this weekend as her plus-one."

The younger detective—Falson—checked his notebook. "But you don't actually work for her?"

"No, not officially. But I was coming along as her assistant —in case she needed, you know, assistance."

"Right, but just to be very clear, you are not a PR professional. Correct?"

"Not per se. My background is in market research. But I have worked for PR firms doing research."

"Got it."

Then they asked about Gina's movements yesterday. They inquired where she was, who she was with, what she was doing, and why.

Gina attempted to answer everything in a straightforward way and fought against her natural inclination to joke—even though she was extremely nervous.

Next, they asked her about her relationship with the Schaeffers and whether she had known them before this weekend.

Finally, they posed the question of who she believed might have been involved in Stanley Schaeffer's death and why.

"Just your opinion, Ms. Biletti," Detective Waverly said.

This was the question Gina had dreaded the most. Despite all her suspicions, she didn't want to throw anyone under the bus without more evidence—especially Becca, who the cops must be looking at as the top suspect. At the same time, she knew that this was her chance to help bring the killer to justice.

She was torn.

In the end, she decided to stick with the facts:

1) She had heard various rumors that Stanley and Vanessa's marriage was on the rocks.

2) She had seen a woman who looked like Vanessa meet with a man who might have been Tomas early on the

morning of Vanessa's death. The woman passed a thick envelope to the man.

3) She had stumbled upon Stanley Schaeffer and Amadora, the wine rep, in a compromising position last night.

4) Because of this, she had wondered if Vanessa's death was suspicious.

5) Including the Schaeffers, four groups were competing for a very valuable alpaca at this auction: Becca and Catherine Hill, Édouard Orville, and Frankie Roth.

She stressed she wasn't really up on the alpaca industry and the various ranches, and Yvonne Loneskum would be the best person to ask about that.

Detectives Waverly and Falson asked a few perfunctory follow-ups and then told her they would be in touch should they have any more questions.

Gina was then handed off to another cop who took her to a different room where a technician took her fingerprints, did a DNA swab, and took fingernail, hair, and urine samples. All on a voluntary basis, he stressed, even though it was pretty clear that not volunteering would be cause for suspicion.

"How long will it take to get the results?" she asked.

"A few days at most, but I'm guessing the brass will do everything they can to expedite it."

No one had said so explicitly, but Gina got the strong impression that none of the guests were leaving Maidenwell until all the evidence had been analyzed. It was like Reeve had said. The murderer was here—with no way out.

After all the poking and prodding, the cop escorting her told Gina that she was free to go—but recommended that she find a buddy if she was planning on leaving Haverford Hall.

GINA WONDERED if Millicent counted as a buddy.

With a little remedial instruction from the gal at the front desk, Gina used her keycard to contact Millicent and fifteen minutes later, her card chimed with a message.

I'm out front.

As Gina got into the vintage car, Millicent asked, "Are you okay?"

"Yeah, it wasn't a concussion."

"What?"

Gina realized Millicent was asking about the murder.

"Yeah, sorry. Things have been pretty intense."

"I'll say. Everyone I know is stunned. No one thought that something like this could happen in Maidenwell."

"Yeah, well, if it makes you feel any better, my guess is that this is all connected to the alpaca people. I don't think anyone in the village had anything to do with it."

"That's pretty much a given. Have they found the guy that did it?"

"Not yet, but there's a very limited pool of suspects."

Gina asked Millicent to drop her off at Berenstein's Books, which thankfully looked open. As she exited the car, she asked if Millicent could pick her back up after lunch.

"No problem. Text me."

As Gina pushed her way inside the bookshop, the bell over the door tinkled. There were no customers and no sign of the proprietor. Or his cat.

"Berenstein?" she called. Maybe he was in the back, stocking shelves, or whatever you do when you own a store.

"Larry?" she called again, winding her way through the stacks.

This is weird. The door had definitely been unlocked and there was no "Sorry We're Closed Because I'm Taking a Nap" sign in the window.

"Yoooo-hooo, Larry Berenstein—anyone home?"

Gina continued to explore the store. It wasn't that big, so she was able to examine the entire space. Still no sign of Berenstein.

A tickle of apprehension ran along her spine. Not full-blown fear, but close.

She spotted a curtained doorway against the back wall. It probably led to the back room.

"Berenstein?" she called out again. "It's Gina. No, I haven't come to buy your store. I just want to talk."

Cautiously, she poked her head through the curtain. *Yup, definitely a back room.* There were shelves and a long work table filled with books and stacks of boxes. At the far end of the room was a tiny little kitchenette with a grimy-looking coffee maker and one of those cube-like dorm fridges. Beyond the kitchenette were two doors. Between them stood a vacuum cleaner and a bucket filled with brushes and cleaning supplies.

Maybe he's talking to the maid out back.

In the front corner of the room stood a modern-looking desk that looked like it was from IKEA. Definitely out of place. And on the desk was an open laptop. Its screen displayed a screensaver of animated colors and wavelike patterns.

How come everyone gets a computer besides me?

Gina ambled over to the desk. She couldn't help but wonder what Berenstein was working on. It was probably something super boring, like taxes or sales reports. But maybe he was writing a novel or something. Surrounded by all these books all day long, how could you not be tempted to throw your hat in the ring? If she worked at a bookstore, she'd definitely write a novel.

"Ahem."

Gina jumped and whipped around to see Berenstein, wiping his hands with a paper towel.

"You know you get access to all the financials once you

tell me you're serious about buying."

"Where the hell were you? I thought the serial killer got you."

"I was indisposed."

Gina wrinkled her nose. "Oh."

"You know, you're not supposed to be back here. Didn't you see the sign, kiddo?" He ushered her out into the main part of the store.

"No. I didn't see Waldo, either. I was experiencing very dark thoughts."

"Well, I'm touched, Biletti. Really touched. I was worried about you, as well. Bad business up at the manor."

"Bad business?" She blinked in disbelief. "A guy got his femoral artery yanked out of his leg and bled to death. I'd say that's a little more than 'bad business,' wouldn't you?"

"I was trying not to contribute to your obvious state of panic."

"Thanks."

"Anyway, it looks like you were correct about the murder."

"Yeah, but very wrong about the murderer. Anyway, can you lock up and grab a bite with me? It's not like you have any customers."

"Normally, the place would be packed. Packed, I tell you. But what with the—"

"Save the sales pitch. Where are we going for lunch?" She headed out the front door and Berenstein locked up behind them.

"You like Thai?"

"I could do Thai. Is it, like, normal Thai, or Thai fish and chips? Or Thai bangers and mash?"

Berenstein chuckled. "Just normal Thai." He led her past the pub and the White Horse Inn to a small restaurant emblazoned with a sign that read 'Queen of Siam.'

"Looks like a good place for lunch," Gina said.

"It is," Berenstein said. "Very private."

As she passed through the ornately painted doorway into the restaurant, all kinds of delicious aromas hit her.

"Ah, Mr. Larry." An older Asian woman greeted Berenstein. "Eating in or takeaway?"

"Eating in today, Dolores. Perhaps a booth."

"No problem. Who's your girlfriend?"

"This is Gina Biletti. She'll be buying my shop when I retire."

"Oh?"

"Not buying his shop," Gina said quickly. "Just in for the weekend. Nice to meet you."

"The weekend, huh? You're not going anywhere now. They shut down the train."

The booths were separated by brightly colored walls of patterned fabric hanging from the ceiling and draping down to create mini tents around the tables. The fabric probably didn't block out any sound, but it looked cool and gave the illusion of privacy. Luckily, it was a little early for lunch and the restaurant wasn't very crowded.

Gina ordered some veggie spring rolls and a bowl of Tom Kah soup, and then, in hushed tones, filled Berenstein in on what had gone on.

"Unbelievable," he said between bites of Drunken Noodle. "Have the fuzz made any progress?"

"Fuzz? Really?"

"Don't be ageist. That's what we used to call them back in my day."

"Back in Woodstock, huh? Anyway, I imagine the *detectives* are still interrogating people."

"What about you?"

"They're done with me. I hope."

"No, I meant, have *you* made any progress?"

"Me? I told the detectives what I knew." Gina nibbled another bite of her spring roll and mumbled, "More or less."

"I heard that, young lady."

"I love it when you call me 'young.'"

"Yes, still buttering you up, so you'll buy my shop."

"Not going to happen."

"So, what did you tell them? More or less?"

"Possibly a little less than I could."

He shook his head. "Biletti—"

"I didn't want to get anyone in trouble," Gina said with a sigh.

"Even the murderer?"

"Oh, I want to get him in trouble. Or her. It's just that there's one person who might—on the surface—have a pretty powerful motive."

"Ah ha!"

"Don't ah-ha me. I don't think she did it."

"But this mystery person could reasonably be the murderer?"

Gina thought for a moment. Becca hated Stanley, that was for certain, but would she actually benefit from his death? There was no way the auction would happen now. Even Frau Loneskum wasn't as cold-blooded as that.

"I'm not completely sure about a motive," Gina admitted.

"Then you have to keep digging. Find out who really had a motive."

"Yeah, easier said than done."

"Oh, I don't know about that. Remember what we discussed? It usually comes down to love or money. Or sometimes both."

After her conversation with Berenstein, Gina felt more confused than ever. He was right, though. Someone out there had a motive for killing Stanley. And if it wasn't Becca, maybe the motive wasn't so obvious.

She needed to find out who would benefit from Stanley's death and why.

The problem was, Gina really didn't know much about Stanley. She had heard bits and pieces from Becca and Catherine and Noelle. But there was one person in Maidenwell that knew Stanley's secrets. And that person was his shifty little assistant, Ian.

Okay, he wasn't exactly little, and he wasn't all that shifty, but Ian definitely enabled Stanley: stealing wine for him and guarding his door while he shtupped the wine lady.

If anyone knew what was going on with Stanley, it was Ian. She would have to find him and get him to spill the beans.

Finding Ian turned out to be pretty simple. On the way back from the Thai restaurant, Gina spotted the young man entering the pub.

"Sorry to dine and dash, Berenstein, but I think I just saw someone who might shed some light on those motives we were talking about."

Berenstein glanced back to where Gina's gaze was fixed.

"By all means. Go get your man!"

fifteen

. . .

IAN WAS NOT happy when Gina plopped down at his table.

"Oh no. Not you." He snapped closed his bright red hard-bound designer notebook and gripped his fancy pen tightly.

"Relax," Gina said. "I don't want to cause any problems. I just wanted to say how sorry I am about Stanley."

"Thanks, but you have to leave me alone. I'm in enough trouble."

"Well, the cops told me that we should buddy up when we're out and about. And what trouble?"

He stared at her. "Are you serious right now?"

"Okay, I can see you need a drink. I'm buying. What'll you have?"

"I don't know. An IPA if they have it."

"Coming right up."

Gina went to get the drinks, keeping an eye on Ian the whole time, in case he decided to bolt. But thankfully, he just sat there, rubbing his eyes and flipping manically through his notebook.

"Here you go." She placed his beer and her wine down on the table, then eased into her seat, trying to get a glimpse of what was written in the book. But Ian was too fast. In a swift motion, he closed the book, scooped up his beer and took a swig.

"So, what do you want?"

"Why do I have to want anything? I just saw you alone, and I was alone and I remembered the cops said we should not walk around by ourselves, so I thought maybe we could be alone together."

"We're in a village of several hundred people right now. I don't think that qualifies as being 'alone.'"

"Probably not."

"What do you really want?"

Gina took a deep drink of her wine. It wasn't as good as the wine lady's Pinot.

"I just want to talk about Stanley. I feel so bad about what happened."

"Why? Did you kill him?"

"No, of course I didn't kill him. Why would you even say that?"

"You're right. I have a pretty good idea who did it."

"Oh?"

"It's obvious, and I told the cops so."

"Well, spit it out."

"That Rebecca chick."

"Becca?"

"Yeah. She hated Stanley, and everything he was trying to do."

"Yeah, sure, I'll give you that, but she doesn't strike me as someone who would sever someone's artery with a pointed weapon and—"

"What?" All the color drained from Ian's face.

"What do you mean what?"

"His throat was slit?"

It dawned on Gina that Ian didn't know how Stanley had died.

"No," she said softly. "It was the artery in his leg. Severed."

"Jesus." He turned away. "Who the fuck would do that?"

"That's what I intend to find out."

"You?" he scoffed. "You're just a PR lady."

"No, I'm not."

"Then who the hell are you?"

"Someone who's pretty good at asking questions and getting answers."

"Right." Ian took another long drink of beer, draining the rest of his glass. "Okay, I'll play along. If it wasn't Rebecca, who was it?"

"I don't know. Yet."

"Who do you suspect?"

"Everyone," Gina said evenly.

"Everyone? Me? If that's the truth, you picked the wrong person to buddy up with. Big time."

"I don't think it was you, Ian."

"Good, because it wasn't. I hated that son of a bitch Stanley, but I didn't want him dead."

"Of course not." Gina was doing her best to sound agreeable. "Hold that thought."

She hustled back over to the bar and ordered some shots of tequila and another beer for Ian. Might as well keep him lubricated, so he'd keep talking. She had to make two trips to carry all the drinks, but Ian didn't seem to care that he was being plied with alcohol.

"Shots?" he asked.

"Tequila," Gina said. "I figured we should toast Stanley."

"Sure." Ian raised his shot glass and held it up unsteadily. "To Stanley."

"To Stanley," Gina echoed.

"Always making more work for me. Even after he croaked." Ian downed his shot, while Gina sipped hers in what she hoped was a ladylike fashion.

She wasn't really a shot kind of gal. Not since her bachelorette party in Lake Tahoe, anyway. And those were Jägerbombs, so they didn't count.

"More work? What do you mean? You're a free man, Ian." Gina pushed the pint glass of beer towards him.

"You'd think so, but no way. I'm not a free man. Not by a long shot."

"Well, I'm reasonably certain that indentured servitude is frowned upon in this day and age, so—"

"I'm the executor for Stanley's estate."

"Oh..." The word dragged from Gina's mouth as the implication dawned on her. "I see."

"I don't think you do. His estate's a mess and he doesn't have a full will."

"How could you be an executor without a will?"

"I know, right? Stanley kept dragging his feet about the will because he thought he was basically invincible. Asshole. Two months ago, he started putting together the outside financing to help buy Florentine and expand Schaeffer Family Farms."

"Two months ago? That's pretty cocky. He was sure he was going to win the auction?"

"Yeah. Cocky. But the private-equity firm required that he have certain provisions in place, business documents, and an estate plan determining what would happen to the ranch's assets—including Florentine."

"I still don't get it."

"Stanley fudged it. He had a partial will drawn up—with me as an executor."

"Oh," Gina said again. She had hoped that this information about Stanley's will would shed some light on who might have a motive to murder him. But it sounded like Stanley was going to have the last laugh. "So, who inherits everything?"

"I have no idea. Vanessa's dead. They had no kids. Stanley was an only child."

"Are his parents still alive?"

"Nope."

"Relatives?"

"He was adopted."

"What about the investors?"

"That's the ironic thing. They never closed the deal. They wanted to make sure that Stanley got Florentine before funding him." Ian drained the last of his beer. "I don't know why I'm even telling you this."

"Sometimes, it's good to talk about things. Get the weight off your shoulders."

"I guess." He pushed his glass towards Gina. "One more."

"You got it."

"And another shot."

When Gina returned with the drinks, she found Ian staring morosely at his book.

"So much to do," he muttered.

"Listen, Ian, I have to ask. What about the wine lady?"

"Stanley was screwing her."

"I know. I was there. Remember?"

"Oh, yeah."

"Could she have had anything to do with his death?"

"I doubt it. There were lots of women. Amadora Seville was just the latest."

"He wasn't planning on putting her in his will, was he?"

"God, no. The biggest gesture he made to her was to get her this catering gig."

"Well, someone wanted him dead."

"I told you, it was probably Becca. Or her aunt."

"Catherine? No way."

"She had a reputation as a ruthless businesswoman in her time. I'm sure Becca got all the hard-ass genes. Don't let her pretty face fool you."

"Pretty?" Was there something going on between them?

"She kind of looks like Taylor Swift, don't you think?"

"I guess." Gina took another ladylike sip of her tequila. Sure, she was tempted to knock it back. But she needed to keep her wits about her.

"What about that guy Tomas?" she asked. He was her last lead.

"The Fixer."

"What?"

"That's what Stanley called him. The Alpaca Fixer."

Gina recalled what Noelle had told her. "Is it true that Tomas smuggled in that girl alpaca for Stanley?"

Ian said nothing. Just stared into his beer.

"It is, isn't it?"

"You don't beat around the bush, do you?"

"I told you, I'm good at asking questions. So did he smuggle in the alpaca, or what?"

"I guess it doesn't matter now."

"Is that a yes?"

"It's a 'I-don't-know-for-sure-but-I-think-so.' Satisfied?"

"I'm getting there."

"Anyway, there was some kind of drama going on between him and the Schaeffers. Maybe he wanted more money now that he knew what Magdalene was being used for."

"You said 'Schaeffers,' plural. Was Vanessa involved in this smuggling scheme as well?"

"I don't know. Maybe. I only know that she was in the meetings with Stanley when Tomas came to the ranch."

This seemed like the most promising lead. All kinds of scenarios were buzzing around in Gina's head. And they all ended with Stanley being dead. "Okay, Ian. You've given me a lot to think about. Thank you."

"Just keep my name out of this. I've got enough trouble on my plate."

GINA MADE a beeline to Berenstein's shop and started gushing to him about everything she'd learned.

"Whoa, slow down, woman!"

"I'm not going to slow down, Berenstein. This could be it. Maybe that's who I saw on Saturday morning. Tomas and Vanessa in the garden. She was paying him off."

"What? Then he killed her? That doesn't make sense."

"I did just have several shots and a glass of wine, so—"

"So maybe you need to take some time and mull this over. You don't want to be rushing to the fuzz smelling like the back alley behind Studio 54."

"What?"

"Never mind."

Gina cupped her hand to her mouth and breathed into it. "I don't smell that bad, do I?"

"No comment."

"Well, I stand by my theory. Even if Tomas didn't kill Vanessa, it doesn't mean he couldn't have killed Stanley."

"What, now we have *two* murderers stalking the moors of Maidenwell?"

"What moors?"

"It was a figure of speech."

She began pacing around the cluttered bookstore. "You know Stanley was killed in the stables."

"And?"

"And Tomas has a room there."

"He lives in the stables?"

"It's a little compound of buildings. Haven't you been up there?"

"I fear my riding days are long over."

Gina shot him a glance.

"It was a joke," Berenstein said. "Nevertheless, you

slowing down a bit and really thinking this through might be a better plan at this point."

"Maybe you're right." The thought of a nap did sound pretty good right about now. Although she felt bad about resting when there was a killer still on the loose.

"I'll call you a cab. You want some tea while we wait?"

"No, I'm good."

"Well, I'm having one."

Gina followed Berenstein into the back room, where he had a little electric kettle As he made his brew, Gina glanced around the room again. Her eyes settled on Berenstein's computer.

"How come you get to have a computer?" she asked.

"What do you mean?"

"They took all our devices at the train station."

"Yes, because you're a Guest, not a Resident."

"I don't understand. Residents can have computers?"

"We're vetted. They don't want Guests to take pictures or videos of Maidenwell and send them out into the world. You're a PR person. You should know that."

"I told you, I'm not really a PR person."

"Well, those kinds of skills would come in handy, don't you think? For promoting the store."

Gina ignored him. "Well, if you've got the Internet here, you can do a bit of online sleuthing for me."

"What did you have in mind?"

As she rode back up to Haverford Hall with Millicent, Gina asked if there was any fresh news.

"Not that I've heard," came the younger woman's reply.

"Is that a good thing or a bad thing?" Gina pondered aloud.

Millicent just shrugged her shoulders, "Everyone's on pins and needles. Big time. We all thought that we'd be getting away from all that bad stuff by coming to Maidenwell."

"Yeah."

"Damn alpaca people," Millicent said with a bitter laugh.

"I know, right?"

They rode in silence for a while, with Gina just staring out of the window at the honey-colored stone cottages and the winding lanes. Maidenwell truly was a magical place. The whole murder thing cast a shadow on it, though.

Once Millicent dropped her off, Gina trudged back to her room, all set to sleep off the booze. But her mind kept circling back to Tomas. What if he really was the murderer? What if he made a run for it? She hadn't seen them yet, but rumor was there were horses in the stables. Tomas, being a bona fide Peruvian cowboy, could easily swipe one and gallop off into the badlands.

She decided she should probably find Reeve and maybe let him know about her suspicions and what she had learned from Ian. At the very least, Reeve could coordinate with the state detectives and keep an eye on Tomas.

Gina texted Reeve that she had something important to discuss. Then she stretched out on her bed, waiting for a reply.

At some point, the shots and wine and big Thai lunch all conspired to cause her eyelids to droop and within two minutes, she was sound asleep.

Gina didn't dream—or if she did, she didn't remember her dream. A sharp knock on her door pulled her from her slumber.

"Come in." Her voice was thick with sleep.

Reeve pushed open the door. "How come you didn't answer any of my texts?"

"Good morning to you, too." Gina sat up drowsily.

"It's four o'clock in the afternoon."

"Yeah, as you can see, I was napping."

"Did you misplace your keycard again?"

"No, I must have slept through its chirps."

"You want me to come back?" he asked.

"No, I'm fine. Just give me a second." She tottered off towards the bathroom.

"I don't have a lot of time," Reeve called after her.

In the bathroom, Gina freshened up. She frowned at her face in the mirror. *Dealing with a murder is really murder on the bags under my eyes.* Oh well, there wasn't time to look pretty.

When she returned to the bedroom, Reeve had made himself comfortable in one of the brocade chairs. He looked as ragged as she did.

"Long day?" she asked.

"What do you think?"

"I can imagine. Any more news?"

"Not that I can share."

"Fair enough. I have something to share, though."

"I'm all ears."

So Gina told him about Tomas, including what she had heard from Noelle and from Ian. She also reminded him of what she had seen early on Saturday morning in the garden—including the fact that the woman had passed the man a thick envelope.

As she spoke, Reeve jotted down some notes in his little notebook.

"Interesting," he said.

"Well, what do you think?"

"I know the state CID guys have been questioning Tomas Villanueva, given his proximity to where Stanley's body was found. But I don't think they had this background info. Good work, Biletti."

"Just doing my duty." She beamed at him.

"Much appreciated."

"Do you think I could get a deputy badge or something?"

"Are you serious right now?"

"No, I guess not."

"Good." He got up to leave.

"You have to take off so soon?"

"Yeah, there's still a lot going on. State needs all the help they can get." He snapped his notebook closed. "But thanks again for this. Continue to keep your ears open. Especially at the dinner."

"What dinner?"

"Frau Loneskum is throwing a dinner for all the guests tonight. I'm sure you're invited." He looked around the room, and his eyes settled on an envelope on the floor near the door. "There it is."

Gina took the envelope from him, opened it, and read the note aloud. "*Frau Yvonne Loneskum requests your presence to honor the memory of the Schaeffers this evening at 6 p.m. in the dining hall.* Short and sweet. You going?"

"Me? Not invited."

"You want to be my plus-one?"

"I have to work. Besides, I don't think people will be as free to talk if they know there's law enforcement around."

"You're probably right."

"You need to keep your eyes and ears open. Contact me right away if you learn anything that might be relevant to the investigation."

"Will do." Truth be told, Gina felt a nervous wave pass through her at the thought of attending a dinner party with a murderer. What if he freaked out and went on a killing spree right there in the dining room?

"Will any cops be around?" she asked.

"Sure. There will be a few detectives in the wings. Why? Are you worried?"

"Of course I am. And while we're on the subject, is anyone going to do anything about this?" She motioned to the door—which still did not have a lock on it.

"Yes, against Frau Loneskum's objections, we're installing security chains in the morning."

"Why wait? I'd feel a hell of a lot better knowing that someone can't just waltz into my room while I'm asleep."

"Hey, I knocked!"

"I wasn't talking about you. I doubt the murderer will be so polite."

"Well, we didn't have them in town, so we're sending someone to the Home Depot in Bend."

"You guys should really rethink your facilities planning. Maybe build a warehouse or something."

"Yes, that's actually in the works. If it makes you feel any better, we do monitor the geo-location of all the keycards within this building."

"How does that help me?"

"If someone were to enter your room, we'd know it."

"Oh great, so if I get strangled or something in the night, you'd know who did it."

"Hopefully."

"That really doesn't make me feel better. At all." Then a thought occurred to her. "Did you check keycards coming into Vanessa's room the morning she died?"

"Of course. And the night before."

"And?"

"No one else besides Stanley entered the room."

Gina made a dismissive snort. "You do see the glaring weakness in your high-tech security system, don't you?"

"What are you talking about?"

"What if the killer deliberately left his keycard in his room?"

"No one would do—" Then Reeve caught himself and a grim smile played across his face. "I see what you did there."

"Uh huh."

He looked over at Gina's door. "In the meantime, you

could wedge a chair under the knob right before you go to sleep."

"Does that really work?"

He shrugged. "Better than nothing."

"That makes me feel so much safer."

Gina kicked Reeve out, then lugged the chair over to the door and tipped it so it was wedged beneath the door handle. Then she went to the bathroom to take a shower. At least the bathroom door had a lock on it.

sixteen

. . .

THE MOOD at the dinner party was somber, despite the free-flowing wine in the salon before dinner—courtesy of the wine lady herself, Amadora Seville. Gina did her best to steer clear of her. *Hashtag awkward!*

Gina had arrived fashionably late, but immediately felt inappropriately dressed in her cowl-neck sweater dress and thigh-high boots. It didn't help that her dress was robin's egg blue instead of a more respectful black, or at least dark gray.

Still, looking around the room, the only two people who seemed to understand the assignment were Édouard Orville, dressed in a dark suit and speaking to Tomas (who wore jeans and a flannel shirt)—and mistress-of-the-manor Yvonne Loneskum, resplendent in a long-sleeved black number that amped up her orange hair.

Speaking of orange hair—even though it wasn't really orange—Gina spotted Noelle (sans mom and son) engrossed in conversation with—of all people—Ian.

Across the room, Danielle caught her eye and gave a shy little wave before turning back to Peyton Grier. The two of them looked like they were still working.

On the other side of the salon, the owners of the other

ranches clustered in a small knot, talking among themselves: Becca, Catherine, and the artist Frankie Roth (whose bright pink oversized glasses *really* looked inappropriate).

After snagging a glass of red wine from a tray, Gina made a beeline to Frau Loneskum, just as the older woman dispatched a staff member—probably to check on dinner.

"Frau Loneskum, I am so sorry," Gina said.

Frau Loneskum took a moment to assess Gina's dress, her face settling into a slight frown, before nodding. "You do not have much to be sorry for. You didn't even know Stanley."

"Yes, of course. I only had the opportunity to speak with him a few times."

Frau Loneskum looked away. "I understand you are here under false pretenses, Ms. Biletti."

Gina's stomach tightened. "I'm not really sure what you mean."

"You don't really work with Danielle LaTour, do you?"

"Danielle and I are old friends. And we have worked together in the past."

"You didn't answer my question."

"Technically, I'm between jobs right now."

"You were terminated from your position at Weber Fields & Associates, weren't you?"

How does she know where I worked?

"I, uh, was offered early retirement." Gina stumbled over her words.

Frau Loneskum leaned in and patted Gina's arm. "We tell ourselves all manner of falsehoods, don't we?"

Who the hell is this woman? Before she could say something she would regret, Gina forced a smile and said, "Again, I'm so sorry for your loss."

Then she walked away, feeling the daggers from Frau Loneskum's eyes with every step. *Why the hell was she coming at me like that? I never did anything to her.*

"Hey, girl."

Gina turned to see Becca and let out a deep sigh of relief.

"Whoa, you look like you straight up need a drink," Becca said.

"I've got one, but it's not doing the job." She drained her wine.

"What happened?"

"Oh, I just had a run-in with the Frau."

"What kind of run-in?"

"She basically accused me of being here under false pretenses."

"What?"

"And then she was all in my face about my former company."

"Hey, Gina, relax, okay?"

That was pretty much impossible. "How did she even know where I worked?" Gina scanned the room for more wine.

"She knows a lot of things. Don't forget who her son is."

"I know. It shouldn't surprise me. But it's extremely rude."

Becca shrugged. "The rules don't apply." Then she smiled. "Let's find you a drink. Unless you want something else." She mimed taking a puff.

Gina was tempted—for purely medicinal reasons—since she was so keyed up right now. But she quickly realized it wasn't a good idea. "I don't think we have time for that right now."

"Wine it is, then." Becca flagged down a server and snagged two glasses of wine. She handed one to Gina. "Cheers."

"To Stanley," Gina said.

"Seriously?"

"The man died."

"Well, yeah. Since you put it that way, I'll drink to that."

"You're horrible!" Gina whispered.

They drifted to one side of the room, away from the other guests. "So, how are you holding up?" Gina asked.

"Me? Fine, I guess. I mean, this whole thing is so surreal."

"Did the cops talk to you?"

"Oh, yeah. I believe the correct term is 'interrogation.' And they did interrogate me. Big time."

"Me too. How did that go?"

"Fine, I guess. It's a little weird, because it's common knowledge that I knew what Stanley's game was and I called him on it."

"Yeah."

"I'm not going to lie, I'm not shedding a single tear for Stanley. I'm pretty sure the world's a better place with him not in it."

"Maybe keep your voice down just a bit."

"Whatever."

"So, do they, uh, suspect you?" Gina asked.

"Of course."

Gina was surprised by the younger woman's nonchalance.

"They suspect all of us," Becca said.

"Well, they don't suspect me."

"How do you know?"

Gina was surprised Becca would even ask the question. "I have no connection to Stanley."

Becca shrugged, a playful smirk playing on her lips. "Maybe he pissed you off. He's been known to piss off complete strangers."

"If anyone could drive me to the point of murder, it'd be Frau Farbissina. Seriously, the way she talked to me…" Gina shook her head.

"She's a crazy old lady—just hanging onto her power."

"Crazy old lady, huh? Is that what you think of me?" Gina took another drink of her wine. It was really smooth.

"You're not old. I bet we're basically the same age."

Gina nearly spit her wine out. "Oh, you're too kind. Trust me, I've got a good fifteen years on you. At least."

"Well, you definitely don't throw off any crazy old lady vibes."

"Oh yeah? What kind of vibes do I throw off?"

"Hm, maybe a 'cool aunt'?"

"Cool aunt? I'll take that!" Gina beamed at Becca.

At that moment, a bell chimed and all the guests were ushered into the adjoining dining room.

The room was pure Downton Abbey, from its high ceilings and fancy moldings to the luxurious Oriental rug. A gigantic mahogany table that could fit double the guest list filled the room. One wall was taken up by a mammoth fireplace that looked like you could roast a whole steer in it, while the opposite wall was all windows showing off the garden, all lit up like a fairyland. The other walls were filled with massive oil paintings, some as big as a New York City parking spot.

As she moved into the room, Gina got a better look at the paintings. They were all dark and gloomy-looking. Some were barely discernible portraits; others showed dramatic landscapes that were definitely not in Oregon, and probably not even in North America.

Elegantly lettered place cards were arranged on the crisp white tablecloth among crystal and china and silver and candlesticks. Gina found herself seated between Édouard Orville and Catherine, and across from Tomas and Noelle.

Servers buzzed around the table, placing the first course in front of everyone—a green soup with a dollop of crème fraiche.

"Watercress soup, I believe." Édouard must have picked up on Gina's curious expression and her barely restrained urge to sniff the soup.

"I don't think I've ever had that before," she said.

"I think the watercress is grown here on the grounds."

"Then I probably strolled past it."

"Oh? Have you toured the gardens?"

Gina opened her mouth to respond, but the room suddenly went silent, prompted by the insistent clinking of a spoon against a glass.

"Attention, please," Peyton Grier said in her drill sergeant voice. "Our hostess would like to say a few words."

"We're here to pay tribute to our very good friends Stanley and Vanessa Schaeffer," Frau Loneskum said. "The Schaeffers were pillars of the alpaca community and I know that many of you aspired to their success. But I daresay that Stanley and Vanessa attained much more than business success. They lived well, laughed often, and gave the best that they had to all those around them."

Gina caught Becca rolling her eyes.

"Stanley lived life with gusto and even a room this large feels empty without him. And Vanessa's grace and beauty and sharp sense of humor will never be forgotten." She raised her glass. "In the immortal words of Chaucer: *Now let us sit and drink and make us merry / And afterward we will their bodies bury.* To Stanley and Vanessa."

Everyone toasted—even Becca.

Okay, that was bizarre, Gina thought. Thankfully, no one wanted to follow up Frau Loneskum's toast, so the guests hesitantly dug into their soup.

Édouard had been right. The soup *was* watercress, and it was surprisingly good. Light and flavorful, and not too grassy. The soup was served with rustic sourdough bread that must have just come out of the oven.

As she ate, Gina vaguely recalled reading somewhere that guests at a formal dinner were first supposed to speak with the person on their left. In her case, that was Catherine.

"Did you end up catching anything?" Gina asked.

"What?" Catherine seemed distracted by something.

"When you were fishing."

"Oh, god, that seems like a million years ago. Yes, actually, I did. I caught three good-sized trout after you left."

"My reverse luck coming into play, I guess." Gina smiled. "Is that one of the fish you caught?"

The server offered a platter of poached fish with a creamy dill sauce, garnished with sliced cucumbers and chives.

Catherine smiled. "Maybe. Although I released all of mine. Still, I wouldn't be surprised if this fish came out of the streams here."

Gina couldn't tell if it was salmon or trout, but the dish was amazing. Fresh and delicious.

The dinner turned out to be a fairly sedate affair. Most of the guests were focused on not doing or saying anything that might offend Frau Loneskum. And because there was no real opportunity to speak privately, Gina couldn't snoop and ask the questions she really wanted to ask.

After coffee and dessert—a truly scrumptious pear clafoutis—everyone traipsed back into the salon where the Frau broke out the sherry, digestifs, and whiskey.

Gina's head felt as light as a bubble, while her tummy was rebelling like she had downed a kettlebell during the feast. But she felt she needed to soldier on. Who knew if there would be another opportunity to talk to her fellow guests while everyone was so drunk?

"Hello there." She sidled up to Tomas, who was nursing a whiskey and looked like he was trying to gauge when he could safely depart the dinner party without insulting his boss.

"Hola."

"I'm Gina. We didn't really get a chance to speak at dinner, but I met you the day Florrie escaped."

"Ah, yes. Florentine. You were the lady who let him out."

"Actually, no, that was Noelle's son, but I was there."

"Whatever you say, Señora. I am pleased to meet you." He bowed stiffly. "Tomas Villanueva, at your service."

He had a wonderful accent and reminded Gina of a younger, shorter Antonio Banderas.

"I hope Florentine has recovered."

Tomas shrugged. "He is an alpaca." He stressed the first syllable. *Al-paca.*

"So horrible about Stanley and Vanessa. How are you holding up?"

"Holding up, Señora?"

"Coping. I hope you are not too upset."

"Very bad about Señor Stanley."

"You must have known him well."

Tomas shrugged again. "Yes, I see him here. With the alpacas."

"Well, not just here, right?" Gina finished up her sherry. It tasted horrible, but she figured it would get her into less trouble than the whiskey.

"Señora?"

"Well, I understand you did some work with the Schaeffers. Some *animal transport* work." She let her last sentence hang there.

Tomas just blinked a few times, then a huge smile bloomed on his face. He had perfect teeth. "Not me, Señora. I only work for Frau Loneskum."

"That's not what I heard." Gina watched Tomas' face closely. "I heard you were the one who found Stanley's prize female. What is her name?"

"Magdalene."

"Yes, Magdalene." *Interesting that he knew exactly what I was talking about.*

"She is a magnificent creature, yes. But you are mistaken, Señora Gina. I cannot claim to have found her."

She looked right into his eyes. *Shifty. For sure.*

"Sorry, my mistake." She smiled thinly. "I must have heard the story wrong."

Tomas bowed again. "So nice to chat with you. My apologies. I have early duties tomorrow, and I must bid good night to our hostess now."

"Of course. Have a good evening, Tomas."

"And you, as well, Señora."

There's definitely something going on with that guy, Gina thought. She should have asked him if his 'early duties' involved lurking around in the gardens.

A tap on her shoulder caught Gina's attention. She turned to find Noelle, eyes bright, and a big smile on her face.

"Hey, stranger. Just wanted to check how you were doing. Physically, I mean."

"Good, thanks. No sign of a concussion or anything."

"No dizziness or blurred vision or headaches?"

"Not so far. I can't make any predictions about tomorrow morning, though. I drank way too much."

"Me too. I might snag another coffee. You want one?"

"No, I'm good. I don't want to be buzzing all night long."

"I hear you. But I think they have decaf."

"Maybe. But I'll come with you. I never pass up the chance to gawk at fine china."

"You're really funny, you know that?" She led Gina towards a sideboard which had been set up with coffee and tea.

"My therapist says I use humor to deflect," Gina said.

"Deflect what?"

"I don't know. Being nervous. Self-conscious."

"What do you have to be nervous about?" She handed Gina a cup of coffee.

"Nothing really. Although I had the weirdest interaction with Frau Loneskum."

Gina told Noelle about how the Frau basically accused her of being here under false pretenses.

Noelle took a sip of her coffee. "I wouldn't worry about it. No one's at their best right now. Given the circumstances."

Gina nodded. That was a nice observation. Kind as well.

She took a sip of her coffee. It was delicious. Maybe Frau Loneskum grew the beans on the premises. Who knew?

Noelle noticed her smile. "Hits the spot, right?"

"Yes, definitely a good call. Better than smoking pot with Becca."

"Oh?"

"Vaping, I should say. Apparently it's healthier."

"I wouldn't go that far."

"Well, I just did a little. On Saturday in the hedge maze."

"You go, girl."

"I don't make a habit of it. Not since college anyway."

"I'm with you. Give me a glass of wine. Or three. And I'm good." She smiled.

Gina took another sip of her coffee. "So where's Mason?"

"Back in the room with my mom. He wouldn't do well at something like this."

"He's not a little party animal?"

"God, no. He likes to spend time on his own. Reading. Drawing comics. He's super creative."

"That's cool."

"Well, not entirely. But he'll be okay." She smiled again. It was a sad smile, though. "So tell me, how was your interrogation? With the police, I mean."

"Fine. I'm kind of working with the authorities."

"You are?"

"Yeah." Gina lowered her voice. "No big deal, but I'm trying to help them sort things out."

"Do they have a suspect?"

"We're all suspects, technically."

"You know what I mean."

Gina didn't know how much about Tomas she should reveal to Noelle. Then again, Noelle was the one that first told her the rumor about Tomas smuggling alpacas for Stanley. She decided to confide in the vet.

"I think you were right about Tomas being involved in alpaca smuggling."

"Really? Do the police know about that?"

"I told them. They're looking into him. Seriously."

Noelle made a face.

"Don't worry," Gina said. "I kept you out of it."

"I saw you talking with him just now. Does he know he's being investigated?"

"No idea, but when I asked him if he got Magdalene for Stanley—"

"You didn't!"

"Yeah, I did. And Tomas got all weird about it."

"You need to be careful, Gina. If he really is the murderer, he might be very threatened by you asking questions."

"I know."

"And, take it from me, a cornered animal can be very dangerous."

seventeen

. . .

GINA WANTED to walk back up to her room with Danielle, but her friend was still immersed in a conversation with Peyton Grier and the Frau. Gina couldn't wait. She was definitely feeling the effects of all the booze and she had to pee really bad.

As she exited the salon, she half-expected to see Reeve waiting for her in the hallway, but it was empty except for a lone serving trolley stacked with dirty glassware.

Someone's going to get in trouble for that.

She made her way up the grand staircase to the residential floor, definitely a little wobbly as she walked.

I'm way too old for this kind of drinking, Gina thought. She wasn't in college anymore. That was for sure. At least she had the good sense not to sneak out and smoke pot with Becca. *Oh, excuse me. Vape pot.*

As she made her way down the hall, she silently cursed whoever decided that the guest rooms here at Haverford Hall didn't need little signs with numbers on them—or locks on the doors, for that matter.

Where the hell is my room?

All these corridors looked the same: narrow passages with the identical pale wallpaper, framed oil paintings, wainscoting, and brass light sconces. The only thing that was different —barely different—was the subject of the landscape paintings. Sometimes the painting depicted a meadow with a horse (never an alpaca). Sometimes the painting was a slightly different meadow with rolling hills. Sometimes it was rolling hills without much of a meadow.

Every fifty feet or so, there was a little alcove with a pair of big overstuffed armchairs. Presumably so that guests could rest up during their wanderings.

This place is even twistier than the hedge maze, Gina thought.

She continued down the corridor, around a corner, and past another alcove. Finally, she arrived at her room, marked by a horse and hound painting. At least, she thought this was the right painting. *Maybe the lead foxhound has a little more brown on his head. Who knows?*

Gina entered her room and flicked on the light. She stood there blinking for a moment in confusion. Not only was this not her room, but everything looked weirdly tilted. Maybe she was drunker than she thought.

She looked longingly at the bed, thinking it might be a good idea to lie down for just a bit, but the bed had been stripped down to the mattress—which was odd.

The dresser drawers were pulled out as well, like someone had hastily searched the room. Gina made her way into the bathroom and saw all sorts of make-up and toiletries cluttering up the counter around the sink. Bottles of high-end shampoo and conditioner perched on the shelf in the shower.

Gina's eyes flickered in recognition, a thought forming in her woozy mind. *This must be Vanessa's room.*

She poked around the toiletries and discovered several expensive anti-aging serums, including a jar of La Mer that she was briefly tempted to take. *No, bad Gina!*

Back in the main bedroom, Gina looked around some more. If she could only find something that linked Vanessa's death to Tomas. She knew there had to be something here, but it was hard to focus. She felt herself slipping away minute by minute.

After ten or fifteen minutes of looking around, she realized that she really had to get back to her own room—and her bed—before she wouldn't be able to. The only thing she had found were a ton of soda bottles in the garbage. At least a dozen. It was a brand she had never heard of before: Rock River Breeze. In her confusion, Gina snagged one of the empty bottles and teetered out into the hallway.

Things were not good. The hallway was definitely spinning. Gina felt her way along one wall, moving as quickly as she dared.

About forty feet down the corridor, she reached another little alcove. *I just need to rest for a second.*

She swayed and fell back into one of the overstuffed chairs, and took a deep breath. That felt better. She fished out her keycard. Someone had told her it could help her find her room, but good luck figuring that out. She could barely get the thing to send a text.

As she fiddled with the card, she heard the voices of someone approaching. A man and woman were talking in hushed tones, but the hallway magnified the sound of their conversation.

"You need to just calm the fuck down," the man said. Gina recognized Édouard Orville's voice—although the words he used were at odds with his usual polite utterances.

"I'm not going to calm the fuck down, Ed," the woman said. "Once they find out about the money, it will all be over for me. Three bad things!"

A jolt of adrenaline cleared Gina's head a bit. She stood up and pressed herself against the back wall.

"No one's going to find out about the money. You didn't put anything on paper, did you?"

"I'm not stupid."

Gina finally placed the woman's voice. A little nasal with a hint of East Coast accent. *Frankie Roth.*

"Well, then, you have nothing to worry about," Édouard said.

"Are you kidding me?" Frankie scoffed. "What if Vanessa told someone?"

They were getting closer. This wasn't good. Gina thought about making a run for it. But there would be no way she could escape without being seen. *Shit.*

"The only person Vanessa would have told was Stanley," Édouard said. "And that's a moot point."

"I don't know. I feel like we should just come clean."

Gina felt sweat dripping down the small of her back. This was bad. Really bad. In ten seconds, Frankie and Édouard would be at the alcove.

"Are you insane, woman?" Édouard said.

Gina scrambled behind the chairs, squeezing herself against the wall, and trying to make her body as small as possible.

"If Loneskum knew we were working together, she'd never sell us Florentine."

Gina peered around the edge of the chair, watching Édouard and Frankie stride by. Thankfully, they didn't even look in her direction.

"And then all *this* would be for nothing!" Édouard said.

"Hang on," Frankie said, her voice full of apprehension.

They stopped moving.

"What is it?"

"Are we lost?" Frankie asked.

"Of course not. My room is in the next section." Édouard's voice dropped an octave. "You still want that nightcap, don't you, my sweet?"

"Mmmmm, can't wait," Frankie purred.

"And that other thing we talked about...?"

"Ooh la la!"

Gina almost threw up a little in her mouth.

SHE SAT THERE, on the ground, wedged behind the overstuffed armchair, for another fifteen minutes. Maybe longer. It was possible that she had dozed off, because the next thing Gina knew, she was being shaken awake.

"Oh my god, Gina, are you okay?" Danielle was kneeling over her.

"Ugh," Gina croaked out.

"I thought you were dead, babes. I just saw legs sticking out from under the chair. If I didn't recognize your white Gucci Mary Janes, I would have kept on walking."

Gina sat up and tried to shake off the fog. It wasn't working.

"What the hell are you doing on the floor? Did you pass out?"

Gina felt her lips move, but it was as if her tongue was coated in syrup. "Hiding," she managed, her words slurry and slushy.

"Hiding? From who?"

"Bed."

"Hiding from your bed?"

"Need bed." Gina was a lot drunker than she thought. Everything was spinning, and her arms and legs felt like pins and needles.

"Is that what you've been drinking?" Danielle took the empty soda bottle from Gina and sniffed it.

"Keep that. Might be..." Gina trailed off. She was so messed up she could barely speak.

Somehow, Danielle managed to shepherd her back to her room. With the patience of a saint, she eased Gina out of her party clothes and into something more comfortable. As Danielle turned to leave, Gina reached out and caught her wrist. "Stay."

She patted the bed next to her and slumped back on the pillow.

"You want me to sleep here?" Danielle asked.

"Yeah," Gina mumbled, struggling to keep her eyes open. "But no sex."

Danielle barked a laugh. "You have a pretty high opinion of yourself, don't you? And, by the way, *ewww!* You're my friend!"

"Don't you think I'm hot?" Gina asked, her words blending together into a slurred mumble.

"We are definitely not having this conversation, Gina." Danielle headed towards the door.

"Don't leave!"

"I'm just going to get my sweats and my toothbrush. Then I'll be back to babysit you."

"Promise?"

"Yeah, just try not to choke on anything until I get back."

"Okay."

Once Danielle left, Gina inched her body more upright and wedged all her pillows under her shoulders. She tried taking deep breaths, attempting to clear the fog from her mind. But the room refused to stop spinning, making her feel queasy.

What if I've been drugged? Roofied, even? The thought came unbidden, raising a terrifying possibility. She couldn't remember leaving her drink unattended, but then again, she couldn't remember much of anything right now.

She opened her eyes again to see if the room had settled down.

No such luck. If anything, it was getting worse. Now it looked like the walls were stretching apart. The sensation made her stomach flip.

She realized that she still had to pee, and the thought of that made her have to pee even more.

Damn it.

She swung her legs off the bed and tried to stand up, but her legs were like overcooked spaghetti strands. She wobbled, struggling to find her footing in the swirling room, and finally ended up crawling to the bathroom.

I am never, ever drinking anything again. I can't do this anymore...

Miraculously, Gina did her business without falling off the toilet. Then she pulled herself up in front of the sink to splash some water on her face and in her mouth.

The water actually felt good and she finally felt a little bit of the fog clear, but then she made the mistake of looking at her reflection in the mirror.

Oh my god, am I really that old?

Her eyes were bleary and red, her face looked swollen, and her hair was a frizzy over-bleached rat's nest. She wasn't a hot mess. Just a mess.

A soft click from the other room snapped her out of her self-pity. "I'm here," she croaked to Danielle. "Just admiring my gorgeous reflection. I can see why you're not itching to jump in bed with this."

The lights abruptly went out in the other room.

"Danielle?"

Blinking at the threshold of the bathroom, Gina tried to peer through the gloom. *Is she pissed at me for making her babysit?*

The light from the bathroom wasn't enough for her to see much. Especially because the room continued to lurch and shift in her vision.

Why can't I just barf it out?

At her bachelorette party, the last time Gina had been this messed up, she remembered feeling much better once she—

Suddenly, the back of her skull exploded with pain. And she was falling. Either that or the room decided to tilt big time.

Her world plunged into darkness.

eighteen

. . .

WHEN SHE AWOKE, Gina realized she wasn't in her own bed. She was in a hospital bed. In a hospital room. With no one else around.

How…? What…?

Her head was still thick and foggy—and it hurt, but at least the room wasn't spinning.

She took a deep breath. The air was cool and smelled different from the air in the manor house. The sounds were distinct as well: the low hum of hospital machinery and the faint beeps of monitors.

Gina felt the back of her skull. Definitely a bump there, but no blood or anything.

She looked around for some kind of call button near her bed. The last thing she remembered was walking back to her room after the dinner party and overhearing Édouard and Frankie.

What had they said?

Something about working together—secretly—to get Florrie. Oh, and they were making out or something.

Gina pushed the image from her mind.

Still, this was a surprising twist. Édouard Orville and Frankie Roth. In cahoots. *Very interesting.*

She remembered what Becca had told her. Even though Édouard and Frankie both owned large alpaca operations, Becca was convinced that they were not seriously in the running to win Florrie.

A woman appeared at the door of her room, a nurse or doctor judging by her scrubs. She had a round face and long, straw-colored hair.

"Well, well, well. You're awake. Finally." She also had a pronounced English accent.

"Where am I? Am I in England?"

The woman smiled. "Not quite, although I could see how one might think that. You're in hospital. Maidenwell General, to be specific."

"Wow, Peyton wasn't kidding. You guys really do have a hospital."

"We do. And you're here." The woman smiled at Gina. "My name is Jane Dooley. Let me know if there's anything I can do for you."

"Nice to meet you, Jane."

"Please call me Nurse Dooley."

"Ah, formal. Got it. So I guess I should ask. Am I going to live?"

"Most certainly. You're only in here as a precaution. Your friend found you passed out in your room. Quite intoxicated."

"Really? Because I don't think I drank that much."

"Oh, you did, I'm afraid. Your blood alcohol level was .26%. Definitely in the red zone for your weight and age."

"I actually don't feel too badly hungover."

"Well, you've been asleep for nearly eighteen hours."

"What?" Gina thought she misheard the nurse. "Did you say *eighteen* hours?"

"More or less. You've been sleeping it off. We've also had

you on an IV for a bit to help with your dehydration and blood sugar."

"This is crazy. I swear, I really didn't drink that much. I'm guessing maybe six drinks over the course of the entire evening. Could I have been drugged?"

"Nothing in your blood tests indicated that."

"Really?"

"You sound disappointed."

"It's just… bizarre."

"How's your memory of that evening?"

Gina sighed. "Not good."

"Has this ever happened to you before?"

"Not since college. No, wait. I take that back. My bachelorette party got a little out of hand."

"Well, hen parties don't really count." Nurse Dooley smiled at her. "How long ago was that?"

"Fifteen years ago." Gina unconsciously felt for her wedding ring. It was something she used to do a lot during all those years she had been married.

"Well, that hardly makes a pattern, does it? Still, if you'd like to speak with someone about your alcohol consumption—"

"I actually have a therapist back in New York. You can bet she's going to hear all about this. Lucky her."

"That's what she's there for, isn't it?"

"Absolutely. She definitely earns her hourly rate with me." *Although for how much longer?* With no job and no prospects, Gina wasn't sure how much of her old life she could still afford. She pushed the thought from her mind.

"Hey, can I ask you something?"

"It depends what it is," Nurse Dooley said.

"You have any experience with untraceable poisons?"

"What?"

"I know it sounds weird, but I'm just curious. Are there any substances that would kill someone without showing up in, say, a toxicology report?"

"I really am not at liberty to discuss something like that."

"I know. I get it. It's not for me, obviously. It's just that I'm doing some research for a mystery novel I'm working on—"

"Uh huh." Nurse Dooley gave Gina the side eye.

"You know what, never mind."

"I think that's best. I'll get Dr. Kurian for one last look and then we'll get you sorted."

"Oh, do I need to meet with your financial person? I have insurance."

"Not necessary. All healthcare is included here in Maidenwell."

"But I'm not actually a resident."

"I know. That policy extends to guests as well."

"Sweet deal. Can you figure out how to do that for the rest of the country?"

"Mr. Loneskum's working on it." She winked and then left the room.

Loneskum? Who is *this guy?*

About a half hour later, Dr. Kurian entered the room, reading his tablet computer.

"Good to see you again, Doc. I'm surprised you don't have my chart on your keycard."

He smiled at her. "You seem to be in good spirits."

"No pun intended?"

"Well, how are you feeling, Ms. Biletti?"

"Probably better than I have any right to be."

"I would concur. I understand this binge drinking was an isolated incident..."

"You understand correctly."

"Well, good. How's your head feeling?"

"A little sore. But I guess that's the price you pay for having one too many. If that's what actually happened."

"I meant from your fall at the pond."

"Oh, that? With all the booze, I forgot all about that."

Dr. Kurian frowned.

"Kidding. I actually feel great. Thank you for everything."

"Well, let's not make a habit of this, shall we, Ms. Biletti?"

THE FRONT DESK nurse had called a car for Gina, but it turned out she didn't really need it.

When Gina emerged from the hospital foyer and got her bearings, she realized she was only a block away from the Village Green.

Leave it to Maidenwell to hide a full-blown hospital in the center of the village.

The hospital building was deceptive. It was fairly large, but from the outside it matched the architecture of the surrounding buildings, with the same honey-colored stone blocks, gabled roof, chimneys, and lattice windows. It looked almost like a larger version of the White Horse Inn. But, based on the elevator ride from her recovery room to the exit, the hospital must extend six or seven stories underground.

The air was cool and fresh and breezy. As Gina strolled through the village towards Berenstein's bookshop, she felt thankful to be alive. Sure, she was still a little weak and not quite back to normal, but definitely a thousand percent better than last night—or whenever it was that she got so messed up.

The more she thought about it, the more she was convinced that someone had drugged her—despite what the nurse said. She would have to ask Berenstein if he had a book on poisons or something.

The late afternoon sunlight bathed everything in a warm amber glow and the streets were filled with a good number of people going about their business. And, unlike the pedestrians back in New York, these people didn't shove by Gina, glare at her, spit in front of her, or expose themselves to her. Some people actually smiled and said hello. *How odd.*

When she arrived at Berenstein's bookshop, he was just closing up. "Biletti, where in blazes have you been?" He ushered her inside and towards his back-room office. "I've been trying to reach you all day."

"Believe it or not, I've been in the hospital."

"What?"

"In a semi-coma. They said I drank too much. But I think I might have been poisoned."

Berenstein slumped into his oversized desk chair. "Tell me everything, kiddo. But first, would you like a cup of tea?"

"That actually sounds nice. Might even taste better than the IV fluids I've been sucking on for the past eighteen hours."

"Good. While you're up, make me a cup as well. No milk." He motioned towards the little kitchenette.

"You want me to make the tea?"

"Better get used to it. The shop doesn't come with employees—although you are free to hire one if you can make the numbers work."

"You don't give up, do you?"

She found Berenstein's crusty old electric tea kettle and a few mugs in the drying rack near the sink. "You use bottled water for your tea?" There weren't any bottles in the fridge.

"Heathen!" Berenstein cried. "I'll have you know that we have some of the best, cleanest water in the entire country—right here in Maidenwell."

"You don't say."

"I do say, sister. It's our volcanic soil. Acts like a gigantic water filter. That's why our beer is so tasty, as well."

"Okay, as much as I enjoy talking about groundwater, there's something a little more pressing on my mind."

"Such as?"

"Are you senile? SOMEONE TRIED TO KILL ME." Gina shook her head in exasperation.

"Right. You were going to tell me all about it before you got me all distracted about the beverages."

While she hunted around for tea bags and sugar, Gina told Berenstein about the dinner party/wake for the Schaeffers and how she ended up blind drunk despite only having a half-dozen drinks over the course of four or five hours.

"So you think you were poisoned?"

"Yeah. Something happened to me."

"Could it have been something you ate?"

Gina thought about the dinner. It was a formal service and everyone ate the same thing. And most everything was served from platters, except the soup and salad.

"It's possible, but I think it's more likely that someone slipped something into my drink."

"Did you go to the bathroom and maybe leave your 7 and 7 unattended?"

"First of all, I don't drink 7 and 7s." Gina strode over to Berenstein and plopped a mug of tea/no milk on the desk in front of him. "Second of all, I've lived in the City for over twenty years. Do you think I would ever let a drink out of my sight in a public place?"

"Just checking."

"Yeah, well, it was a reasonable guess, but I don't really know how they got to me."

"Ultimately, it doesn't much matter," Berenstein said. "What's much more troublesome is *why*."

"No idea."

He made a face. "I think it's obvious. Someone believes you are a threat. A serious threat." His words hung in the air.

Gina laughed. But it wasn't a laugh of amusement. It was a single, somewhat hysterical peal of laughter.

Berenstein clapped her on the shoulder. "Pull yourself together, Biletti. Good news is that they failed."

"Yeah, for now." Gina tried to take a sip of her tea, but it was too hot. "What am I going to do?"

"You could lock yourself in your room until the fuzz, er, cops find the killer."

"Not an option. None of the doors at Haverford Hall lock."

"Really?"

"Old Austrian tradition, apparently."

"You're welcome to stay with me, but I must warn you I snore and have been known to pass gas in the—"

"Too much information, Berenstein. Too much information."

"Well, you think about it. I've got a fold-out futon from the 80s. It's admittedly uncomfortable, but better than being throttled in your sleep."

"You're really selling this, but I think I'll be fine."

"Well, continue with your story, then. I don't mean to be rude, but you'll need to give me the *Reader's Digest* version."

"What are you going on about?"

"I have a date tonight. In—" He glanced at his big Casio digital watch. It looked like the one Gina's father used to wear. "—about eighteen minutes."

"Who's the lucky woman?"

"Norman. And he's not a woman."

Gina smiled at him. "I stand corrected. But eighteen minutes? Really?"

"I'm not going to stop living my life just because someone's trying to kill you," he said jokingly. "Seventeen minutes now. I suggest you start talking."

So Gina told him everything she remembered about the evening—including her uncomfortable conversation with Frau Loneskum and her tense encounter with Tomas. She also told him how she accidentally stumbled into Vanessa's room, and what she had overheard between Frankie Roth and Édouard Orville.

"I must say, you do get around, young lady."

"Maybe too much, as it turns out."

"So it sounds like your number one suspect is this rogue Tomas…"

"I don't know." Gina rubbed her eyes. How could she be tired? She had slept for over eighteen hours. "I mean, it seemed like he had a connection with the Schaeffers, although he denied it. Of course."

"They always do."

"And, although I can't be one hundred percent sure, Tomas could have been the guy I saw meeting with the woman in the garden—who could have been Vanessa Schaeffer."

"Lots of 'coulds,' my dear."

"I get that a lot, but I have to trust my gut."

"An admirable trait, of course. But the powers that be require more than a trustworthy gut if they are going to make a move against Tomas. You have to find some actual evidence."

"I know, but I looked through Vanessa's room. There just wasn't anything there. Except for a ton of soda bottles."

"Ah, the lady was addicted to the cola nut. Well, that's something—"

"No, it wasn't cola. It was lemon-lime, I think. A weird brand, too. I had never heard of it. River something…"

"RRB?"

"What?"

"Rock River Breeze?"

"That sounds familiar."

"Was there a sailboat on the label?"

"Possibly," Gina said.

"Blue cap?"

"I can't remember those kinds of details. Don't forget, I was drugged. But that name sounds familiar. River Breeze, you said?"

"Rock River Breeze. I'll show you." His fingers danced over the keyboard of his computer as he searched for the soda manufacturer's website. "Here we go."

He turned the laptop's screen so Gina could see the image of a Rock River Breeze soda bottle. She was ninety percent sure that was what she had seen in Vanessa's room.

"It has kind of a cult following," Berenstein said. "RRB is only available in the Midwest."

"And yet, you've got it here in Maidenwell. Through the whims of Yvonne Loneskum, no doubt."

"Au contraire, my dear. RRB is nowhere to be found in our fair village. In fact, most sodas are frowned upon here."

"Well, clearly you are mistaken. There must have been a dozen bottles of the stuff in her room. Unless…"

"Unless she brought it with her!" Berenstein said.

"Vanessa *is* from the Midwest."

"Well, there you go."

"There I go, what? You think the poor woman ODed on lemon-lime soda?"

"Doubtful." Berenstein looked at his watch again. "The good news is that I found quite a lot of information about the other victim." He tapped at the keyboard again. "All bookmarked for you."

"You're going to give me your laptop?"

"No, I'm going to give you this." He produced a key on an Alf keychain. "Lock up when you leave."

"Are you serious?"

"Better get used to it."

nineteen

. . .

AT FIRST, Gina felt distinctly uneasy about being in the bookstore alone. After Berenstein left, she went around to all the doors and made sure they were secure. But then she made herself another cup of tea and settled down at Berenstein's laptop. He had about a million tabs open, with various pages about Stanley Schaeffer.

She spent the next hour or so going through everything Berenstein had collected, and also went down some rabbit holes of her own. Most of what was online about Stanley concerned his alpaca ranch, and it pretty much tracked with what she had heard from Becca and the others. No surprises there. There was a fair amount of IAOF profiles and award coverage for Magdalene featuring lots of photos of the alpaca with Stanley, or Vanessa, or sometimes the both of them posing with a bunch of oversized award ribbons.

Going back in time, she found one or two articles about Stanley's stint as the failed CEO of Janguls, an orthopedic shoe and insole company based in Naperville, Illinois. There was also a lot of press about Stanley's marriage to Vanessa de Avilés and his new position with Blair Hill Fresh Meats, Inc., the meat packing conglomerate that Vanessa's family owned.

Probably the most interesting thing Gina found was a YouTube video of a 2001 local news broadcast about how a 23-year-old Stanley Schaeffer from Decatur, Illinois, had landed the opportunity to be a contestant on ABC's *Who Wants to be a Millionaire*. Unfortunately, he didn't make it to a million dollars, but managed to walk away with $13,300. Not a bad haul for a kid right out of college. The biggest surprise was when the news story showed a clip of the game show episode.

The Stanley from 2001 who bantered with Regis was young, thin, and had a full head of hair. Red hair.

Gina laughed to herself. *I would have never pegged you as a ginger, Stanley, old man.*

Just then, her keycard buzzed angrily. It was a text message from Danielle.

WHERE R U, BABES? WORRIED

She hated when people typed in all-caps.

At Berenstein's place. All good.

JUST FOUND OUT THEY LET U GO
FROM HOSP

I escaped...

WUT????!!!

j/k. I'm feeling fine

SOUP?

Soup actually sounded good. French fries sounded better. Her stomach growled a bit at the thought of solid food.

Sure

BE THERE IN 15.

Gina kept researching Stanley, but found nothing else of interest. Apparently, he didn't spend any time on social media. She couldn't even find a Facebook page for him. Same deal with Vanessa. There were some reviews of dance performances from the early 2000s that mentioned her, but just in passing.

She closed the lid of the laptop and leaned back in Berenstein's rickety old office chair.

Solving mysteries was hard work. Even when you weren't actively being poisoned. There were just so many dead ends, as well as unanswered questions.

Gina got up and washed out the dirty teacups, and made sure the electric kettle was unplugged. As she was drying the cups, Waldo the Siamese cat sauntered in and meowed at her.

"Oh, hello." She felt vaguely guilty that she had forgotten all about Berenstein's cat. To be fair, this was the first she had seen of him all night. "You hungry?" She squatted down to pet Waldo. He arched his back and favored her with a loud purr. "Let's see if we can find your food." She checked in the fridge, hoping to find a half-open can of Fancy Feast or something, but all she found was some ginger ale, a half-eaten strawberry Pop-Tart wrapped in a paper towel, and a few grease-stained take-out boxes Gina didn't bother opening. After poking through the cabinets and drawers, she finally found a bag of dry cat kibble.

"That doesn't look very healthy. I'm going to have to speak to your dad about upping your nutrition, Waldo."

The cat uttered an agreeable *meow,* then swirled around Gina's legs as she poured out some kibble in a little plastic bowl decorated with stylized fish skeletons with Xes for eyes.

"Enjoy!"

Five minutes later, a rap on the front door echoed through the shop. Through the window, Gina saw Danielle wave to her. Careful not to let Waldo escape, Gina slipped out the front door and locked it behind her.

Danielle gave her a big hug. "So sorry I wasn't there when they discharged you, babes. It's been insane. Vanessa's family have threatened a lawsuit."

"What?"

"Yeah. Apparently she had a physical, including cardio tests, in the summer. No issues were found. They're claiming it was something that happened to her here."

"The soda…" Gina's voice trailed off.

"What?"

"We need to find Reeve."

"We're supposed to have dinner. Soup. Remember? I was taking you to the White Horse."

"Fine. Just call Reeve. Have him meet us there."

THEIR ONION SOUP, Caesar salads, and a big plate of fries arrived at the same time Reeve did.

"French fry?" Gina offered as he sat down.

Reeve ignored the food. "You said this was important."

"Potentially." Gina explained the bottles of soda she had found in Vanessa's room.

"And what were you doing in her room?"

"Have you seen those corridors? I'm surprised anyone ends up in the same room two nights in a row."

"*You use your keycard,*" Reeve and Danielle both said at the same time.

"What, do you guys own stock in the keycard company? Anyway, I was drunk—excuse me, poisoned—"

"The hospital said it was just alcohol, hon."

"Yeah, well, we're going to have to agree to disagree on

that particular detail. Anyway, the point is, I found myself in Vanessa's room and came across about a dozen empty soda bottles."

"I remember," Danielle said. "You were obsessed with soda when I found you."

"Doesn't surprise me that you found garbage in the room," Reeve said. "We ordered the staff not to go in there. The place hasn't been cleaned since Friday morning."

"The bottles were of Rock River Breeze soda."

"So? Is that supposed to be significant?"

"Damn right, it's significant." Gina popped another fry into her mouth. "Apparently this Rock River Breeze soda—or RRB to people in the know—"

"Oooh," Danielle said.

"—is a regional brand that isn't sold outside of the Midwest."

Reeve thought for a moment. "So Vanessa Schaeffer brought her own pop with her. Rich people do things like that."

"The thing is, Danielle and I saw the Schaeffers board the train. Everyone did, really. They were late. The train had to stop in the middle of the tracks while the Schaeffers' helicopter landed."

"I heard about that," Reeve said.

"Well, I happened to notice their luggage being brought on the train. It was very nice."

"Okay, I'm still not tracking—"

"I didn't see anyone carting on cases of soda. That was for sure."

"Maybe she called ahead," Danielle said. "Put in a special request at the Hall."

"What, did she have a rider or something?" Gina said. *"Stock my room with green M & Ms and Rock River Breeze, or else."*

"You're right," Danielle said. "I can't see Frau Loneskum being quite that accommodating."

"You said it, not me."

"So you believe Vanessa Schaeffer was somehow poisoned with this Midwest soda?" Reeve asked.

"I'm sure that's easy enough to find out. Just check the bottles in her room."

Reeve jotted in his little notebook. "Anything else?"

"Maybe take another look at Édouard Orville and Frankie Roth."

"In connection with the pop?"

"In connection with each other." Gina recounted what she had heard in the hallway.

"Good work, Biletti." Reeve rose from the table.

"You're leaving so soon? Why not join us for a drink?" Gina raised her mug of chamomile tea.

"Are you kidding? You just tacked on three more hours of work to my shift." He nodded and left the table.

Danielle leaned over towards Gina. "You like him, don't you?"

"Seems like a competent law enforcement officer." She felt a blush rise along her cheeks.

"Ha, ha! I knew it."

"You don't know anything." Gina felt herself getting redder. "Anyway, what about you?"

"He's def not my type."

"No, I meant..." She trailed off. "I don't know what I meant. I'm just tired. Although I don't know why. Apparently, I slept for eighteen hours or something."

"You've gone through a lot. Getting blind drunk can be draining."

"Not you, too. For the last time, I was poisoned!"

"By who?"

"That I do not know." She took one last French fry. "Let's get out of here."

Danielle paid the bill and called for a car. While they waited outside of the inn, Gina's keycard buzzed.

It was Reeve. There were no soda bottles in Vanessa's room.

WHEN THEY ARRIVED BACK at Haverford Hall, Reeve was there to meet them. Before he opened his mouth, Gina asked if Vanessa's room had been cleaned.

"No. That's the thing. Nothing else was disturbed. Just no bottles."

"And you looked everywhere?"

He narrowed his eyes at her, but didn't respond.

"Okay, dumb question."

"There's a bottle in your room," Danielle said.

"What?" Gina and Reeve both turned to her.

"Yeah, you had an empty bottle with you when I found you passed out—"

"Poisoned," Gina corrected.

"When I was trying to get you back to your room, you were very insistent that we take the bottle with us. Like drunk insistent."

"I don't remember any of that," Gina said. "But good on me."

Unfortunately, when they arrived at Gina's room, there was no sign of the bottle.

"This room has definitely been cleaned," Danielle said.

"Where did you leave it?" Gina asked.

"On the dresser." Danielle pointed. "Right there."

The three of them checked the room, including all the garbage cans. No luck.

"I'll check with housekeeping," Reeve said.

"It was here, I swear it," Danielle said.

"I believe you," Gina said.

Reeve had stepped away, and now stared at his keycard intently. "I've got to go."

"What happened?"

"They found the murder weapon."

"What was it?"

"That's what I'm going to find out."

"Can we come?" Gina asked.

Reeve just gave her his look.

"Okay, fine. Well, good luck, then. Whatever."

As he left, Reeve motioned to a fresh addition to the inside of the door.

"A chain lock!" Gina said. "Nice."

"Don't say I never do anything for you." He winked.

After Reeve left, Danielle hung around, and they chatted for a while. Then Gina realized how much she needed a shower and kicked Danielle out.

"You want me to come back, babes?"

"I'll be fine—now that I've got a door that actually locks."

"Well, maybe if you're up, I'll see you in the morning. I have to be downstairs by eight, though. Peyton runs a tight ship."

"I bet."

They hugged goodnight, and once she was alone, Gina chained the door. Then checked the lock. It seemed perfectly secure. *Was that so hard?*

She availed herself of the room's deep soaker tub—even though she wasn't usually a bath kind of girl.

The first five minutes of a bath were always great. Soothing and therapeutic. But as the water cooled, Gina would get more and more uncomfortable. She knew she could refill the tub with warm water, but the spell would always be broken and she'd find herself dripping wet on the bath mat. Cold. Unfulfilled. And vowing never to take a bath again.

But within a year, she'd be back in the tub again.

I just can't quit you, Dr. Teal's.

So she soaked and read her book—until the water got too cold. Then she crawled out and shivered on the bath mat.

Her novel had distracted her for a bit, but she found her thoughts swirling back to the murders of Stanley and Vanessa and the question of who killed them.

As she crawled into bed (after double-checking that the chain lock was still in place), she kept thinking about all the information she had uncovered—and wondering what remained just out of reach.

First, her thoughts went to Tomas. He was still the likeliest suspect. He had had shady dealings with the Schaeffers. He was likely an alpaca smuggler. *And let's not forget that Stanley's body was found in the stables. Right where Tomas lived.*

A distant second in her list of suspects was the team of Édouard and Frankie. While she didn't know much about Édouard, she knew Frankie was on the verge of bankruptcy—because of her involvement with the Church of Triscology. Apparently, Frankie and Édouard were working together to get Florrie. Plus, Gina had overheard some very shady things coming out of their mouths. Especially Frankie's mouth: *Once they find out about the money, it will all be over.*

Also down there on the list was the wine lady, Amadora Seville. She was having an affair with Stanley—which definitely made her suspicious. And Gina could see her bumping off the wife, so she could have Stanley for herself. *Which is disgusting, by the way.* But Amadora didn't have a motive to kill Stanley—as far as Gina could see. It would have been different if he put Amadora in his will or something. But according to Ian, Stanley didn't even have a valid will. Which put a big crimp in the theory that most people kill for money.

She kept coming back to Florrie. There must be something about that alpaca that would push someone to murder.

And as much as she hated the thought, she couldn't help thinking about Becca.

The stakes were super high for the young woman. Not just financial stakes, but ethical stakes. And potentially the well-being of thousands or maybe hundreds of thousands of alpacas.

But was Becca actually capable of murdering another human being? Or two human beings?

That was what Gina thought about as she drifted off into an uneasy slumber.

SHE DREAMT of the talking alpaca again: Florrie. With his big expressive eyes and extra fluffy fur, this Dream Florrie looked much cuter than the real Florrie.

He stood next to Gina on the edge of the pond, where she had hit her head after seeing Noelle naked.

In this dream, it was *Gina* who was naked. She stared into the water.

"You going to jump, or what?" Florrie asked.

"I'm not sure yet."

"Then why'd you drag me all the way out here?"

"All the way out here? It's like a ten-minute walk—which is five for you because you've got four legs."

"Ha ha."

"Besides, I'd thought you'd be grateful to get out of that pen."

"Whatever," Florrie sniffed. "I'm just bored."

"Bored? With a murderer loose?"

"About that…"

"What?" she asked excitedly. "Do you know something?" She had never considered that the alpaca might have witnessed Stanley's murder.

"Not exactly…"

"Well, you either do or you don't. No one likes a cagey camelid."

"Ooh, look at you—using all the big words. You want my help or not?"

"Of course I do! Tell me, who killed Stanley?"

"I can't tell you that—"

"What?"

"Let me finish. I can't tell you that, because you need to discover the answer for yourself."

"If you say *'the journey is the reward,'* I swear I'm going to throw you in the water."

"I'd like to see you try," Florrie said. "I weigh 200 pounds."

"You're a big boy."

"It's all muscle."

"Uh huh. So getting back to Stanley's murder…"

"Like I said, you have to discover the truth for yourself."

"Well, in case you haven't been paying attention, that's what I've been doing," Gina huffed. "That's *all* I've been doing."

"Look closer," Florrie said enigmatically. "Maybe start by checking yourself out in the mirror."

"Yeah, right. A) There're no mirrors here—and B) uh, I have no interest in staring at my own naked body."

"Well, you happen to have a fabulous body—for a human. But I was talking about checking your *face* out. And, as for not having a mirror, what do you think this perfectly still body of water is good for?"

Florrie was right. The surface of the pond was still and glass-like.

Looking down, she could see an indistinct reflection of herself.

Gina squatted down for a closer look and her reflection sharpened.

She gasped. Her hair was red!

And at that moment she lost her balance and tumbled forward—right into the water.

twenty

. . .

GINA AWOKE from the dream with her heart pounding. She lurched out of bed and ran to the bathroom to look into the mirror.

Her hair was its normal color: Madison Reed Medium Neutral Blonde 9N.

Just another weird dream.

Oh well. That would have been the cheapest and easiest color I'd ever had done.

After washing up, she checked her keycard. There was a message from Danielle.

> No time for breakfast. Sorry. See you for dinner? xxxxoooo

Gina sighed. Another day in paradise, and she wasn't sure what she was going to do. Berenstein was probably getting sick of her. Reeve too. Maybe she should check in with Becca.

Before she could ponder any more possibilities, a sharp knock sounded on her door.

Of course there was no peephole, so Gina was reduced to calling out "Who is it?"

"Open the door, at once, Ms. Biletti. It's Detective Waverly."

She knotted up her robe and opened the door. The older detective who had interviewed her was standing there, flanked by two uniformed officers.

"Come with us, Ms. Biletti."

"What's all this about? I haven't even had my coffee."

"We need to ask you some more questions downstairs."

Gina was getting a really bad vibe from this. "Can I at least get dressed?"

"Make it quick. We'll be right outside."

"Fine."

"And we'll need you to keep the door unlocked, please."

This is so weird, Gina thought. She quickly dressed in jeans and a t-shirt and her favorite Rag & Bone cotton shirt jacket and tried to fix her hair a little.

"Let's go, Ms. Biletti," Waverly called through the door, rapping on it for emphasis.

"Coming!"

She brushed her teeth super fast, grabbed her keycard, and headed out.

"So what do you need to ask me?" Gina said out in the hallway.

The cops walked in formation around her, with Waverly just behind and to her left.

"Downstairs," he said.

They took her down to the same interview room with all the recording equipment. The other detective—Falson—was already there.

"Good morning, Ms. Biletti. We have some follow-up questions for you."

At least this guy was being slightly more pleasant. Maybe it was a classic good cop/bad cop routine.

After identifying her and themselves aloud for the recording, they launched into a barrage of questions about her whereabouts during the day Stanley died. Gina found herself giving the same answers over and over again.

Then they focused their questions on Gina's visit to the stables. How many times had she been there? Was she sure? When exactly did her visit occur? Were there any other people there who could verify her story?

"It's not a story, it's the truth." Gina struggled to keep her anger under control. How dare they treat her this way? "Are we almost done here?"

"We're done when we say we're done," Bad Cop Waverly said.

"Just a few more questions." Falson launched into a bunch of questions about the hedge maze.

It was very weird, but he wanted to know how many times she'd visited the hedge maze, when, if she was alone, and how much time she spent there. Slowly, it dawned on Gina what this was actually about.

"You're fishing for information about Becca, aren't you?"

Detective Waverly frowned at her. "We're not fishing for anything, Ms. Biletti. This is an official investigation."

"What's your relationship with Rebecca Hill?" Falson asked.

"I don't have a relationship with her," Gina said. "We just talked a few times."

"At the hedge maze?"

"Yes. We bumped into each other there on Saturday."

Waverly checked his notes. "And then you went to the stables together…?"

"Yes."

They continued to grill Gina about her time at the stables, asking the same questions: how long she spent there, who she saw, even what she touched.

Honesty is the best policy, she thought to herself. So Gina told them everything. Again. She even admitted to snooping around near the video security station.

"And did you disable the security system?" Waverly asked.

"Me? Are you kidding? I can barely get my keycard to text."

"Is that a 'yes' or a 'no," ma'am?"

"No. Big no."

The interrogation continued for another full hour, until somehow they made it through to the end of the questions.

"Can I go?"

"Yes," Falson said.

"For now," Waverly said.

"Thank you for your cooperation, Ms. Biletti," Falson said.

Gina got up to leave. One of her feet had actually fallen asleep, and she limped as she rose from the table. "I have to say, for what it's worth, I don't think Becca had anything to do with this."

"We'll form our own conclusions," Waverly said. "Thank you very much."

"I'm an excellent judge of character," Gina added. "I suggest you focus on Tomas and Frankie Roth and Édouard Orville. They're the ones who are the sketchiest in my book."

"You don't have a book, Ms. Biletti," Waverly said.

"You know what I mean."

After they let her go, Gina called for a car to go into town. It was a beautiful morning, warm, dry, and sunny, and she would have preferred to walk, but she knew that wasn't a good idea.

While she waited for the car to show up in front of Haverford Hall, Reeve drove up on his little golf cart. He didn't look happy.

"Good morning."

"Not really," she said. "So far, it's been a pretty crappy morning. Do you know I just spent nearly two hours in the gulag downstairs being interrogated?"

"They're just doing their jobs."

"I guess."

"And they let you go."

"Barely."

"That's something."

Reeve seemed distracted.

"You okay?" she asked.

"Fine. Where are you headed?"

"Into town. I thought I'd grab some breakfast and visit with Berenstein."

"Hop on. I'll take you. There's something we need to talk about."

A little jolt of electricity crackled down her spine. "I've got a car on the way."

"Let me see your card for a second."

She made a big show of fishing it out of the breast pocket of her jacket. "Yes, I do have it on my person." Then she handed the keycard to Reeve.

He clicked and tapped for a total of three seconds and then announced, "No problem. Ride cancelled. I'll take you."

Gina arched one eyebrow at his cart. "I don't know. Is this thing even street legal?"

"It is if I say it is." Reeve smiled a rare smile.

"Alrighty, then."

As they rode down the main thoroughfare, he said, "We got more info on those pop bottles you saw."

"You found them?"

"Yes, in the recycling area near the kitchen. They had been washed."

"Washed?" Gina's mind raced.

"Yes. We're not sure who washed them. It's not something they normally do. Everyone who's worked for the past week has been questioned. Also, Hospitality says that they don't stock that brand of pop—and it's not available anywhere in town."

"So either she brought them with her—which is doubtful —or someone else did."

Reeve nodded. "Also, I probably shouldn't be telling you this, but we got the info back from the Schaeffers' post-mortems."

"Really?" Gina tried to contain her excitement.

"Yes, Vanessa's blood work came back clean. No sign of poisons or anything unusual."

"So she really did die of a heart attack?"

"No way to know for sure, but so far, there's no other explanation."

"What about Stanley?"

"He died from blood loss."

"The artery?"

"Yes. But they did find something unusual in his system. Pentobarbital."

"I've heard of that..." Gina wished she had her phone so she could look it up.

"There was a partially digested pill in his stomach."

"What's it used for?"

"It's a barbiturate. It used to be prescribed as a sleeping pill."

"Used to be?"

"It was discontinued over twenty years ago."

"Then how did Stanley get his hands on a twenty-year-old sleeping pill?"

"He didn't. These days, the pills are used for assisted suicide."

"What?!"

"It's legal in Oregon."

"Wait, rewind. Stanley committed suicide?"

"It's possible."

"How do you explain the severing of the artery?"

"Based on the angle of the wound, it could have been self-inflicted."

"No way. Who cuts open their own artery?"

"I said it's possible. Not probable. The CID is still treating this as a homicide."

Gina thought for a moment. "You said that they found the weapon."

"Yes."

"Well?"

"Well what? I can't tell you anything about it."

"C'mon, Reeve. It's me. I thought we were partners."

"Partners? Since when?"

A flush of anger colored Gina's face. "Okay, stop the golf cart!"

"What?"

"STOP IT!"

Reeve pulled over to the side of the road. They had just made it down the hill and were on the outskirts of the village proper. "What are you doing?" he asked.

"Leaving."

"Why?"

"You're being shitty. I helped you. I've shared what I learned. Now you're cutting me out?"

"I'm not cutting you out. There are rules I need to follow."

"Oh, bull."

"Gina!" he called after her.

She ignored him and stalked away. She had no idea where she was going. She just needed to get away from him.

But Reeve jumped out of his vehicle and chased after her. He grabbed her shoulder and spun her around.

"Listen, you're a suspect, okay? A serious suspect."

"What?" She couldn't believe what she was hearing.

"You and Rebecca Hill."

Gina barked out a laugh. "That's ridiculous."

"They have your prints and DNA on the weapon."

"*My* prints?" She couldn't believe what she was hearing. "And what weapon?"

"The weapon that killed Stanley."

Gina shrugged wordlessly and made a face at Reeve, waiting for him to continue. You can't unload a bomb like that and not keep talking.

He gave up. "It was a hay hook."

"I have no clue what that is."

"It's exactly what it sounds like. A metal hook about yay-big—" He moved his hands about eight inches apart.

"Still doesn't ring a bell."

"Sharp pointed end. With a handle opposite. It's used for moving hay bales."

"I'm from New York City. We don't move hay bales there." *This must all be a big mistake.*

"They found it in the hedge maze," Reeve said. "Your DNA's on it, and your fingerprints. They also recovered a vaporizer with cannabis oil with both your DNA and Rebecca Hill's DNA."

"So what? We smoked some pot in the hedge maze? It's legal here!"

"I know it's legal—"

"And there were no hooks or hay bales in the maze."

"The team believes the hook was disposed of in the hedge maze at some point after the murder."

Gina shook her head. "Wasn't he killed on Sunday?"

"You know he was."

"Yeah, I also know that I wasn't in the hedge maze on Sunday. Check the CCTV. Or our keycards."

"The keycard tracking was inconclusive," he admitted.

"What does that mean?"

"It means that the murderer could have just left their keycard in their room."

"A-ha! Just what I've been saying. Darn that you guys didn't think of chip implants!"

"Gina—"

"Then you could know for sure who went where. Oh, I

forgot. You *do* know where I was, with you—having breakfast together on the morning Stanley got murdered. Or did you forget?"

"I didn't forget. I'm not stupid. I know you had nothing to do with Stanley's death."

"Well, you don't sound like you know it. Just the opposite." Gina turned away. She was still majorly pissed at Reeve. And those asshole investigators. They must have ransacked her room to find Becca's vape pen.

"I've been trying to get them off this line of inquiry, but they don't pay too much attention to my opinions. I'm just the local rent-a-cop."

Gina's expression softened. Just a little bit. "They're wasting a lot of time looking at me when the actual killer is still at large."

"It's worse than that. Regenschirm's attorneys are saying we have to release all the guests as soon as possible—for legal reasons. Likely some of you will be going home within twenty-four hours."

"Some of us?"

"Probably not you."

"Great. Just great."

"I'm doing everything I can, Gina."

"Doesn't seem like it."

"And I could lose my job just for telling you what I did."

Gina turned to look at him. "Well, I appreciate it. I guess. It's just horrible and frustrating. I thought these people were professionals?"

"They're trying to be methodical."

"Whatever." She strode away.

"Where are you going?" Reeve called after her.

"Enjoying my last few hours of freedom."

"So, I'm in the presence of a major murder suspect, eh?" Berenstein regarded her over a very large coffee mug emblazoned with a 1980s *Far Side* cartoon featuring cows in a suburban living room.

"Don't you start with me."

"It sounds like you have an alibi, though."

"More than one." Gina looked around the bakery. No one was paying attention to them. Still, she lowered her voice. "Depending on when exactly Stanley was murdered."

"Do tell."

"They think it was between roughly 6:45 and 7:30. I had breakfast with Reeve in town at 6:30 and then chatted with Noelle at the pond."

"And how much time between?"

"I don't know. I wasn't timing myself. But I said goodbye to Reeve right before seven, I think."

"And when did you gawk at the naked vet?"

Gina felt herself redden. "I did not gawk!"

"That's fine. No judgment, kiddo."

"I don't know when I saw Noelle, but I'm guessing it took me twenty, thirty minutes to get to the pond."

"That sounds about right. It's pretty far up there—well southwest of the road."

"You've been there?"

"Of course. It's a beautiful hike. So thirty minutes unaccounted for, hmmm? Within the murder window. Plenty of time." He inched his chair back away from her.

"Shut up."

"I'm teasing. Buck up, Biletti. I think you're close to finding the killer."

"Close? I've got no clue. No pun intended."

"Ha ha. Did you say that someone took those bottles of Rock River Breeze?"

"Took and washed. But no one knows who did it."

"Are you sure about that?"

"Yes, all the staff were questioned. There's nothing there."

"*Au contraire,* my dear. The absence of something can be a significant clue. Don't you remember your Sherlock Holmes?"

"I preferred the TV show. With what's-his-name."

"Heathen! If you are going to embark on this journey as a sleuth, you must familiarize yourself with the classics. But I digress."

"You sure do—"

"My point is that if the bottles of Rock River Breeze were insignificant, someone would have copped to taking them from the room. The fact that they appeared—mysteriously washed of any telltale evidence—suggests that there was something there to find."

"Poison!"

"Yes, poison."

"The problem with that is there wasn't any poison in Vanessa's system."

Berenstein took another sip of his tea. "That doesn't mean anything. There are plenty of poisons that are virtually undetectable without very specialized tests. Especially after a few days. Remember what I told you about digoxin?"

A thought struck Gina suddenly. "What if I was poisoned with the same substance?"

"Well, if it was digoxin, you'd probably be pushing up the proverbial daisies right about now. The point is, Biletti, you're right on the edge of figuring this out. And, unfortunately, the murderer knows it."

"You're not really cheering me up."

"Sorry, kiddo. I just want you to be careful."

"I am careful."

"Extra careful. Maybe you should just hole up for twenty-four hours. Until everyone leaves. You can stay with me. Invitation's still open."

"Thanks, but I can't give up now. The cops are trying to tie me to Stanley's murder."

"That's ridiculous. They have nothing that will stand up in court."

"Doesn't matter. People have been put away for life based on flimsy evidence. Remember that kid from *Serial*?"

"They let him go."

"Yeah, after twenty-three years in prison. No thanks."

twenty-one

. . .

GINA WANTED to walk back up to Haverford Hall to clear her mind and think, but Berenstein convinced her to call for a ride.

When the car arrived, Millicent stuck her head out of the window and waved to Gina.

"How *are* you?" Millicent asked as Gina climbed in. "It's been a minute."

"I know. This is like a nightmare."

"They still haven't arrested anyone?"

"Besides me?"

"*What?!* They arrested you?"

"Not really arrested. But apparently I'm a person of interest."

"Should I be worried that you're in my car?" Millicent asked with an uneasy smile.

"Should I be worried about your driving?"

"What?!"

"Kidding."

As they headed through the village, Gina quickly filled Millicent in on some of what was going on with the investigation—sticking mostly to tidbits that were more or less public knowledge.

"I don't get it. Where do you fit into all of this?"

"It's stupid. I was in the place they found the murder weapon."

"Oh…" Millicent sounded worried.

"It was *the day before* the murder."

"How is that relevant, then?"

"It's not."

"Well, do you need a lawyer or anything?"

"No," Gina said automatically. But the fact was, she didn't know whether she needed a lawyer or not. "You know someone?"

"I know a patent attorney."

"I'm not accused of stealing intellectual property."

"Yeah, but he might know someone. I'll beam you his info."

"Thanks."

When they parked at the front of Haverford Hall, Millicent sent the info to Gina. They chatted for a little while longer before saying goodbye.

"Everything will work out," Millicent said. "Just be brave."

"Easier said than done, but I get your drift."

"Call me tomorrow. I'll drive you to the train."

"That's pretty wishful thinking."

"C'mon, don't be negative." Millicent smiled at her.

"I'll try." Gina waved as she walked towards the front entrance of the manor. *Yeah, right.*

Before she went inside, she decided to take a walk instead. There were a bunch of people outside enjoying the early October sunshine, so it wasn't like she would be alone and vulnerable.

Gina circled around to the West Gardens where she had seen the woman in white her first morning in Maidenwell. It seemed like a lifetime ago, even though it had been less than five days. Of course she had lost a day in there somewhere, what with the whole being poisoned thing.

As she strolled down the wide stone steps into the formal gardens, she caught sight of an older woman sitting on a bench. Not far away, a little boy was playing with a stick. *Mason Garland.* But the woman wasn't Noelle. It was her mom.

"Morning," Gina said as she walked over.

"Oh, hello."

"You're Noelle's mom, right? I'm Gina Biletti. We met near the stables."

"Yes, I'm Leah. Good to see you, Gina. Have a seat."

"Don't mind if I do. It's a beautiful morning."

"It's the afternoon now."

"Oh, really? Without my phone, I've completely lost track of time."

"Your keycard has a clock on it," Leah said.

"Of course it does." Gina smiled and nodded toward her grandson. "How's Mason holding up? With all that's been going on, I mean."

"He doesn't really understand it, thank goodness. I think he's just eager to get home to Idaho."

"Idaho? I thought Noelle said you guys lived in California."

"We did. But we moved back to Boise over the summer. Noelle liked Mason's doctors in Idaho better."

"What about you? Do you like Idaho better?"

"I actually like Michigan better. That's where Noelle grew up. Although you really can't complain about California's weather, can you?"

"I'm not going to argue with you there. But I'm used to crappy weather. I'm from New York."

"Whereabouts in New York?"

"The City."

"That must be exciting. To live in New York City."

"It can be. But mostly it's expensive."

Leah turned away, focused on what her grandson was doing. "Mason! Stop that!" she called.

The kid was smashing his stick against one of the life-sized stone statues on the edge of the garden. It looked like Mason was on a mission to take out one of the Greek gods.

"Excuse me." Leah rose from the bench. "I'm afraid he's going to break something."

"Kids." Gina followed Leah over to where Mason was still assaulting the statue. He was bashing it all around the upper thighs and waist with his stick.

"Ooh, careful there, champ," Gina said. "You're getting awful close to his loincloth. One wrong smack and his days of making little statues are over."

Leah shot her a look. "I'll handle this."

"Sorry."

Leah patiently—and probably wisely—waited until Mason paused to catch his breath, then she swooped in and disarmed him. The boy complained and whined, but then Leah steered him over to one of the squared-off flower beds where a lone butterfly perched on a mostly dead flower.

"Were you looking for Noelle?" Leah asked.

Gina definitely got a 'harried grandma' vibe from her now. "Sure. I wanted to check in and see how she was doing."

"I think she's at the stables, doing something for Frau Loneskum."

"Oh, okay. Maybe I'll take a walk over there."

"Good, you do that. Tell her that I'm taking Mason in for lunch."

"Will do."

Mason gave a feral bark that might have been a laugh. Gina and Leah turned back just in time to witness Mason catching the butterfly. It looked like the kid was about to tear the wings off the hapless insect. But as Gina watched, Mason smiled and gently held the butterfly up to the breeze, and let it fly away.

Okay, that was weird.

All the coffee from breakfast made Gina need a pit stop back in her room. As she trundled up the main staircase, Ian was going down—his nose stuck in his red notebook—and they nearly bumped into each other.

"Oops. Sorry." He looked up and recognized Gina.

"How are you doing?" she asked.

"Still freaking out. This estate situation is getting worse and worse."

"I'm sorry."

"Not your fault. Unless you were the one who killed Stanley." He smiled wanly.

"Why? What have you heard?" She smiled back, although it was kind of twisted to be joking about this—especially in light of her being a prime suspect.

"The good news is that we're going home tomorrow," Ian said.

"Has that been confirmed?"

"Yes. Ten a.m. train to freedom."

"I wonder if there's going to be a farewell party."

"No, I think Frau Loneskum just wants everyone out of here."

"I don't blame her."

"Well, I'll see you later." Ian continued on his way.

"Wait a sec!" Gina realized Ian could clear something up for her. "I need to ask you something about Vanessa."

He paused, but didn't look especially happy about it. "I don't think I'm allowed to talk to you about the Schaeffers."

"I just need to know if she drank Rock River Breeze soda."

"Yeah." Ian sighed. "She was addicted to it."

"So you brought a supply with you? Here to Maidenwell, I mean."

Ian shook his head. "Nope."

"You sure?"

"I was always having to order her soda. There's a distributor we work with to get it wholesale."

"But you didn't bring any with you?"

"I told you once, we didn't."

Gina obscured the truth a bit. "Well, someone saw her drinking it."

"Well, then she arranged it with Guest Services here. Why do you care? Are you addicted to it as well?"

"No. Just curious."

"Well, talk to Guest Services. I'm sure they have plenty left over now. Sadly."

Gina returned to her room, unable to stop thinking about the soda. It was so weird. Why couldn't anyone give her a straight answer about where the soda had come from?

She freshened up and was about to head out to the stables when someone knocked on her door.

Leaving the chain in place, she opened the door and peered through the gap.

"I'm not here to murder you," Becca said. "I just want to talk. Can I come in?"

"Sure." Gina unlatched the door and motioned for Becca to enter. "Sorry, I don't have any weed to offer you, because apparently it's been confiscated."

"Yeah, that's what I wanted to talk to you about." She flopped into one of the brocade chairs. "Are you getting hassled by the cops, too?"

"A little bird told me I'm their number one prime suspect."

"You're number two. I'm number one."

"This is crazy." Gina sat down on the edge of the bed.

"I know. It's like a nightmare."

"Where were you when it happened?"

"That's part of the problem," Becca said. "I was alone. Walking."

"Where?"

"In the gardens—near the fern building."

"The fernery?"

"Fernery?" Becca smiled. "You're making that up."

"No, I swear. That's what it's called. One of the old guys that works in the greenhouse told me."

"Well, whatever. That's where I was on Sunday morning."

"What time?"

"I don't know. Early. Before seven, I think."

"That's weird. I was kind of near the gardens—also going for a walk. I had just come from breakfast and I needed the exercise."

"Me too. I didn't sleep the night before because I was so keyed up about the auction and my pitch to the Frau."

"I'm surprised we didn't bump into each other."

"Do you think that's why they suspect us? Maybe they have video of us walking around in the area."

"I was nowhere near the stables on Sunday. Were you?"

"No."

Gina shook her head. "From what I understand, they found the murder weapon in the hedge maze. And they knew that you and I were together in the hedge maze on Saturday."

"That doesn't make sense. Nothing happened on Saturday."

"Well, Florrie got loose, and a kid was missing for a while, so a few things did happen on Saturday. Also, the same little bird told me that both our DNA was on the murder weapon."

"I don't even know what the murder weapon was!"

"A straw hook," Gina said.

"Straw?

"For moving bales."

"Oh, a hay hook."

"That's what I said."

"Close enough."

"So you know what it is?"

"Of course. Hay hooks are all over the place in barns."

"Well, that might be true. But I've never seen one—let alone touched one."

Becca glanced away, like she was thinking of something. "I can't remember touching one here either."

"I'm thinking that our DNA samples got contaminated or something. Maybe sloppy crime scene work."

"Could be," Becca said. "Or someone is trying to frame us."

"What, like snip off some of our hair and rub it on the weapon?"

"I don't know. All I know is that I didn't kill Stanley—even though I wanted to."

"Well, I didn't either. But someone did."

"I guess."

"Do you think it could be Frankie and Édouard?"

"What?"

Gina leaned forward. "I need to tell you something."

A worried expression played across Becca's face, but she said nothing.

"Remember the night of the dinner party?" Gina asked.

"Sure. I got kind of wasted."

"Please. Nothing compared to me. But on my way back to my room, I accidentally heard Édouard and Frankie talking in the hallway near their room."

"Accidentally?"

"If you must know, I was in the process of passing out in one of those little alcoves."

"Nice."

"But I heard them, clear as day. They were talking about how they were worried that the Frau might find out that they were working together."

"What? No way!"

"It gets worse. They're together."

"I don't—"

"*Together* together."

"TMI."

"Yeah, well, I heard Frankie say that she was concerned about—quote—*finding out about the money*."

"What money?"

"She didn't spell it out, but both of them sounded super sketchy."

"So you think that Frankie and Édouard killed Stanley?" All the color had drained from Becca's face.

"I don't know. What do you think? You know them better than me."

"They had me fooled. Working together? Really?"

Gina nodded.

"And, like, having sex? Did you actually see them?"

"What? No. Gross! I just heard them."

"They were doing it in the hall?"

"Would you stop! They were just talking. With a bit of making out. But they were worried that if the Frau knew they were working together, she wouldn't sell them Florrie."

"This whole thing is super weird," Becca said. "I didn't think either of them had any chance of getting Florrie. I mean, they are obviously second tier. Everyone knows it."

"Frau Loneskum, too?"

"Of course."

"Well, what changed, then?"

"I don't know. Maybe Frankie stepped up. Presented a breeding plan. Although she's not very sharp in that area."

"Maybe Édouard helped."

"Could be." Becca sighed. "I don't know. I just want this whole thing to be over."

"Well, it's not going to be over for us until we figure out what really went on."

"Maybe you should talk to Frau Loneskum," Becca said.

"Me? Why me?"

"You could tell her what you heard."

Gina shook her head. "She hates me. I told you."

"I remember."

"*You* could talk to her," Gina said. "Give her a heads up."

"No, it can't come from me. She already thinks I'm maneuvering to get Florrie."

"How's that going, by the way?"

"Everything's on hold," Becca said glumly. "My aunt is telling me to just be patient."

"You think that Frau Loneskum will go ahead with the sale?"

"Of course. She's getting out of alpacas altogether."

"What? I didn't know that! How come? I thought alpacas were the best thing since sliced bread."

"She thinks she's too old. Who knows? Maybe she is. This actually is a young person's business. You can't hurry genetics, you know. It takes time. Many multiple generations. I think the Frau realized that."

Gina nodded. "Seems like this might play out some time in the future."

"I don't even know that I have a future." Becca looked away.

"Come on. Buck up. They really don't have anything on us—besides some janky DNA evidence that would get thrown out of court within thirty seconds."

"You think so?"

"I'm no legal expert, but I do watch a lot of TV," Gina said with a straight face.

"What if they don't let us leave?"

"I think they would have already arrested us. The fact that we're both running around leads me to believe that they don't have enough to hold us."

"I think my aunt is trying to get a lawyer over here."

"Really?" It sounded like Catherine wasn't as optimistic as Gina was.

"It's not that easy—logistically speaking. No trains going in or out."

"If they arrest us, then they're required to give us access to a lawyer. But, honestly, let's not go there. Be positive. Who else could have murdered the Schaeffers?"

"I have no idea," Becca said. "Maybe Stanley's assistant. But I'm just guessing."

Gina shook her head. "I don't think that Ian had anything to do with it. I've talked to him a bunch and Stanley's death means a ton of work for him. He's the executor of Stanley's estate."

Becca snapped her fingers and her eyes went wide. "The will! Yes! Who inherits all his money? That should point to the killer."

"If only it were that straightforward. Turns out Stanley was in the process of writing a will. As of right now, he doesn't have one. So no one is set to inherit."

"They didn't have kids."

"Also, no siblings or living parents or other relatives. That's why Ian is so overwhelmed."

"I wonder if they're going to liquidate Schaeffer Family Farms," Becca mused. "They'll have to—if no one's going to inherit it."

"I don't know. This isn't my area. I'm guessing that the state of Idaho might have a claim if there's no one to inherit."

"Vanessa has a big family. Plenty of relatives on that side."

"Yeah, who knows?" Gina said. "Changing subjects, do you know Tomas?"

"Frau Loneskum's guy?"

"Yeah. He seems sketchy to me."

Becca made a face. "How so?"

"Well, a couple of things. There's a rumor going around that he's an alpaca smuggler."

"What?!"

"You haven't heard that one before?"

"No."

"You know Stanley's prize female?"

"Sure, Magdalene."

"Noelle mentioned that people think she was smuggled out of Peru illegally."

"I don't think so. She has a certificate with the IAOF."

"Doctored," Gina whispered.

"No."

Gina shrugged. "That's just what I heard."

"From Noelle?"

"Yeah."

"I wouldn't put much stock in that. She's not a fan. They had a big blowout a few years ago."

"Noelle and Stanley?"

"Yeah."

"What about?"

"No idea. All I know is that she used to work for him. And then they had a big fight. She either was fired or quit."

"How long ago was this?"

"God, I don't know. A long time ago. I was in high school."

"So you've known Stanley for a while?"

"I used to help my aunt at shows and work at her ranch during the summers. So I've probably known him for ten years. But I hated him at first sight."

"Really?"

"Yeah, he was creeping on some young girl at a show. And Vanessa was there with him. He's such a pig."

"Hey, don't disparage pigs!"

"You're right. A pig is a million times better than Stanley."

"Okay, so getting back to Tomas..."

"Cross him off your list. My aunt saw him Sunday morning."

"When?"

"Around seven. He was outside of the machine shop in the back."

"Machine shop?"

"Yeah, she saw him on his quad thingie."

Gina didn't really know what that was, but remembered the machine shop in back of the manor, when Reeve took her there the first day she met him. "She's sure?"

"Positive. Her room overlooks the courtyard."

If that was true, Gina had to strike her prime suspect off the list. "Hmm. Did she tell the investigators?"

"I don't know. She didn't say."

"Okay, who else, then?"

"We're running out of people."

"Have you heard anything about Amadora?" Gina asked.

"I don't know who that is."

"The wine lady. Braids. Very pretty. She was shtupping Stanley."

"Shtupping?"

"Having sex with her. Geez, haven't you ever been east of the Mississippi?"

"They were doing it?"

"Absolutely. I burst in on them."

"You what?"

Gina quickly recapped the story, and Becca laughed out loud. "I wish I had seen that!"

"No, you don't," Gina said. "You really don't."

"Well, cross her off the list too," Becca said.

"Why?"

"I saw her when I was heading out for my walk. We even said hello."

"When?"

"Not sure. Before seven, though. She was with one of her workers, packing stuff up. Wine cartons. Displays. Stuff like that. I thought it was weird to be doing that so early, but maybe she thought she was going to leave on the morning train."

Gina never really considered Amadora a suspect, but now she could really cross her off the list. And the list was looking pretty bare.

"Maybe we're totally missing something," Becca said. "Maybe it's not an alpaca person at all. Maybe it's someone from the village."

Gina rubbed her eyes. Was she getting a headache—on top of everything?

"You have to admit that it's possible that it wasn't one of us, after all."

"I guess," Gina said. "Although Danielle told me that everyone who is accepted as a resident has gone through an intense screening process, psychological profiling, and god knows what else."

"So? People hide all kinds of secrets. Maybe a serial killer slipped through the cracks."

"That's a scary thought."

"I know, right?"

They spent the next half hour gabbing, and then Becca said she needed to get back and check on her aunt.

'"How's Catherine doing?" Gina asked.

"Not good. I think she's more worried than I am."

After Becca left, Gina wondered if there was time to catch Noelle at the stables. She drifted over to the window and looked out.

Leah and Mason were still out there in the garden—even though Leah had mentioned that they were going in for lunch. Maybe they ate and went back out. Gina could see how it might be easier to keep Mason occupied outside—instead of cooped up in a small guest room.

Gina glanced over at the clock. A little after 2 p.m. Maybe she would head over to the stables.

She looked out the window again.

Mason was back at it, smacking the statue with his stick. Granted, she hadn't spent a lot of time around kids, but Mason struck her as particularly...

She froze.

Violent.

twenty-two

• • •

AS SHE WALKED along the bridle trail to the stables, Gina's suspicions went into overdrive. All kinds of pieces of the puzzle started to fall into place.

The picture that was emerging was horrific—and there were so many questions that she couldn't even begin to make sense of everything.

But she kept coming back to certain inescapable facts.

1) Mason had tried to push that little girl off the edge of the rest stop. Gina had seen it with her own eyes.

2) He was violent towards animals. She had seen him whip Florrie and drive him out of the pen.

3) He was also violent towards her, whipping her arm with surprising strength for a ten-year-old.

4) Reeve had told her that Mason was troubled—a special needs kid. And he didn't talk to anyone besides his mom and grandmother.

5) Stanley's wounds were right below his waist—at the same point at which Mason attacked the statue. The fact that Stanley was attacked on his inner thigh had always struck Gina as unusual. But now it made perfect sense. That was arm-height for Mason.

Gina had to stop and lean against a tree, she was hyperventilating so much.

Maybe she had been unable to figure out a motive for Stanley's murder *because there wasn't one.* The killing was random. Or at least not premeditated. It was the work of a psychopath.

A ten-year-old psychopath.

Mason had run into Stanley at the stables—and maybe vented his rage on Stanley. Like he had vented his rage on Florrie and Gina the day before—in the same place. Maybe Mason surprised Stanley—struck him with the hay hook out of the blue. No one expects a ten-year-old kid to murder them.

Then a little tickle of doubt crept into Gina's imagined scenario.

What about the drug that was in Stanley's system? The pentobarbital?

It was doubtful that Mason could have forced Stanley to take a pill.

Unless…

Gina took a deep breath, trying to keep her head clear.

Unless the pill had nothing to do with Stanley's death. Reeve had said that pentobarbital was used as a sleeping pill. Sure, the drug might have been discontinued—but rich people could usually get their hands on whatever they wanted, especially when it came to drugs.

What about Vanessa? Was she murdered or not? Was that just another weird coincidence? A red herring?

Gina's head spun with the possibilities. She kept coming back to something she talked about at work a lot when her team was faced with a thorny research question with lots of conflicting data points.

Occam's Razor.

It was an oddly named logic principle that meant that when you were considering several competing theories or explanations, the simpler explanation was nearly always the correct one.

Boil the problem down to its essentials.

Someone killed Stanley. Was it more likely to be someone with an esoteric motive—or was it more likely to be a disturbed, aggressive kid who was very strong for his age? A kid who had been in close proximity to Stanley in the same location the day before?

There was only one way to get to the truth about Mason. And it would not be easy.

Gina would have to confront Mason's mom.

Noelle would have to have known.

There would have been blood.

And Mason only spoke to his mother and grandmother.

Another thought sent a chill through Gina. *Does Leah know about this?*

The older woman had been acting a little weird when they spoke in the garden. Maybe she wanted someone to know about Mason—what he had done.

WITH HER HEAD IN A FOG, Gina continued down the bridle trail. She barely registered where she was or where she was going. Everything around her looked surreal, especially the patterns of dappled light filtering through the trees and the long shadows that shaded the trail in darkness. At one point, she got the distinct feeling that she was being watched, but when she whipped around, no one was there.

I need to pull myself together.

But she couldn't help it. A million thoughts raced through her mind at light speed.

She stopped again and took a deep breath, forcing herself to calm down and focus. *Away with you, monkey mind!*

What would she say to Noelle? How could she bring up

her suspicions without the other woman completely shutting down?

She would just have to go for it. See what Noelle's reaction was. Maybe she'd be relieved. After all, she was a rational person—a vet. Maybe she had even diagnosed what was wrong with Mason.

Gina glanced over her shoulder again, not sure if she had seen anything.

Oh god. What if I'm wrong about the kid? What if the actual murderer is stalking me right now?

She picked up her pace, panic welling up inside her. *How far are those damned stables?*

When she had come here with Becca, it seemed like a short five-minute walk. Now it felt like she had been on the trail for twenty minutes.

And on top of everything, Gina was getting a cramp in her side from race-walking. *Great.*

She pushed through the pain and kept walking, still looking back to see if she could see anyone following her. But there was no sign of life—other than some birds.

Finally, through the trees, she spotted the big arched entrance way with the clock tower.

Gina paused to look around. The courtyard of the stable block was quiet, so she entered the main barn through the door she had gone through the last time she was here.

"Hello?" she called. "Noelle?"

No one answered, and she didn't see any humans inside either. A few alpacas were milling around in their stalls. For the first time, Gina noticed that several of the stalls were connected. Maybe the alpacas got lonely and didn't want to hang out on their own.

The Great Florentine was not in his stall, but the door to his outside pen was open, so he was probably outside. Maybe Noelle was with him. Or maybe she had left and was back at Haverford Hall and Gina had walked out here for nothing.

Gina looked around again, walking from stall to stall. *No one's home.*

She decided to check the outside pens, and if Noelle wasn't there, she'd get the hell out of here. *Why isn't anyone around? There should be people feeding the alpacas, shouldn't there?*

Outside, she found Florrie nibbling hay from a long black plastic trough. She shaded her eyes from the afternoon sun and looked around at the other pens. There were maybe another dozen alpacas—all colors—but no people. There was even a mom alpaca with a little baby nursing from her. The mom was all black, but the baby was a deep reddish-brown color. It struck Gina as a little odd.

Wouldn't a black-furred mom alpaca have a black baby? She wondered if alpacas passed down hair color like humans. Supposedly, 97% of humans on the planet had brown or black hair. 2% had blonde. And less than 1% were redheads. She wasn't sure, but she vaguely remembered reading that you needed both parents to be blonde to produce a blonde child. Or was that for redheads? Something about recessive genes.

She looked around the various pens and shaded her eyes, and peered into the pastures beyond. No sign of Noelle or anyone else.

Great. Now she would have to walk all the way back by herself. And who knew if there was someone out there stalking her? This was not a good idea—coming out here all alone. What had she been thinking?

Now that she was coming off the buzz of her theory that Mason might be the perpetrator, doubts seeped into her mind. A lot of doubts.

The more Gina thought about it, the more she realized that Berenstein had been right. Someone was on to her. Between the disappearing soda bottles, the mysterious meeting in the morning, and the attack on her Monday night, things just didn't add up. A kid couldn't have been involved in all that.

Neither could Stanley, because he had already been out of the picture.

"Gina?"

She spun to see Noelle emerging from the main building behind her. The vet smiled. "I thought I heard someone. What are you doing here?"

"Oh, hi…"

Noelle's red hair caught the autumn sunlight, and it reminded Gina of how surprised she had been when she saw the photo of young Stanley Schaeffer on the old news story. He had red hair too—once upon a time.

A weird thought popped into her mind. Could Stanley and Noelle be brother and sister?

No, that was wrong. Becca had said that Stanley had been *involved* with Noelle, way back when. Which was very weird.

"I was actually, um, looking for you…" Gina said. But she could hardly string two words together, her mind was racing so fast. *Could Noelle have gotten pregnant by Stanley? Was he Mason's dad?*

"Well, I'm flattered." Noelle stepped closer. "How come?"

"Oh, I don't know. I just ran into your mom and she mentioned you were here." The few times Gina had seen Stanley and Noelle together, he made it very clear that he didn't like Noelle. *Maybe the affair went off the rails. Maybe Stanley didn't like the idea of having an illegitimate child.*

"Hmmm. So you thought you'd take a walk?"

"Yup." Then it hit Gina. *Stanley had no children—which meant no heirs. Except maybe he actually did. Mason.*

"Are you okay, Gina? You look pale." Noelle moved even closer.

"Uh, I'm not sure. I might be having a relapse."

"Right. You were in the hospital, weren't you?" A strange look flickered in Noelle's eyes. "Tetrahydrozoline overdose, wasn't it?"

"Did you say tetrahydrozoline?" The drug sounded

vaguely familiar. Gina wondered if she had done a focus group on it at some point.

"It's a vasoconstrictor."

"What?" Gina backed away. "The doctors said it was just alcohol poisoning."

"Tetrahydrozoline is kind of hard to detect—unless you are specifically looking for it."

Gina glanced around frantically. She was up against a fence. There was nowhere else to go.

"It builds up in the system—and mimics a heart attack. Of course, there's no time for that now."

"I don't understand," Gina gasped—even though, deep down, she *did* understand. It was Noelle. She was the one who had murdered Stanley and Vanessa.

Noelle moved closer—and something glimmered in her hand. *Is that a knife?*

"From the look in your eyes, I think you know what's going on," Noelle said, her voice perfectly calm. "I always thought you were a smart woman. Smart and beautiful."

Wait, did she just call me beautiful?

But before Gina could process anything further, Noelle lunged forward.

Everything seemed to move in slow motion.

Gina glimpsed what was in Noelle's hand: a hypodermic needle—big enough to tranq a horse. The vet raised it like a dagger and it caught the light.

Heart pounding, Gina struggled to get away—but Noelle grabbed the front of her shirt jacket with surprising strength and pulled her close—coming in for the kill.

"You won't feel a thing," Noelle murmured. Then she plunged the hypodermic needle right into Gina's heart.

"Stop!" Gina heard a voice yell. But it wasn't her own.

Then Noelle's body slammed into hers and Gina felt herself topple backwards.

Everything went black.

"You did it this time." Florrie looked down at Gina with his big brown eyes.

Gina sat up, rubbing the back of her head. She was in a green pasture that seemed to stretch forever in every direction. The sun was warm and the faint aroma of juniper hung in the gentle breeze. There was no sign of Noelle—or even the stables, for that matter.

"What happened?" She was pretty sure that she was dreaming. Or dead. The talking alpaca was a big clue.

"Didn't you learn anything from watching all those murder shows?" Florrie asked. "You never confront the killer on your own. *Never*."

"In my defense, I didn't know she was the killer when I went out to see her."

"Uh huh." Florrie seemed bored by the discussion. "You figured it out pretty quickly."

"Not quickly enough."

"It depends who you ask."

"So I *am* dead." Gina inspected herself. "She must have injected me with some kind of poison."

"Tetrahydrozoline. Which, by the by, is what's in eye drops."

"Eye drops?"

"Yeah, the stuff you use to get the red out when you've—I don't know—been overindulging."

"Ah, gotcha." Then, like a bolt, the memory of the party on the first night came back to her. After she had confronted Ian about stealing the wine for Stanley, she found a bunch of empty little plastic bottles. Bottles of eye drops.

"Ian?" she gasped.

"Don't get your panties in a bunch, girlfriend. He had nothing to do with this. It was all Noelle."

"I was right, then. She wanted Mason to inherit Stanley's money."

"Bingo."

Gina scrambled to her feet. "I have to stop her."

The alpaca actually laughed. The sound was even more unsettling than hearing him speak. "Look at yourself. You're in no position to do that."

He was right. Gina felt like someone had taken a sledgehammer to her ribcage.

She tentatively felt her chest where Noelle had stabbed her with the hypodermic. There was something hard there—rectangular. It was in the breast pocket of her shirt jacket.

Her fingers closed around the object, and she pulled it free.

Her keycard.

Her goddamn keycard.

And then she heard herself laughing—with Florrie joining in.

twenty-three

. . .

WHEN GINA AWOKE, she was in a hospital room—the one she had been in before. She blinked and looked around the room.

Reeve sat in a chair nearby, flipping through his little notebook.

"Ugh," she croaked.

"You're awake." He smiled at her.

"Am I?"

"How are you feeling?"

"It depends. Was I injected with a big hypo filled with eye drops?"

His eyebrows quirked. "You knew about that?"

"Noelle's one of those super-villains who likes to talk."

Reeve clicked his little walkie-talkie and spoke into it. "She's awake."

Within a minute, her hospital room filled with people, all talking at once.

"Babes, I am so glad you're okay." Danielle leaned over her and hugged her. "We were so worried."

Becca set a vase of flowers down on Gina's night stand.

The flowers were the same pink color as the tips of her hair. "It was so brave of you—to face Noelle down like that."

"Yeah, you totally could have been killed," Millicent said.

"She was just trying to get out of buying my shop," Berenstein huffed. "Nice try, kiddo."

"So anyone want to bring me up to speed?" Gina asked.

"Well, you're here for observation," Nurse Dooley said. She was the last one to arrive. "We just want to make sure you don't have a concussion."

"Again," Danielle added helpfully.

"I actually meant bring me up to speed about the whole being-attacked-by-a-murderer-with-a-hypodermic-needle thing."

"Noelle Garland's in custody," Reeve said. "I witnessed her attacking you."

"More than that," Danielle said. "He pulled her off you and disarmed her."

"She was going for your neck next," Reeve said. "But the needle broke after it impacted with your keycard."

"My keycard? I thought that was a dream."

"Saved your life, missy," Berenstein said.

"This is insane."

"No, you're very lucky, Ms. Biletti," Nurse Dooley said. "If she had injected you in the heart, there wouldn't have been enough time to—"

"Okay, okay." Danielle ushered the nurse away. "She doesn't need to hear about that."

"Was I right about Mason? Is he Stanley's son?"

"What?" at least three people exclaimed simultaneously.

Gina explained how she had made the connection between Mason's hair and Stanley's hair and how it prompted her to theorize that they might be father and son.

Reeve furiously scribbled in his notebook as Gina shared her idea that this whole thing had been an elaborate plot to ensure that Mason would inherit Stanley's estate.

"Anything else?" Reeve asked.

"I don't think Vanessa died of a heart attack. I think Noelle poisoned her—with tetrahydrozoline in her soda."

"Ah, Rock River Breeze," Berenstein said. "I knew that stuff could kill you."

"She said something about it taking time," Gina said.

"That's true," Nurse Dooley said. "A drug like that builds up in your system and could cause your heart rate and blood pressure to drop to dangerous levels."

"And it could kill you?" Danielle asked.

"Absolutely. Or put you in a coma."

"During the party on the first night, I found a whole bunch of empty bottles of eye drops," Gina said. "I bet the stuff in the soda wasn't working fast enough, so Noelle spiked Vanessa's drink at the party."

"Okay, I've heard enough," Reeve said. "I need to get this information to the state investigators pronto. They'll want to interview you now that you're awake."

"Might as well get it out of the way."

"I'll let them know." He turned to leave, but then stopped and turned back to Gina. "Oh, and good work, Biletti. Really good work."

"Any time," Gina beamed. "You know where to send my check, right?"

But Reeve was gone.

"So how did she kill Stanley?" Becca asked. "I don't get it. He didn't die of a heart attack. He bled to death."

"He had another drug in his system," Gina said. "Pentobarbital."

"It's used for euthanasia," Nurse Dooley said.

"They found the remnants of a capsule in his system," Gina said. "But I wouldn't be surprised if she injected him first. I think that's what really killed him."

"Injecting would be a lot quicker," Nurse Dooley said. "Depending on the dose, he'd be out of it in less than a minute and probably dead within three."

"But why the leg wound?" Becca asked.

"As sick as it sounds, I think she was trying to frame Mason for the murder. Maybe she thought he wouldn't serve time because of his age or his, uh, disability or whatever. Who knows? She was obviously really messed up."

They chatted for several more minutes until Nurse Dooley kicked them all out because she needed to get the room cleaned.

"That's it?" Gina asked. "I'm free?"

"You're perfectly healthy."

"Thanks to her iron-hard noggin, no doubt," Berenstein said.

"And, hopefully, we won't ever see you back here," Nurse Dooley said.

"Not much chance of that," Danielle said. "We're out of here. For good."

Gina turned to her friend. "You mean…?"

"Ten a.m. train tomorrow, babes," Danielle said.

THE STATE INVESTIGATORS met Gina when she returned to Haverford Hall and whisked her downstairs for ninety grueling minutes of interrogation. Besides relaying all the facts of what had happened at the stables, she also told them all her theories about what might have been going on behind the scenes. Waverly and Falson both seemed impressed, despite doing their best not to show it.

After collecting all her contact information, they finally dismissed her without so much as a word of thanks. *Oh, well.*

Gina headed back up to her room to wash up and change. Danielle had asked if she might be up for a farewell dinner. Gina said that was exactly what she needed.

So an hour later she found herself at The Feathers pub

with Danielle, Becca, Catherine, Millicent, and Berenstein. Danielle had also invited Reeve, but apparently he was still working.

It was a wonderful dinner, and although Gina stuck with non-alcoholic cider for the evening, everyone ended up being loud and laughing a lot. It felt good to have a release after all the stress over the past four days—not to mention the attempts on her life.

They tried their best to avoid talking about the murders and the fallout from them. Of course, Gina was intensely curious about the PR implications, but she knew Danielle wouldn't talk about work in front of the others. She would just have to wait until the ride home.

Home.

Did she really even have a home to go back to? She couldn't afford her apartment, that was for sure. Or probably any apartment in Manhattan. Where would she go? What would she do?

"You okay, babes?"

"Fine. Just tired, I think." Gina smiled wanly.

"You had a big day. We probably should get you back."

"Last chance, Biletti," Berenstein said. "Buy the bookstore and I'll even pick up the tab for dinner."

"Tempting, Berenstein, tempting."

"I already paid the bill!" Danielle said.

"You sneak!" Berenstein said.

At the end, there was a lot of hugging and preemptive declarations of missing one another—even though Gina would see Becca and Catherine on the train and Millicent would be driving them to the station in the morning.

Gina actually found herself a little teary when saying goodbye to Berenstein, though. He held her tight and said, "I have a feeling you'll change your mind about the shop. Call me anytime."

Gina slept like a baby that night, and she didn't dream of

Florrie or any other alpacas. She almost overslept as well, barely having time to shower and pack up before Danielle knocked on her door.

The train ride back was bittersweet. Despite all the murder and mayhem, there was something special—magical, even—about Maidenwell, and Gina knew she was going to miss the village. A lot.

She said her final goodbyes to the alpaca people as they disembarked at Aune Station, exchanging info with Becca so they could keep in touch—even though, deep down, Gina knew she'd probably never see the young woman again.

At the station, Gina and Danielle traded their keycards for their personal electronic devices, and Gina actually kissed her phone. "I missed you so much, baby!"

"You're such a freak," Danielle laughed.

"Uh huh." Gina was already digging into her unread texts and emails.

The drive back to Portland went quickly. And, although Gina peppered Danielle with questions, her friend had little information to share.

"There's no way we can keep a lid on the death of the Schaeffers," she said. "Best we can hope for is to keep Regenschirm out of it."

"Good luck with that. People are going to want to know where and how they died."

"We'll try to go with 'an unnamed Oregon resort.' It might work."

Two hours later, Danielle dropped Gina off at Portland International Airport.

"Thank you for this," Gina said, as she hugged her friend goodbye. "It was amazing."

"Seriously? You almost died."

"True. But I think I was in worse shape *before* I came to Oregon."

Danielle nodded, understanding exactly what Gina meant.

Gina smiled. "But next time, *I* get to pick where we're going for our girls' weekend."

epilogue

. . .

IN THE WEEKS THAT FOLLOWED, Gina and Danielle spoke often, and Gina managed to get the scoop on what had happened since they left Maidenwell.

The cops had enough evidence to charge Noelle Garland with murder, and when they began investigating her mother Leah as a possible accessory, Noelle confessed to murdering both Vanessa and Stanley and said that her mother knew nothing about it.

Several of Gina's theories turned out to be right.

Noelle and Stanley had a relationship a decade ago, and Noelle got pregnant. Stanley paid Noelle a hundred thousand dollars to never see him again, but over the years—as Mason's health challenges became more and more apparent—Noelle went back to Stanley asking for more money.

He kept putting her off, telling her he intended to make Mason the prime beneficiary of his estate. That mollified her for a while, but this past spring, she had heard from an investment banker friend of hers in the Bay Area that Stanley didn't actually have an estate plan.

That was when she decided to murder Stanley and Vanessa.

She used a tetrahydrozoline cocktail to induce Vanessa's fatal cardiac arrhythmia, and initially planned on murdering Stanley at the stables that same day, but her plans were spoiled by Gina's presence. Noelle had brought Mason to serve as a distraction on Saturday afternoon, but he got confused and thought that his mom was going to kill Florrie. That was why he chased the animal away.

When Gina heard that last bit from Danielle, she felt like she had been punched in the stomach. *Mason was trying to save the alpaca. He was a good kid.* How could she have been so wrong about him?

Noelle had admitted to trying to frame Tomas Villanueva for the murders. She knew all about the smuggling operation. Pretending to be Vanessa, she set up the early morning meeting with Tomas—to offer him more money to keep his mouth shut during the auction. She suspected that the manor's security cameras might record the meeting and provide some evidence about an extortion scheme that led to murder.

Noelle lured Stanley out to the stables on Sunday morning, telling him she had discovered something about Florentine that he needed to know before the auction. Having disabled the stable security cameras the day before, she struck quickly when Stanley arrived, injecting him with a high dose of pentobarbital, and then—thirty seconds later—delivering the fatal blow with the hay hook to make sure he couldn't be revived. To further confuse the police, she used a veterinary piller to force a pentobarbital capsule down Stanley's throat.

Because there was some blood on her clothes and body, Noelle decided to clean herself in the pond on the far edge of the estate. It was there she ran into Gina, and while Gina was unconscious, Noelle seized the opportunity to put Gina's fingerprints and DNA on the murder weapon—which had already been marked with Becca's DNA. Then she later hid the hook in the hedge maze.

"And she did it all for her kid?" Gina asked.

"Apparently so."

In the days ahead, Gina found herself thinking a lot about Noelle and Mason. She couldn't get them out of her head, and she was gripped by a strong feeling of despair. Noelle obviously suffered from some sort of psychosis that caused her to believe that murder was the only way to take care of her son. It was so sad.

Eventually, Gina had to focus on her own problems, the chief of which was moving.

The sad truth was that Gina had to be out of her apartment by the end of October. She had been lucky enough to connect with a former work friend who had also recently gone through a divorce. In Marsha's case, she kept the family home and received alimony and child support. But she was willing to rent out the basement of her 1960s ranch house in Rockland County to Gina. It was a long commute into Manhattan, but the price was right, and it was better than being homeless.

So Gina was in a mad rush to sell furniture and other possessions that she couldn't move out to the 'burbs.

On a Thursday afternoon, she went down to her lobby to meet a woman who had texted her she was interested in Gina's seven-foot-long vintage teak sideboard that she had inherited from her aunt. It was a classic mid-century modern piece, but there was no way Gina could get it out to Marsha's house without hiring a truck and a bunch of guys.

Downstairs, there was no sign of the woman, but a well-dressed man approached her. He was older and had kind of a rough-looking face that didn't fit with his tailored Martin Greenfield suit.

"Ms. Biletti?" he asked.

"Who wants to know?" She wondered if this guy was a detective, but quickly realized that a detective wouldn't be dressed so well.

He murmured something to himself. Gina couldn't be sure, but it sounded like "she's here." Which was weird.

She glanced around the lobby. There were a few people milling around near the mailboxes and Mr. D'Agostino, the doorman, was around here somewhere.

Hopefully, if this guy tried anything, she'd be able to get some help.

The man reached into his jacket pocket and withdrew something, which he offered to Gina.

It was a Maidenwell keycard.

"What's this for?"

"It's an invitation."

"What do you mean, an invitation? I just got back from—"

"An invitation for employment," another man said. He had just come in through the front door and he looked incredibly familiar—

Then it clicked. *Matthias Loneskum.* In the flesh.

Gina's heart jumped, and she felt her face flush.

"Nice to meet you, Gina. I'm Matthias." He offered his hand.

"I, uh, saw your video." *Oh my god, what a stupid thing to say.*

"The Maidenwell one? It was a little cheesy, but I think it got the message across."

"Yeah. Definitely did." Matthias Loneskum was a lot shorter in person. Maybe five seven or eight.

"Well, I know you're probably in the middle of something, so I'll be brief. I'd like to offer you a job at Maidenwell."

"I don't understand."

"You were the one who got to the bottom of what happened." He looked around to make sure no one else was listening. "The… unpleasantness. Excellent work."

"Thank you, but I still don't understand."

"My mother spoke very highly of you, and—"

"Your mother? Really?"

"Yes. You seem surprised."

"I'm very surprised," Gina said. "Extremely surprised."

"Well, we could use someone of your talents on staff."

This whole thing was surreal. Gina wondered if this was some delayed concussion or something, but she decided to just play along.

"You know I'm a market researcher, don't you?"

He smiled quizzically. "I know you *were* a market researcher."

"So, you need a market researcher at Maidenwell?"

"I have plenty of market researchers. I need someone to keep an eye on things."

"Isn't that Reeve's job?"

"He spoke highly of you as well. You'd be working with Mr. Reeve, and Ms. Grier as well."

"Have you asked her about that?"

"I don't need to ask her. She works for me."

Ah, a bit of the Loneskum arrogance slipping through the polite veneer. "I still don't know what exactly I would be doing."

"But you're interested?"

"Of course I'm interested!"

"Good. We can figure out the rest once you arrive." He clasped her hand again. "Fantastic to meet you, Gina."

"Arrive where?"

"To your orientation." Then he turned to leave.

"Wait," Gina called after him.

He hesitated at the lobby door.

"Can I ask you one last thing?"

"Sure."

"Who ended up with Florentine?"

"Hill Alpacas, of course."

"Becca?"

But he was already gone.

Gina looked helplessly at the guy in the suit.

He just shrugged and said, "You'll get used to it." Then he left too.

She looked down at the keycard in her hand and smiled to herself.

and then there was nun

Gina returns in her second Murderwell Mystery.

Welcome back to Maidenwell, where the Christmas snow is falling—but so are the bodies.

Hired as the eyes and ears of globe-trotting billionaire Matthias Loneskum, Gina Biletti expected a peaceful life amidst cozy tea shops, quaint cottages, and harmless village gossip. Little did she know that the holiday season would bring a chilling turn to Maidenwell's idyllic charms.

As Christmas approaches, an engagement party for Matthias' overachieving sister, Beatrix, sets the stage for murder and mystery.

Among the guests, a tapestry of intriguing characters emerges: a mysterious and beautiful young nun, an ex-con, an enigmatic foreign businessman, and a group of ambitious young tech entrepreneurs competing for a $5 million start-up prize. But when a gunshot shatters the tranquility of a Christmas hunt and tragedy strikes with a shocking "suicide," Gina's cozy world is turned upside down.

A massive winter storm seals the village up like a snow globe, and Gina faces a dreadful realization. She is trapped with a cunning and cold-blooded killer. Can she unravel the truth before another body falls, or will this be her first and last Christmas in Maidenwell?

The second book in the Murderwell series, *And Then There Was Nun*, is a riveting Christmas mystery that promises shivers, twists, and a hefty dose of holiday charm.

Library of Congress Cataloging-in-Publication Data
Name: Wood, B.G., author
Title: A Floof to a Kill: a novel / B.G. Wood
Description: First edition | Oregon: Bogwood Press, 2023
Subjects: GSAFD: Detective and mystery fiction

ISBN: 978-0-9851943-5-2

murderwell.com

v. 2.01

www.ingramcontent.com/pod-product-compliance
Lightning Source LLC
Chambersburg PA
CBHW061119100726
47911CB00013B/603

* 9 7 8 0 9 8 5 1 9 4 3 5 2 *